CU00729628

I FEEL HIM WATCHING

Can you feel him watching?

T.A MCKAY

Unsuspected

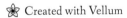 Created with Vellum

DEDICATION

To all my readers. Thank you for your continued support.

PROLOGUE

THE CAMERA WHIRS AS IT ZOOMS IN A LITTLE CLOSER. Now I can see the expression on Nicolai's face clearly so I snap a few pictures. He looks beautiful as he concentrates on his workout, his skin shiny with sweat and his cheeks tinged red with exertion. I imagine it's what he looks like when he's in the throws of passion, what he would look like leaning over me as he pushes into my body. I clench my arse as I imagine exactly how that would feel, how good it would burn as he claimed me as his own.

I get down on the grass lying on my stomach and angle my camera up towards the French doors on the back of Nicolai's house. They cover nearly the full wall of his home gym and it gives a great view as he does his workouts. He might be an older guy but he has the body of a twenty year old and I can't get enough of it. I click a few more pictures as he bench presses his weights, the muscles in his arms bulging with effort. I love those muscles, they have almost become an addiction for me now and I have hundreds of photos of them in my room. Truthfully it's more than his arms that have my attention though, it's everything about him. I just can't seem to get enough of him.

Nicolai drops his weights and sits up, dropping his head as he breathes heavily. His elbows are resting on his knees and he looks tired but sexy. He's been working out for about an hour so far and I know he will be finishing up soon, it's why he's doing weights, it's how he ends a workout. I take more photos, my finger just pressing the button as the pictures mount up. I will go through them later and get rid of any I don't want. Nicolai's head comes up and I hold my breath. He is looking directly at the dark bush I'm lying under and I can almost feel the touch of his eyes, but I know it's just my imagination. He doesn't know I'm here, he never does.

The camera continues to quietly whir as it takes photograph after photograph and I know there will be hundreds when I get home, but I don't care. As his eyes search the area around me the intense look on his face captures my attention. It's a look I want him to use on me before he kisses me, to prove to me that he wants me as much as I want him. I know he probably does but he's afraid to let me know, scared that I will turn him down. I won't though. I want him more than anything else on this Earth.

When he gets up from the bench and stands in front of the glass door I can feel myself getting hard. He is just wearing a pair of tight workout shorts and nothing else. His muscles are defined and shiny with sweat and I want to take my tongue and lick him dry. He has a little chest hair and it greys slightly as it disappears into the top of the shorts, but it makes me want to follow its path to see how grey it goes. Nicolai looks around his back garden, the darkness covering my presence but I know he can feel me watching. He knows that I'm out here watching him, he can feel the caress of my eyes against his body. I know he doesn't know it's me but he will. One day I'm going to take what's mine and that's him. One day Nicolai will be mine, no matter who I have to go through to get him.

CHAPTER ONE

NICOLAI

I SHIVER AS I RUN THE SPONGE OVER MY BODY AND LEAVE SOAP all over my chest. The last few weeks I've had this strange feeling that someone's been watching me. Nothing obvious, just the small hairs on the back of my neck stand up on end and it feels like there is a tingle all over my skin. I know I'm imagining it, no one is out there, but I can't seem to shake the strange feeling. It hasn't only been when I've been at home, and that's proof that I'm losing my mind. Supermarket, the local pool, even at work in the local secondary school, I feel the strange electricity on my skin all the time.

Ducking my head under the water, I let the heat ease the tension in my muscles. I overdid the weights tonight and I know I'm going to feel it in the morning. The burn from the water helps though, and I stand there longer than I should just letting it soothe me. When I've pushed it as long as I can, I turn off the water and grab a towel from the rack next to the tub. I really should have been asleep about an hour ago because I'm up at the arse-crack of dawn tomorrow for a trip with my students, but I couldn't relax and needed to burn some energy. Now I think maybe I should have given it a miss, then I wouldn't have to sit on a bus for too many hours while my muscles scream in protest. Nothing I can do about it now, but I can try and get to sleep before I am tired and sore tomorrow.

I throw the damp towel over the heated rail to dry it out and turn off the bathroom light. I head into my room still naked and make my way towards the window. The room is lit with a tiny little bedside light, so I know no one will be able to see me as I close my curtains. The window is open because of the stupidly hot weather this month, and I stand for a moment and let the breeze blow gently over my heated skin. It isn't a cold breeze, more like a warm breath from a lover as they lean over you. I feel my dick twitch at the thought, and I roll my eyes. I haven't felt anyone else's touch for so long that a fucking wind gets me hard. Nope, not pathetic in the slightest.

I close the curtains with a little more force than intended before climbing into bed, still completely naked. It's far too hot to even attempt to wear anything below the duvet, and to be honest I'm beginning to like the freedom. I turn and grab my mobile from the bedside unit and set the alarm for five in the morning. I'm glad that it's June so when my alarm goes off in the morning it will be light already, and I won't feel like it's the middle of the night. I could sleep an extra hour, but I want to go for a run before I spend all day stuck in a museum with a group of uninterested teenagers. I need that hour to clear my head and set me up for the day, even if it will steal an hour from my sleep.

I put the phone back on the unit and turn off the light, plunging the room into darkness. I refuse to look at the time because I have a feeling it will make me want to change my alarm, but if it's dark outside I know that it's later than I'd planned to go to bed. I push the duvet down over my hips so I don't feel like I'm boiling from the inside and I stare at the dark ceiling. My brain is working overtime making sleep hard to come by. I wish it would just turn off, but that doesn't seem to be a possibility. I take a deep breath and close my eyes, refusing to let my thoughts take over. There is nothing that is important tonight, and I purposely think of nothing, concentrating on my breathing and nothing else. Just when I think it isn't working, I feel my body relax completely, and sleep takes me away.

I GRAB MY BAG FROM THE BOOT OF MY CAR AND RUN TOWARDS the front entrance of the school. I can't believe that I slept in this morning, and not just by a few minutes. Over an hour after I silenced my alarm I finally opened my eyes, and that's when my morning started going to shit. I ripped the t-shirt I was putting on after it got caught on my bedpost, I lost my mobile phone even though I hadn't moved it from the unit beside my bed, only to find it in my dirty clothes hamper, and now my chest muscles are screaming at me because I missed the run I had planned to ease my muscles out. The only thing going in my favour is even though I'm late, I'm still arriving before the kids, so I have a few minutes to make myself a coffee.

Rushing down the hall, I head straight to the staff room. I should probably go to my classroom first, but the thought of coffee is pulling me to the coffee machine. I open the door and jump about a foot in the air when Gareth jumps out from behind the door with a shout. "You stupid fucking idiot."

Gareth bursts out laughing, grabbing his stomach as he doubles over and struggles to breathe. I hate it when he does shit like this to me, which is all the bloody time, but he always finds himself so funny. I met him four years ago when I first started working here, and it didn't take us long to become really good friends. He feels a bit like a brother now, and his girlfriend Claire is like my little sister. He's about five years younger than me, even though he acts like a teenager most of the time, but he has two kids and is as good as married which is a lot more than I have in my life.

"I hate you. You know that, right?" I push past him, shoving him with my shoulder on purpose and making him topple slightly.

"You love me so don't kid yourself. You're late, does that mean you had a good night last night?" He wiggles his eyebrows at me, and

I roll my eyes at him. This is a common question I get from Gareth because he seems to think that because I'm single, I should be out there fucking anything that moves.

"The only good thing that happened last night was a good work-out... and before you ask, I mean with weights." He looks disappointed with my answer, but I ignore him so I can fill the travel mug that I retrieved from the cupboard.

"You need to get out there and live a little, my friend."

"I know, but nothing has changed since the last time you told me that. So just let me get my coffee because I'm gonna need it to survive today." Gareth going on this trip is the only thing that will stop me going insane. He's an English teacher, and even though I'm in the science department, we seem to get paired up a lot for the trips. I would like to think that it's because we're mature and sensible, but I think it's more that we are the newest teachers here and no one else wants to do it.

Gareth grabs his backpack and own coffee cup and waits for me by the door. I quickly add some caramel macchiato creamer and stir it in. I eat pretty healthily, but this is the one treat I allow myself. Some might say I was slightly addicted to the flavouring but I don't agree, even if I do buy it in bulk from Amazon. Grabbing my bag after putting my lid on my cup, I rush to the door to try and limit how late we will be. I take a detour via my classroom and catch some papers I need to grade and then head out to the car park. There is already a large group of students waiting there, but the bus is still missing. I slow slightly as we reach the kids and a few of the girls turn to face us, broad smiles on their faces.

"Good morning, Mr Morgan." Tilly smiles at me and her cheeks redden. I groan internally because I know that Gareth will be loving this. Tilly's crush on me seems to be common knowledge, and Gareth finds the whole thing very amusing.

"Morning, Tilly. Are we all ready to leave?" I purposely turn to talk to the group of kids, ignoring Gareth as he laughs behind me. A few mumbled groans come from the boys, but the girls at least seem a little more enthusiastic.

The complaining is just dying down when the bus pulls around the corner and stops a few feet away. I take out the register and mark off the names of all kids who're meant to be attending today. There's only one kid missing, and that's Simon, which really isn't a shock. I don't think that kid has made it to school on time more than five times since I started here. I hand the list to Gareth, and he rolls his eyes when he sees who's missing.

"Right kids. I want you all on the bus as quickly as possible. All bags under seats and seat belts on. You can sit with whoever you want, but if there's any drama then I'll follow the seating chart." That piece of news is met with some eye rolling and even more muttering, but as they start to get onto the bus, there's very little drama and bickering.

I drop my bag onto the front seat as I watch the kids get organised, only looking away when Gareth drops into the space next to me. "Nope. Go find somewhere else to sit."

He snorts and doesn't move. He balances his coffee cup on the floor between his feet as he throws his bag into the luggage rack opposite us. "Not gonna happen. If you think I'm sitting on this bus for the next ninety minutes without someone to talk to, then you have lost your mind."

"You could do some grading like I'm gonna do?"

This earns me another snort, and I can see all the work I had planned going straight out of the window. What is it about today that just isn't going in my favour? "You are such a nerd. I know you're an old man, but you could relax just a little. You aren't that close to dying."

I glare at him, but he's immune to my frustrations now. Well, either immune or just doesn't care. I resist the urge to slap him in the back of the head because that really wouldn't be a good example in front of the kids, but it takes a lot to keep my hands to myself.

A noise on the at the door has me turning to see Simon hurrying up the bus stairs, his cheeks red and no two bits of hair sticking up in the same direction. The other kids let out a cheer and applaud him as he smiles at me on his way to sit next to John. I mark his name on the register before turning to the driver. "That's us all accounted for now. I'll check seatbelts, and then we can go." He nods, and I take a few minutes to walk down the aisle to check that all the kids are buckled up. There are comments from them about not being kids and that they know how to use a seatbelt, but I don't let it deter me. At the end of the day these young adults are my responsibility, and I've met some of their parents. They're scary. If something was to happen to their little darlings, I don't think they would think twice about suing me or punching my lights out. I don't want either to happen, so I take a few minutes to make sure they are locked in.

Giving the driver a nod I get back into my seat, which is now missing my backpack and coffee. As soon as I'm buckled in my coffee appears in front of my face. I take it out of Gareth's hand and take a large drink. I sigh as the flavour covers my tongue and I can almost feel the sugar giving me energy. Feeling a bit more relaxed, I turn and look at Gareth. "Where's my bag? You might not want to work, but I was planning on marking while we travelled."

He snorts and points across the aisle to the luggage rack, and there it is, sitting behind Gareth's bag and very much out of my reach.

"Would you stop that snorting thing, you aren't a teenager even though you spend all day with them. Do you do that shit to Claire?"

"Do I look stupid? If I laughed at her, there would be a chance that there would be no more kids in my future."

"More kids?" Gareth already has two little girls, both under the age of four, and I would have thought that would be enough for anyone. I've never felt the need to have kids, working with them is more than enough, but his daughters are the cutest things ever. I know he loves his kids, but he's never mentioned having another.

"Don't know. It's being talked about at home, but nothing's been decided. I keep imaging that we would end up with triplet girls or something. You know, five kids under the age of five. That's the sort of luck I have."

It's my turn to snort, and he glares at me. I try to cover up the outburst by taking another drink of coffee.

"Mr Morgan, how long until we get there?" A voice shouts from the back, and it's the first clue that this is going to be a very long journey.

"I know I teach science but let's try a little math. If we left five minutes ago and the whole journey is going to take ninety minutes, how long do we have left?"

Giggles come from who I suspect is Tilly's group, but it's the loud male voice that makes me laugh. "You could have just said a while."

I face the front again, and I find Gareth smiling at the interaction. "They think you're a dick now."

"Probably not the first time. Might stop them asking every five minutes for the rest of the journey."

He nods before drinking his coffee. "So you going to tell me why you really slept in this morning?"

"I swear this isn't some big adventure that I'm keeping from you. I overdid the weights last night, and then I couldn't sleep. By the time I did fall over it was probably after midnight and apparently, my body didn't like my five o'clock alarm this morning. I'd planned on a run before work, but that didn't happen."

There's that look of disappointment again. "Seriously? What's the point in having a single friend if you don't have a life I can be jealous of? You need to get out and sow your wild oats a bit more."

"You know I'm not into that. Show me where I can find a guy who wants more than a quick ..." I look around and make sure there are no kids within earshot, but still whisper, "fuck, and I'll be right there."

I expect Gareth to say something funny, but instead he goes into his pocket and pulls out his phone. He unlocks it before handing it to me, and I'm left looking at a dating app. It's not one I've seen before and not any I've heard of. This one's called 'Back To Basics', and the logo is nothing but two hands entwined. I hand Gareth his phone back and pretend I haven't seen anything, but it doesn't stop him from talking. "Don't look like that. I researched this one, and I think it will be perfect for you."

"You researched a gay dating site?"

"Shut up. I needed something to do while I was up all night with Clara. I swear her teeth are coming through metal instead of gums. Anyway, this site is geared more towards the dating aspect of relationships, not just the hookup. I'm not saying you wouldn't find that on there, stay away from the for one night only section, but most of the guys I saw were professional types who don't get a chance to go out much. They're looking for relationships but don't want to go through the whole scene thing."

I'm still trying to get my head around the fact that he was on a gay dating site, but he's moving past that quickly.

"Give me your phone."

I know I'll probably regret it, but I hand it over without any complaint. I've found that sometimes it's just easier not to argue with Gareth. If I don't like the app, then I'll delete it when I go home. The truth is no matter how dodgy the app might be, I can't deny how freaking lonely I am. Maybe I could meet someone on it that will become merely a friend, someone I could spend time with and have some fun. He might not be Mr Forever but even finding Mr For-A-While would be great.

Gareth spends a few minutes downloading things, and I make a mental note to change the password for my phone because apparently, Gareth knows it. When he hands it back to me, I don't bother looking at it before I lock the screen and put it back in my pocket. I don't know if I'll bite the bullet and make a profile, but even if I do it won't be done on a bus full of kids.

"Don't just humour me, okay? Just have a look tonight, it might be something that you want to do. You need to get out there and meet someone, Nic. I worry about how alone you are."

Shit, if Gareth is mentioning me being alone, I know my life has officially become pathetic. "I will think about it, promise. And just so you know, you're right. I really should do something while I still have the looks to attract a guy."

This gets a snort from Gareth. I'm really starting to hate that noise. "I wouldn't go that far, but maybe get on it before you pull your pension."

I'm just about to give him a dead leg when the children scream from somewhere up the back of the bus. "Oh my god, Simon's just puked everywhere!"

Shit. This is going to be a long day.

CHAPTER TWO

NICOLAI

I CLOSE THE BOOT AND TURN TOWARDS MY HOUSE, ONLY TO LET out a shout when I come face to face with my next door neighbour Dillon. "Holy shit."

"I'm sorry, Mr Morgan. I just wanted to say hi."

I take a step back since I'm standing far too close to the young man who I used to teach, and take a moment to let my heart rate return to normal. I wish people would stop trying to give me a heart attack. "We've spoken about this, Dillon."

He blushes and looks down at his feet. "Sorry, Nicolai." I taught Dillon for two years when I first started at Beechwood Academy but that was over two years ago, so he doesn't need to call me by my full name anymore. He must be about twenty-one now, and it makes me feel older than my thirty-five when he calls me Mr Morgan.

"How are things at college?" He started at the local college when he left school, but to be honest, that shocked me. Dillon is super smart, and I would've expected him to go on to university or at least one of the more prominent colleges, but he stayed local and is now training to be a care assistant. That again is another shock. He always spoke about possibly going into medicine, and I honestly thought he would. He had the grades to get into medical school easily, and when I found out he was doing something else, it was a huge surprise.

"It's good. A little boring sometimes but ... well, it's worth it to be at home." He points with his thumb to the house that he shares with his dad.

"Is your dad home?" In the four years since I moved into my house, I think I've seen his dad maybe a dozen times at most. He works away, and I don't think he comes home, which leaves Dillon in that house alone. I spent the whole time he was in school worrying about him being on his own, but it never seems to bother him. I still worry a little, but now that he's older I don't let it get to me as much.

"He's travelling just now. I think he said that he would be home in a week or so." He says the words to his feet and I can't help but smile. Dillon's always had a problem looking me in the eye. Gareth says it's because Dillon has a crush on me but I don't believe that. I think he's just a shy young man.

"Well, remember if you need anything just let me know. I'm going to grab dinner and then go to bed. It's been one of those days."

He finally looks at me even though it's through his fringe but I can see his smile. "At least it's Friday."

I sigh. "Yeah, thank fuck." I still feel a little awkward swearing in front of an ex-student, but I'm sure he hears a lot worse than that. "Have a great weekend, Dillon." When I say his name, I swear I can hear him inhale deeply but I ignore it as I make my way around him and up my front steps. I look over my shoulder and see Dillon standing on the pavement still staring at me. Okay, so maybe Gareth is right with the crush thing, but I have no plans on telling him that.

I wave once more over my shoulder before going in through my front door and closing it behind me. I drop my bag on the floor, kick off my shoes, and head straight towards the shower. The whole day I've felt as though I've had the smell of sick ingrained in my skin and it's turned my stomach in the worst possible way. As soon as I'd cleaned up Simon and the bus, all I had wanted to do was come home and scrub myself clean but that hadn't been an option. Nope, I had to spend the rest of the day in an overheated museum, which hadn't helped the smell at all.

I strip off my clothes as I walk down the hall towards my room, throwing them all in the clothes hamper as soon as I get through the doorframe. I don't even miss a step as I do it, just keep moving towards my goal. I get into the tub and turn on the water, barely stepping back in time before the freezing cold water hits me. As soon as it heats I'm under the stream with my sponge in my hand. I scrub my body twice before I feel that the smell might be gone and turn the water off. I grab the towel from last night and give my body a rough dry before wrapping it around my waist.

A gentle breeze hits my still damp body when I enter my room, and I instantly look at the window that's slightly ajar. I approach it slowly while looking around my room to see if there's anything out of place. I'm pretty sure I closed the window before I left for work this morning, but now that I'm standing looking at it, I'm not sure. It's part of my morning routine. Get up, go for a run, shower and then close the window. No, I'm not so sure I remembered to do it this morning because I had been running so behind. Did I close the window? I try to think back and even though I can almost picture myself doing it, I might be imagining it. No, I couldn't have. I must have thought I did it in my rush but forgot. Grabbing the bottom of the window I open it wider and lean my hands on the windowsill. The breeze thoroughly blows over my skin now, and I enjoy the feeling.

This room was one of the biggest selling points when I came to view the house. I wanted something that was a little set back from the other houses on the street, and something that offered me privacy towards the back of the house. This little detached bungalow was perfect for everything. The large back garden gives me the full privacy that I craved, and the older home has a lot of character. I would love to say that I kept all the original features, but the first thing I did when I moved in was to get my brother Andrei over to refit a lot of the rooms. The bathroom, kitchen, and my bedroom were the first to be redone. I wanted them as modern as I could get, and my bedroom was extended to give me more space. It's pretty much my perfect house now, or at least until I can convince my brother to build me that sunroom I want.

I turn away from the window and drop the towel as I move across the floor to my dresser. I'm only planning on lounging the rest of the night, so I grab a pair of shorts and put them on. I forgo a top because it's too warm, but bend down to grab the towel I dropped. As I bend over, I get that tingling feeling over the back of my neck again. I grab the towel and slowly stand, my eyes going directly to the window as I scan the back garden. It's bright sunshine out there so I can see the whole area and nothing looks out of place. I shake my head at my stupidity. Why the hell would someone be watching me in my own house? Throwing the towel into the dirty washing hamper, I leave my room and head to the kitchen to make myself something to eat.

I LIE BACK ON THE COUCH AND RUB A HAND OVER MY BELLY. I probably shouldn't have eaten the entire large pizza myself, but after the crappy day I've had, I thought I deserved it. Now as the dough swells up in my stomach, I think I might have made a mistake. Groaning as my stomach rebels, I get up from my position on the couch to get a drink. Common sense tells me that I should settle on a bottle of water, but my whole day has made the need for a beer a real thing. I'll make sure I work out longer tomorrow.

I snort because I know I'm lying to myself about being able to work out. Tomorrow there will be grass cutting and maybe a gentle walk to the local bakers to get something sweet, but there will be no workout. I cringe when I notice that I've picked up Gareth's stupid snorting habit. I spent all day listening to him doing it, and now I've brought it home with me. Great. Opening the fridge, I grab a bottle of beer and open it. The first cold mouthful makes my teeth ache but in the best way. By the time I take the bottle from my lips it's nearly finished, and I don't regret it for a single second.

I see my mobile sitting on the dining table, mocking me with the stupid app that's on it. I promised Gareth that I'd at least have a look at it tonight, check it out even if I didn't make an actual profile. I down the last dregs of beer and take another one from the fridge. I stroll to the table like I'm expecting the phone to jump up and attack me. Taking a seat while still staring at the offending object, I place my bottle on the table while I try to decide what to do. When I finally pick up the phone, I twirl it through my fingers, turning it over and over again until I can no longer put off doing something with it. Maybe Gareth is right. I mean there's no harm in having a simple look at the site. I don't even have an excuse for not becoming a member. My sexuality isn't a secret, so I don't have to hide it from anyone.

Biting the bullet, I unlock my phone and press the app. I crack my neck while it's loading, preparing myself to do battle with the thing. As soon as the sign in screen appears I see my first hurdle. It's not going to let me in without setting up an account, which means that Gareth either set up his own account or he lied about looking around on it. Doesn't matter either way just now though, and I spend the next five minutes adding personal information to my profile. Most of it is basic stuff, age, height, weight, profession, hair and eye colour, but then it starts getting more personal, and it gives me a small pause. If I put this stuff down on the app, then everyone will see it, and I'm not sure how I feel about that.

Fuck it. If I'm going to do this, I may as well jump in with both feet. I give them all the personal information that I usually keep to myself until the fifth or sixth date, and when it asks for a photo, I don't even hesitate as I choose the last decent selfie I took. It's not exactly the most amazing picture I've ever taken, but it's a real enough likeness that I know that men won't complain. My finger hovers over the complete button. If I press this then it's done, there will be no going back. Seriously, no going back? I'm pretty sure if I get over the rather dramatic moment I will register the fact that I can delete the entire profile if I don't want to meet anyone. I press the button to complete the process, and I watch as the screen changes in front of me. It loads up a menu section, and I remember what Gareth told me and click on the 'trying to meet' section.

I spend nearly an hour looking through pictures and profiles of some pretty hot men, and when I finally look up, it's starting to get dark outside. I don't even know when I moved to the couch, but I'm now lying with my feet up on the armrest. It took a while, but I think I'm getting the hang of this app. On the bottom of the profiles, there is a little flag that you press if you think you might want to make a connection with a guy, they then get a notification from your profile, and they can decide if they want to make contact. I've pressed a couple of the flags but probably not as many as I should have. I don't want to go overboard to begin with until I see how the first few go.

My phone buzzes and I close the profile page. I've had several buzzes that I think are notifications, but I haven't bothered checking anything before now. I open up the message section and see that I have a few requests sitting there. Some are from men who have flagged me, and I spend some time checking out their profiles. I have two replies from people I have flagged, and the one that catches my attention is the reply from James. I feel butterflies in my stomach as I open his message and read what he's written.

Hi. Thanks for flagging me. I'm James ...obviously... and I'm looking to connect with someone who likes long walks on the beach and nights in front of a fire. ← Too much? Haha. I'm honestly just looking to meet someone who I can laugh with and maybe spend some time getting to know. If you're that guy feel free to write back ... I promise my jokes get better... maybe.

I'm smiling by the time I've finished reading, and I don't even think before I'm replying to James.

Hi James. I do indeed like walks on the beach and nights in front of the fire, but there must be hot chocolate with marshmallows. Okay, that didn't sound so lame in my head. I'm new to all this, so I hope I don't do anything stupid. I hope to hear back from you, and maybe we can catch a drink or something (If that's how it's done... if not ignore this part of my message.)

I send the reply and close the app. A notification will come through if he replies, and I refuse to sit here waiting like a loser who needs attention. In an attempt to distract myself I head to my room and grab my dirty washing before taking it to the washing machine. Once the machine is filled, I put on the timer so the clothes will be ready when I wake up in the morning. There is no way I will be able to stay up long enough to hang the load up to dry tonight, and I refuse to have my clothes smell by leaving them wet overnight.

The task doesn't take as long as I'd hoped, and in a few minutes, I'm heading back to my room to collapse onto my bed. I stare at the ceiling while I decide if going straight to sleep is a good option, but my phone beeping catches my attention. When I see that it's James replying, my heart jumps in my chest. I bite my lip while I read his message, a smile growing on my lips as I read his words.

Don't worry, it sounded nice in the message too. I mean, who doesn't love hot chocolate? If you are new to this I'll make sure I'm gentle, don't want to leave any bruises ;) I see from your profile that you're a teacher, I don't know if I admire you or feel bad... all those kids in one place *shudders* From that comment you can tell I have no children, do you have any of your own? I think a drink would be nice. I prefer doing this face to face like the old days. You know when you actually met people in person. Let me know when you're free, and we can organise to meet ... and just throwing it out there. I have nothing on this weekend.

My pulse is racing when he says he wants to meet. I open up his picture again, and I'm met with a warm smile and dark eyes. James looks a little older than me even though his profile says he's a few years younger, but he's handsome. His super blonde hair is a complete contrast to the darkness of his eyes, but on him, it works in a way that makes my dick twitch. Part of my brain wants me to close the app and say nothing else, but I channel Gareth and type out a reply.

Isn't that a coincidence... I'm not busy this weekend either. I don't know exactly where you live, but I live near Beechwood Academy. There's a little wine bar not far from there where we could meet tomorrow night. Let me know if you want to, and we can organise a time, or a different place if that doesn't suit you.

I press send before I chicken out, feeling proud for actually reaching out to someone tonight. I took the bull by the horns and made a connection with a guy who isn't just hot, but from the first few messages sounds like he might be a lot of fun. If nothing else, meeting James will get me out of the house for a change. We might not hit it off when we do meet but I will never know if I don't take the leap, and James looks like someone I might want to leap with.

CHAPTER THREE

NICOLAI

"There's no way you can prefer chocolate over pistachio. Sorry, I won't accept that."

I watch James over the top of my glass, and he looks so serious as he talks about ice cream flavours. He's shown passion with any subject we've spoken about in the last two hours, and even though I was worried before he arrived, there is now no part of me that wants to leave. While sitting waiting on him I'd been tempted to run, but I'm so glad I hadn't.

Sitting alone at the table had been an act of courage. I sat and played through dozens of scenarios in my head, the wine only making me more anxious. I imagined him walking in and seeing me, only to turn on his heels and run away before actually meeting me. Or what if he turned up and looked nothing like his picture? Is it possible that someone could be that beautiful in real life and be single? And why is he single? What's wrong with him if no one has stuck around to be in a relationship with him?

All these thoughts silenced instantly when I looked up from my glass and my eyes connected with James who had just entered the bar. It wasn't just my thoughts that stilled. It was my whole body. I'm pretty sure that my heart forgot how to beat for several seconds because yes, he was as beautiful in real life as he was in his picture. His smile relaxed me instantly and then as he led the conversation, I felt like I'd known him for years. He took over the conversation but not in an obtrusive way, and I was happy just to sit and listen to him talk. He is smart and funny, and as I stare at him over the table, I'm struggling to see how he could still be single.

Every single part of him makes my body react. From his deep sultry voice to the way his clothes fit against his body. He is wearing simple dark blue jeans and a shirt, but he has the sleeves rolled up past his forearms, which gives me a delicious preview of toned arms. The material is fitted all the way up to his shoulders, and it's taking everything in me not to drool all over his lap. His arms are toned but not overly large, but even without the build of a bodybuilder, I know that he must spend time working out. It takes a lot of work to get a body like his.

"What can I say, nothing beats chocolate. I try not to eat it because if I gave in to my cravings, I would be the size of a house, but chocolate in any form is perfect."

James' eyes run over my body, and I can feel their path like it's his fingers leading the way. "Don't think that's possible, but if it makes you feel better, you're winning that fight." His voice takes a slightly huskier tone, and I shiver slightly, trying to cover it up by taking a drink of my wine.

"Thank you." I cringe as my voice comes out on a squeak. If there's a better way to sound unsexy, I can't think of it right now.

"No, thank you. I've met a few guys on the app, but I have to be honest and say none of them holds a candle to you. If you don't mind me asking, what's wrong with you?"

My heart starts racing but not in a good way. This feels like it might be a brush off and I don't want that to happen. "What do you mean?" I bite the inside of my cheek to stop myself from doing something stupid like begging him not to leave.

"Well, you're sexy, funny, and smart. I'm not sure why you need an app to meet someone, so I'm thinking there must be something wrong with you."

I snort with laughter because it's the same thoughts I've had about James. The noise comes out loud, and I cover my mouth instantly as my cheeks heat. James points at me with a wicked smile on his face.

"There's your flaw. I knew you had to have one." His eyes gleam, and they draw me in.

"So same question to you. I've been trying to work out why you're single and I can't work it out. Do you have dead bodies in your attic I need to worry about?" I feel myself leaning in closer to him over the table as I wait for his answer.

"No dead bodies yet. But I have many flaws that you are kind enough to overlook."

I sit forward again, using my movement as an excuse to run my eyes over his body. "Like?"

"Well, I have fewer muscles than you. My body would only be a five compared to your ten."

"Liar." He raises his eyebrows, and I can't help the smile that it brings. "Someone with arms like yours can't be a five."

His lip twitches up, but he never breaks eye contact with me. The intensity is making my stomach somersault, and I don't want it to stop. "Okay, you got me there, I have toned arms. But truthfully, if you're expecting a hard muscly body, you're gonna be disappointed."

James tries to sound flippant, but I can hear the change in his voice. I wonder who has put doubt in his mind about his body because I would like to meet that person and show them the error of their way. I break eye contact with James as I let my eyes take a slow journey down over his body. I go slowly so he knows exactly what I'm doing. His body looks perfect to me, and even though he is slightly thicker than me around the waist, the only thought in my mind is holding onto him while I ride him. My dick starts to take an interest in the view, and when I meet James' eyes again, I can clearly see the lust in them. "Don't see anything to be disappointed with."

James' mouth opens like he's about to say something, but the waitress appears next to us and puts our bill on the table. I look at the clock on the wall and can't believe that it's nearly midnight. I had only planned to stay for a couple of drinks, but three hours later it feels like we've barely spent any time together. I grab my wallet and hand my card to the waitress, who winks at me as James tries to tell her not to take it. I add a nice tip to the total since we have probably stayed longer than the staff wanted, and as soon as we step outside, the door locks behind us.

"I'm surprised they let us leave before locking that. I think we might have outstayed our welcome a little."

I laugh at James' comment, and when his hand accidentally brushes against mine, I struggle to hold in the groan that wants to escape at the simple touch. We walk to the car park in silence, but you can feel the electricity in the air around us. By the time we reach the parked cars, my heart is racing in my chest like I've run a marathon. I might be reading more into this than is healthy. Just because I like James doesn't mean he feels the same. I need to calm down so I don't make a fool of myself.

When we reach a dark BMW, James stops walking and leans against the side of the car. "This is me." He puts his hands in his pockets and stares at his feet as he kicks the small stones on the ground. He looks as nervous as I feel and for the first time tonight there's an air of awkwardness between us.

I point aimlessly in the direction of my car, suddenly feeling light-headed. "I'm over there." I only had one small glass of wine, certainly not enough to be feeling any effects from it, but standing next to James has got my body reacting like I'm a teenager. I don't remember ever feeling this way about someone but I've been on my own for so long I might have forgotten.

James suddenly looks up at me, his eyes boring into my own. "I want to kiss you."

My stomach tumbles with excitement, and I wonder if he's able to hear my heart trying to beat out of my chest. I don't know what to do so I go with the only thing I can think of. "Okay." It's maybe not the most eloquent of responses but it makes him move away from the side of his car so I'm more than happy with it. His hands grip my jaw, and he spins our positions until I'm pressed up against his car. My pulse is beating erratically as he moves closer and there is no way he can't feel it under his fingertips.

"You are so fucking sexy." His words are breathed against my lips before he lowers them and finally closes the distance between us. The second he touches me I melt into his body, letting him take full control. He's persistent with his kiss in a way that makes my toes curl. I open to him immediately, and I moan when his tongue touches mine. He tastes of wine, and I don't want him to ever stop kissing me.

Pushing my hips forward, I rub my now painfully hard dick against him. It's only after I've done it a few times that it hits me what I'm doing and I start to worry. Just because I'm kissing him doesn't mean he wants me to use his body for my pleasure. I might be taking his kiss and turning into some sexual thing that he isn't comfortable with. I'm about to pull away from him and apologise when I feel the evidence of how he's feeling. His erection is now pressing against mine, telling me he's perfectly happy with what's happening.

Grinding against him while he kisses me out in public feels a bit risky, a little more exciting that we could be caught at any time, and when I feel James pulling away, I try to chase his lips. He's making me feel excited and sexy, and I don't want him to stop.

"If I don't stop I'm going to take this somewhere I shouldn't." He drops his head to mine, and I feel his laboured breathing against my electrified skin.

"I think you should do that."

He puffs out a laugh, but he doesn't take me up on my offer, instead stepping back to put distance between us. "I want to get to know you before I give in to my urges. I have a feeling I could like you, so I don't want to rush it. Is that okay with you?"

Just when I thought he couldn't get any better, his words have me almost melting. "That's more than fine. I want to see you again."

James brushes his lips over mine briefly again, and I savour the feeling while I can. "You have my mobile number so call me."

I nod my head because I don't trust my voice to sound normal, and he kisses me once more before I step away from his car so he can get in. James drives away, and I watch him go before I dreamily walk to my car and get in. I lean my head back against the headrest and stare out of the windscreen. My body feels all tingly, and I swear I can still feel James' lips on mine. I'm tempted to send him a message before driving home, but I resist the urge, and it's probably a good thing. I'm acting like a lovesick fool, and I need to get control before I make a complete arse of myself. I've had one date with him, and I can't go falling so quickly. We're at the getting to know each other phase, so I need to slow everything down. Falling for the first guy to show me any interest in months is pathetic.

I've never been the kind of guy that falls for a guy so quickly, but being out of the dating scene has apparently made me desperate. I think that I should have taken Gareth's advice a long time ago. I'm sure I'm just missing all the obvious flaws that James has. There is no way he is as perfect as my mind is making him. No, I need to sleep and then message him tomorrow when I have gotten over my urges.

Glad that I've managed to talk myself down from the cliff edge, I start the car and head home. Even if nothing comes from my date with James, I don't regret the night one bit. It's later than I planned on staying out, but it was fun. The sexual attraction might fade when I've let myself calm down, but I can't take away the fun I had with James. He has a warped sense of humour but it matched my own perfectly, and even when he was trying to be all PC about something, he failed in a hilarious way. I could spend hours just listening to him, and that's precisely what I did tonight. I pull into my driveway and turn off the engine. I sit in the dark for a few moments and enjoy the quiet. Tonight was fun, and I'm desperate to do it again. I resist the urge to text James again, telling myself that being desperate isn't a good look on anyone.

A flash of light from my side garden catches my eye, and I

instantly sit up straight. I don't have a good view of the area from where I'm sitting but I know I saw something. I open my door slowly and get out, holding my keys between my fingers in case someone jumps out on me. I think of the strange feeling I've been having for the last few weeks, that constant feeling of being watched, and wonder if I'm not imagining it as I thought. Then there is a chance I'm imagining the whole thing, and I've just finally gone insane.

I approach the area, and I can't settle on a plan of what to do. Part of me wants to say something in case someone is in the area, but then the rest of me doesn't want to make a noise in case someone is in there. I grab my mobile and use the torch function to light up the offending area as I approach it. I'm holding my breath in fear, but when my head starts to get fuzzy, I let a sigh out and try to relax a little. I light up the side of my house, and I huff out a stuttered breath when I'm met with nothing but an empty rose garden. Apparently, I'm losing my mind. It was probably a reflection from a car light or something, and my overactive imagination made it into a stalker who was after me. I roll my eyes at how pathetic I'm being, but as I turn to go into my house, the light from my torch reflects off something on the ground. It's a small square lying in the dirt. I scan my eyes around me constantly as I bend down to pick up the item. It's a little SD card like you put in a camera or phone. It doesn't belong to me, and there's no way that someone who was passing by could have dropped it this far into my garden.

Giving in to my earlier panic, I rush up my front steps and after a brief struggle with my keys, I finally get my door unlocked. When I'm inside I slam the door loudly and use both locks to secure it. I take a few steps back but my eyes don't leave the door like I'm expecting someone to come barging through it at any second. When nothing happens for a few minutes I start to calm down a little, the sweat that was running down my spine drying against my skin and making me itch.

I keep the lights off as I walk down the hall to my bedroom. I go straight to my bed and sit down, grabbing my laptop off the bedside unit. As it's booting up, I look at the SD card that I found under the bush. I can't think of a reasonable reason for it to be in my rose garden other than someone was there, in the place I saw the flash. That option worries me more than I thought possible.

When my laptop is finally booted up fully, I try to press the SD card into the slot on the side. When it becomes clear it won't fit, I let out a frustrated groan. I need a card reader, but there is no way I'm going to get one tonight. I will ask Gareth and Andrei tomorrow if either of them have one I can borrow, if not I will buy one. I will find out what's on that SD card.

I look up from the paper I'm marking when the door to my classroom opens. Gareth comes in before closing it behind him again. He looks really happy, and I will admit that it scares me a little. Nothing good ever comes from my best friend looking so bloody happy.

"Who sucked your dick?"

He gives me the finger as he grabs a chair from behind a desk and collapses into it. "I have a teething child. There's not enough money in the world that would make me ask Claire for a blowjob. She would probably say yes so that she could bite it off." He shudders at his statement, and I feel my dick shrink a little at the thought.

"Is that why you're here? I love you like a brother, Gareth, but I'm not gonna suck your dick."

He glares at me but chooses to ignore me completely. "We have exactly one month until the summer holidays and I can't fucking wait. I need to get out of this place and be able to nap. I miss sleep."

I look at him, like really look, and I see the dark circles under his eyes. I can only imagine the pain he's suffering from Clara being up all night, and then him working all day. Being a teacher is harder than most people realise, and not just because we spend all day with kids. Going home doesn't mean we are off the clock. There are teaching plans and term outlines to organise, and once all those are done, you have the fun of all night paper grading to keep you busy. Apparently, it's starting to take its toll on Gareth. "Clara still up all night?"

"Yeah, and I hate having Claire up all night with her. She spends all day dealing with it and she needs to get a break. Thank god Libby is a good kid, she tries to entertain Clara whenever she can, not that it works. Truthfully I'm glad to get to school for a break from it."

I can only imagine how that feels and thankfully I won't ever have to experience it. I love Gareth's kids, and they call me uncle, but that's as much fatherly instinct I've ever had. Thankfully James seems to be in agreement with me over that, so there won't be any problems in that area.

"What the hell has you smiling like that?"

I touch my lips and realise that I'm smiling. It wasn't a conscious thought but apparently just thinking about James makes my lips react. "I had a date."

This gets Gareth's attention, and he leans forward until his elbows are leaning on my desk. "Like a *date* date?"

I purposely didn't tell him about meeting James before the fact because he would've tried to be helpful and it would have made me more nervous than I already was. "Yeah, a proper date."

"I can't believe you are gonna make me ask. Who was it and how did it go?"

That's the good thing about Gareth, he's always interested. When we first met, I wondered if being gay would be a problem between us. I've had friends in the past that didn't want to hear anything about who I was dating because they felt awkward, but with Gareth, it's never made a difference. He's always interested in who I'm dating. "His name is James and I met him on that app thing you downloaded."

"I told you it was good. So what happened?"

"We met at Toby's and had a drink. We stayed until they kicked us out, and then he kissed me." My lips tingle as the memory assaults me. I wish I could see James again tonight to remind myself that the perfect kiss wasn't just a dream.

"A kiss? That's it?"

"That's it. But it was perfect. The whole night was, and we're planning on seeing each other again this weekend." James messaged me yesterday and asked if I was free on Friday night. Now we have a date to go to the cinema, and I'm stupidly excited about it because I haven't been out on a proper date in years.

"I'm happy for you, I really am, but even when you finally have a life you're kinda boring. I really should have picked a better friend."

It's my turn to give him the finger, but he shakes his head at me like he's disappointed. I look back down at the test in front of me and start to mark the answers. I'm about to sign the bottom of the sheet when it's ripped out from under my pen, and I end up drawing on the table. "Really?"

"Entertain me. Claire's at her mum's with the girls until bedtime, and I don't have anything to do."

The corner of my lip twitches up. "Okay, let's go."

CHAPTER FOUR

NICOLAI

I can hear Gareth complaining from behind me as I pull myself out of the water to sit on the edge of the pool. I run my hand through my hair to slick it back from my face and watch Gareth as he approaches. When he reaches me, he grabs the edge of the pool and leans his elbows on the side.

"This isn't exactly what I meant, dick. I was thinking maybe a pint and a meal. Or anything that wasn't exercise."

"Swimming isn't exercise, it's relaxing. I thought you might want that tonight." I put my hands behind me and lean backwards, kicking my feet in the water gently.

"Not as relaxing as a pint." He sighs, but as he rests his head on his arms, he closes his eyes, looking more at ease than he did earlier. "At least I should be thankful that it's not a public pool."

I look around at the private pool that I pay to be a member of, and I still don't regret the money it costs. I don't allow myself many luxuries, most of my money going into my savings to pay from future renovations on my house, but this one I am more than happy to indulge in. Public pools drive me insane because they are so busy. I tried with our local pool, but after coming up behind the second group of old ladies chatting, I decided to pay for here. Since I use it mainly at night I rarely see anyone else, so swimming lengths is easy. "You're welcome." I lie back on the tiles and close my eyes, finally feeling cool for the first time in days.

A noise catches my attention, and I open my eyes and look towards the door that leads to the changing room. It takes me a second to see what the noise was but when I spot him, I sit up. Dillon's eyes don't leave mine as he approaches.

"Hi, Mr Morgan."

I raise my eyebrows, and he blushes when he gets what I'm trying to tell him.

"Sorry, Nicolai."

"Hi, Dillon."

Gareth raises his head and looks at Dillon like he's a stranger. He hasn't been over to my house in a while, especially since the girls came along, so he probably doesn't remember that Dillon lives next door to me.

"Hey, Mr Downes."

Gareth's forehead screws up, and I can see the moment that recognition hits him. "Shit, is that you Dillon? I haven't seen you in years."

I shake my head at Gareth. I've spent two years building up to swearing in front of Dillon even though he's an adult, and Gareth jumps straight in there like they used to hang out.

"Yeah, it's me. Are you two just out for a relaxing swim?" Dillon's speaking to Gareth, but his eyes never leave me. I suddenly feel very naked in just my trunks, but if I move to get into the water, it will look strange.

"Yeah, just getting some time off from the kids. Doesn't happen very often so this guy here brought me to the pool ... even though the pub would have been better." I look at Gareth as he speaks and he gives me a strange look, his eyes darting between Dillon and me.

"The pool's nice. Maybe Nicolai knew you would enjoy it better here?"

Dillon finally looks away, and I take the opportunity to slip into the water while they two of them talk, feeling more protected as soon as the water slips up to my neck. "He's pretending not to enjoy himself so ignore him. Anyway, we won't hold you up any longer, Dillon. Enjoy your swim." I smile at him as I push off from the side of the pool and swim quickly to the other side. I want to get straight out and get dressed, but I know that it will look suspicious if I do. I stop at the other side and tread water as I watch Gareth approach. I'm happy to see that Dillon has gone to the steam room that's at the back of the pool area.

As soon as Gareth stops he turns to me. "What the hell was that about? Do you have something going on with your very young neighbour?"

"Fuck off. You know I don't."

"Does he know that? I swear he looked like he wanted to lick you dry. He always did have a thing for you. I forgot he lived next door to you until I saw him just now."

I feel myself shudder at the knowledge that he's probably right. It's wrong on so many levels. Not only is Dillon my neighbour and a former student, but he is also about fifteen years younger than me. I've never looked at him as anything other than a young man that I know, but apparently he doesn't look at me the same way. "The last few times I've spoken to him I've noticed that he's looking at me differently. I think you might be right about him liking me."

"Oh, don't make that mistake, Nic. He doesn't just like you. He wants to eat you alive."

I splash water at Gareth, making sure I cover him entirely before I boost myself out of the pool. I won't be able to relax now so I may as well get out. As I walk to the showers, I can feel a tingle on my back, and I turn to find Dillon standing at the opposite side of the pool watching me leave.

"You sound tired."

I lie back on my bed and balance the phone on my shoulder. After leaving the pool, I took Gareth home and had coffee with him. I knew that it was time to go when Claire walked in with both girls, and they were both having some sort of meltdown. Yeah, that was my goodbye, and I practically ran out of the door and into my car. Now I'm in bed while chatting to James and it's the perfect end to a strange day. "Long day at work, then I went swimming with Gareth."

"Sounds fun, well the swimming does. Work is a necessary evil." James works at a local lawyers office and most of his day is taken up with meetings about wills and estate legislation. He says he likes his job, he just finds it a bit tedious at times.

"You love your job, and you know it. Swimming was great, but I bailed on Gareth when both his kids went into meltdown." I decide to leave out Dillon turning up. As much as it would be interesting to get James' take on the whole thing, I don't know him well enough to talk to him about Dillon. It wouldn't be fair on Dillon no matter how strange he was acting.

"See, that's why I don't want kids. I panic when the screaming starts." He laughs, and I relax into the mattress more at the sound. There's something very calming about listening to James, something that settles me.

"I had enough screaming when my brother was born. And I don't think he's stopped having temper tantrums since then." I laugh at my own joke knowing that if Andrei were here, he would have me pinned to the ground so he could give me a dead arm. He might be younger than me, but he got his build off our dad, which means he's enormous.

"I'm sure you're lying about that."

"I suppose Andrei isn't that bad, for a younger brother." I smile as I talk about him because now I'm not lying. Andrei is probably the best brother anyone could ever have. He's supported me throughout my entire life, even when I was a scrawny teenager and couldn't stick up for myself. There are only eighteen months between the two of us so we pretty much grew up together, but we couldn't be any more different as children. He was larger than me all my life, and when I was into experiments and reading, you would always find Andrei playing football or rugby. It's probably why I got bullied so much. I was the geeky Morgan brother, but whenever Andrei found out it was happening, he'd make sure it stopped.

"So, I have a question."

"That doesn't sound ominous in the slightest." I try to sound like my heart hasn't just suddenly skipped a beat at his statement, but I feel nerves spreading through my body as I wonder what the question is.

"Sorry, it's nothing bad. I was just wondering why you and your brother both have such unusual names. I mean, you don't exactly look Russian, but I might be wrong."

Relief has me laughing at James. I've spent my life explaining my name, and I'm surprised it took so long for him to ask. It's usually one of the first things people want to know. "My mum is a huge fan of War and Peace. She told me she got so ill when she was pregnant with me that she was confined to bed for most of it, so she read the book. She named me after one of the characters in it, so when my brother came along, she said she had no option but to name him after one of the others in the book."

"I imagined many answers to that question, but honestly, that was nowhere on my radar."

"What can I say, my mother is a character."

"And so are you apparently." James finds his words hilarious because he bursts out laughing and I end up laughing right along with him. His sense of humour is strange but infectious. "Your mum sounds fun."

"She really is. She's the complete opposite of my dad but the two of them together just work. Mum is more freethinking and fluid, dad is a bit rigid, but both of them love my brother and me fiercely. Mum is the kind of parent who would turn up at the door of someone who was picking on Andrei or me and demand something be done."

"Don't mess with mama bear."

I think back to the times I thought my mum might go full-on Frank Bruno with another parent. She didn't ever care about what anyone thought of her. Her only concern was her family and what happened to them. Her attitude rubbed off on me though, and I will be forever thankful to her because it made coming out a lot easier. "You don't know the half of it."

"I'm glad you had a family that would go to war for you, not many people have that." James sounds sad, and I have the urge to reach out and hold him. If only he was here just now and not just on the phone.

"Didn't you have that?" James is silent, and I wonder if I've asked a question that he isn't happy to answer. "I'm sorry, you don't need to tell me anything."

"No, it's fine. I'm an only child so I don't know what it was like to have a sibling. I did have a lot of cousins that lived close though. I have one cousin, Amy, and we were almost like siblings. There are only a few months between us, so we grew up close. It was nice, but truthfully, I was always happy to go home alone when the fighting started."

"Oh, the fighting is the worst. At least you could escape it occasionally." I don't have a large extended family, a few cousins on each side but we don't live near them, so my immediate family has always been the most important thing to me.

"It used to drive me insane until I didn't have it any longer."

I swallow loudly but stay quiet because I honestly don't know what to say. I knew this wasn't a happy memory for James, but he had seemed willing to talk about it. We've barely known each other for five days, and it's not the deep conversations I usually have so quickly. That's what it's like with James though, nothing seems to be off-limits, and we end up speaking for hours most nights. I think I know more about him than my last two boyfriends and I spent months with both of them. James is easy to talk to, and I find myself wanting to tell him things that I probably shouldn't.

James starts speaking before the silence draws out too long. "My mum and dad split up when I was ten. My mum moved us both here, and I had to leave all my family behind. I still saw my dad for the holidays and things, but my cousins grew up without me so when I did see them it was great, but I didn't really know them. The only one I speak to regularly is Amy, but even then it's only a few times a month."

"I'm sorry." It sounds dumb, but I can't think of anything else to say to him. What do you say to someone who just told you how sad his life had become as a kid? I can't imagine how he felt, so I can't offer him anything other than how sorry I am.

"Wow. I brought that conversation down didn't I? Let's change the subject before you think I'm too depressing to be around."

"Never, but I'm all for making you sound a bit happier. Tell me what can I do to make you happy?"

James groans loudly, and it stirs my dick into action. I imagine that's what he sounds like as he pushes into my body, and god I suddenly want to experience that sooner rather than later. "You're a tease, Nicolai. You can't say things like that when I'm trying to be good and romance you."

I close my eyes and imagine what he looks like lying there in bed. Does he wear boxer shorts or does he sleep naked? He would look sexy as sin either way, and I know that one day soon I need to see him in all his glory. "What if I don't want to be romanced? What if I have another idea?" My voice has dropped to a husky whisper, and my dick is fully hard with the ideas running through my head.

"Nicolai."

James only says my name, but my dick reacts as though he whispered a hundred dirty words into my ear. I groan as I reach down and grab my dick, holding it tightly to try and ease the ache in it.

Suddenly my bedroom light goes on, and I close my eyes against the brightness.

"What the fuck, bro?"

My brother's voice acts like cold water to my libido, and I hear James shouting from the mobile I dropped. I pick it up quickly and speak into it. "I'm sorry, James. That annoying little brother I told you about has dropped in. I need to go."

James chuckles, and I'm glad that he finds this whole thing amusing. I would hate for him to feel I want to get rid of him just because my brother turned up. "Sounds like he found something interesting. I have to say I'm a little jealous."

I groan again, but because my brother is still standing in the middle of my room, I move on quickly. "You're mean. Maybe I will show you next time what he found."

"And who's being mean now? I'll speak to you tomorrow, sexy. Sleep well."

I say goodnight to James and hang-up, glaring at my brother the whole time. Just as I press the disconnect call button, Andrei leaves my room and heads down the hall. Fucker. He could have done that while I was saying good night to James. Throwing my mobile on my bed, I stalk out of my room and towards my kitchen where I find my annoying little brother making himself a coffee.

"Where's that creamer stuff you love so much?"

"It's hidden because you like to drink it."

He looks at me over his shoulder before turning to the little cupboard above my cooker and opening it. He grabs the creamer and pours far too much into his coffee. "You need a better hiding place."

"Noted. Now, wanna tell me why you're here so late?"

He grabs his mug and walks to the small kitchen table where he takes a seat. I stare at him for a few seconds before joining him. Andrei plays with the mug in his hand, and his silence is not like him at all.

"Okay, so you have me sufficiently worried. Want to tell me what's wrong?"

"I need your help."

"Anything. You know that." I don't know what Andrei could need from me, but whatever it is I will give it to him if I can. He spent his life helping me so I owe him.

"Can I borrow some money?" He doesn't look at me when he asks, and his cheeks redden with embarrassment.

I reach out and still his hands that are still messing with his mug. "Andrei, talk to me."

He finally looks up, and when he does, he doesn't have the usual cocky glint in his eye that I'm used to. Instead he looks worried, and with dark circles around his eyes, he looks like he hasn't slept in a few days. "I made a mistake, and I need to make it right before I get into trouble."

This isn't like my brother. He's always so careful with everything he does. He has a sensible head on his shoulders, and he's usually the one helping me sort out my problems, so this change of roles scares me. "Andrei, spit it out."

"I loaned one of my employees some money, and he did a runner. Now I don't have enough to cover the wages this month, and with the tax year just starting, I can't touch any of my savings yet."

My stomach drops as he explains everything. That sounds like my brother. He's always willing to help people no matter what they ask, but I'm so fucking angry that someone took advantage of him. "How much are you short?"

"Five grand. I know it's a lot of money, and you might not have it, but I don't want to have to ask mum and dad unless I have no other option. You know how mum worries about us."

Yeah, asking our parents isn't what he wants. Mum would want to go after the worker who bailed with his money, and dad would lecture him about trusting someone with that sort of cash. Dad's life happens in black and white, there's only wrong or right, and this would be classed as very wrong. He wouldn't look down on Andrei for trying to help, but he would be disappointed that Andrei didn't take measures to protect himself. "I can get you the money, but it will take a few days. I'll need to move it out of my savings, and it takes two working days to clear."

"Thanks, Nicky. You don't know how much this is saving my

arse." He looks back down at the table, but I can see the tension leaving his shoulders.

"Hey, look at me."

He does, and I prod him in the forehead as I speak, just like I used to when I was a kid.

"I love you, you stupid idiot. I'm always here if you need me. Are you listening? Always."

This gets a smile from Andrei, and it finally meets his eyes. I return one before stealing the coffee from his hands.

"But this is my coffee creamer. Touch it again, and I break your fingers."

His laughter follows me as I get up from the table and walk away.

CHAPTER FIVE

NICOLAI

It's finally Friday, and I get to see James tonight. This week has dragged by, and even though we've spoken nearly every night, it's not the same as actually seeing him. I've been standing at my front window for almost twenty minutes waiting on James arriving, even though it's still five minutes before I'm expecting him. I'm so excited to see him that I've been ready for nearly an hour, proving that I'm turning into a desperate guy when it comes to James. I hear a car coming up my quiet street, and I'm practically hanging out the window when a familiar dark BMW pulls in behind my Honda. Before he even has a chance to get out of the car, I'm racing for the front door. I would feel embarrassed about my eagerness, but when I reach James halfway to my house, he cups my face and pulls me in for a kiss. He lingers on my lips, and I sigh into his mouth as his familiar taste covers my tongue.

"God, I missed you. I don't know how that's even possible, but I did."

His words are whispered against my lips, and I nod but don't speak. To reply would mean I need to stop kissing him and I'm not willing to do that.

A cough from behind has us pulling apart like our parents have caught us. I see Dillon standing on the pavement as he stares at James. The staring stretches on, and the whole encounter starts to become awkward. I'm not sure what's happening right now, but I know I need to do something to stop it.

I kiss James lightly on the lips. "I'll just be a minute. Get in the car, and I will be there soon." I turn away when James gets into the driver's seat so I'm facing Dillon. "What's up, Dillon?"

"Sorry to interrupt ...*that* ... but I was wondering if you've seen my cat? I haven't seen him since last night, and I'm a bit worried."

I didn't even know Dillon had a cat and I certainly haven't seen one hanging around. "Sorry, I don't think I have. What does it look like?"

"It's a tabby with a blue collar."

He looks sad, and I feel bad for him, the weirdness from a few minutes ago completely forgotten about. I remember having a cat growing up, and I loved that bundle of fur more than all my friends. I couldn't imagine him going missing and not knowing where he was. "Hopefully he'll come home tonight, if not I will help you look for him tomorrow. I need to get going, or I will be late for my date, but tomorrow, okay?"

His face lights up, and I like the fact he doesn't look upset now. "Thanks, Mr Morgan."

I don't bother correcting him this time, eager to get back to James. "You're welcome, but I'm sure he'll turn up soon." I smile and turn away, rushing to the car and getting in. As soon as the door closes behind me, I lean over and kiss James. He laughs against my lips, and we separate.

"I need to get us moving or we're going to miss the movie."

"And that would be such a shame. If that happens, I'm sure we can think of something to do." I wiggle my eyebrows, and James smirks before reversing out of the driveway. I wave at Dillon who's still standing on the pavement. He returns the wave and watches the car as we head down the street.

"Friend of yours?"

"Neighbour and former student."

He nods but doesn't say anything else.

"What?"

James looks over at me a few times as he drives. "I think that maybe he has a thing for you. And I don't think he likes me."

"Well yes, I've been told he might have a small crush on me. But I promise to not run off with him since I barely see him ... also there's the fact that he's almost half my age." I don't mean to sound so defensive, but the whole idea of Dillon being attracted to me creeps me out.

"Hey, I'm not judging. I don't blame the kid, I mean you're kinda nice to look at."

This gets a small smile from me, but I don't reply, not knowing what to say to him. Instead, I think about how great it is to be in James' company tonight. I was worried that seeing each other after speaking all week would be awkward, but there was none of that. From the minute he held me, I felt relaxed and at peace. In my head I know it sounds completely insane, but being in James' arms made me feel at home.

"Did I upset you?"

I turn instantly to face James when his voice brings me out of my head. He looks worried so I reach out to grip his hand. "God no. I'm just... I don't know how to say it without sounding dumb."

"Just say it."

"I like you, like really like you. We've been speaking for less than a week, and I feel I know you better than my last serious relationship. I enjoy your company, and when I call you, I want you there with me. But I know it's too much, and I don't know what to make of it." I don't do insta-love, and I know this isn't what this is, but I can honestly say that I have a serious case of insta-lust. Maybe it's a good thing that James is being the sensible adult and making sure that we don't give in to our urges.

"I like you too. I get what you're saying about being comfortable with each other, talking to you feels easy. You're so fucking sexy too, and that's why I don't want to jump into bed with you. The moment I saw you in that bar I knew I wanted you, and that's why I can't have you. I have a habit of falling into bed with men, and then they vanish. I don't want that with you. I need something real in my life, something long term, and this feels like a good start to that."

My heart swells as he speaks. I get what he's saying about wanting something more than a fuck. Maybe it's because I'm older, or I'm just jaded with the whole hooking up thing, but I want something more, just like James does. I've never felt that instant connection with someone and that's possibly why the whole thing is confusing me. "So, we take it as it comes? If it goes fast, then we go with the flow, or if we want to slow it down at one point, then that's fine too?"

"I think that sounds like a great plan. Let's just enjoy each other. What will happen will happen, and in its own time."

I relax because knowing that James understands what I'm trying to explain means I might not be losing my mind. I think I'm putting too much importance on everything that I'm feeling, and I should chill out about it all and enjoy the ride. "Okay, are we going to go watch this film?"

"Lead me to the popcorn."

We both laugh as we get out of the car, James coming around to my side and taking me by the hand. I try to pretend that the butterflies in my stomach aren't there, but I can't ignore them no matter how hard I try.

I GRIP ONTO THE FRONT OF JAMES SHIRT AND KEEP HIM CLOSE to me. "Can't you come inside for a little while?"

I can feel the vibrations from James' groan resonate through my chest, and it does fantastic things to my dick. "Stop." Even though he tells me to stop, he grips my hair tighter as he licks my lips, tasting the area he just nipped at gently.

We've been standing in the same spot for about twenty minutes now trying to say goodnight, but we're no closer to finally going our separate ways. The whole night's made me feel like a teenager again. From kissing in the cinema to feeding each other ice cream at the café after the film was finished, it's all felt like one long session of foreplay. Now with the prolonged make-out session at the front door, I'm happily stuck back in my younger days. "I'm serious. Just come inside."

"I can't. I need to go home."

I moan in disappointment, but again, I don't let James move away from me. "When can I see you again?"

"Tomorrow?"

My heart jumps with joy that this time tomorrow I'll be back in his arms. "That works for me. Dinner?"

"What do you like to eat and I'll make a reservation."

I smile but keep the dirty reply that's on the tip of my tongue silent. "You come and pick me up. I'll book something for us. You just need to let me know what *you* like to eat." I smirk when James' eyebrows rise slightly.

"I will leave that to your imagination. Behave tomorrow night, and I might come in for coffee after dinner."

Okay, that gets my dicks full attention, making it push painfully against the zip of my jeans as it tries to get closer to James. "I'll be the model of a perfect gentleman, and I'll make sure I have plenty of coffee, so there are no excuses. I had a great time tonight, but you need to leave before I drag you inside and have my wicked way with you."

"Yeah, I'm getting close to saying fuck it to all my good intentions."

"I wouldn't have a problem with that."

"I know you wouldn't, and honestly neither would I. I don't want to rush it though, no matter how much I want to. So goodnight and I'll pick you up tomorrow."

A few kisses later and I let myself into my house as James drives away. My body is thrumming with energy, and I know that I won't be able to sleep. It's late but I know I need to do something or I'm going to be restless all night. I go to my room and search my drawers for my favourite shorts, but they aren't there. I remember wearing them last weekend, but I haven't seen them since. Maybe they've fallen down the back of the machine or something. I don't plan on looking for them tonight so I grab another pair along with a vest and get changed into them before putting my trainers on.

When I'm fully dressed I grab my running earphones from the charger and put them in my ears. I put my mobile on to charge since I don't need it while I'm out, and lock the front door, putting the single key in the small pocket at the back of my running shorts. I take a few minutes to stretch out my muscles so I don't hurt myself, and as Brave by Sarah Bareilles starts playing in my ears, I take off on a gentle jog. I usually start slowly, building up to a run by the time I hit mile two, and I'm in no rush tonight, so I keep my pace gentle. I take my usual route, feeling no need to mix things up when it's later than my usual running time. I usually go first thing in the morning when the heat hasn't built up yet, but tonight is cool enough that I'm still feeling comfortable by the time I hit mile three.

My feet pound against the ground as I let the music in my ears take me away from everything around me. I know the dirt track I'm running on like the back of my hand so I don't need to concentrate, but as the night darkens around me, I decide that I should probably head home. Darkness isn't a hindrance when I hit the pavement at the end of the track, but while I'm running on the dark dirt, the risks are high that I'll trip on something. I turn to the right and head towards the last stretch of track that leads to the gate that will take me to the main street again. I watch the ground closely so I don't end up on my face, but I pick up my pace a little.

About half a mile from the end of the path, I get that strange tingle on the back of my neck again. I look to the side of the track, but there's only darkness around me. I slow my pace as I struggle to see into the shadows of trees around me. I turn the music off and slowly pull the earbuds from my ears, the whole time my eyes are straining to see into the darkness. Tingles erupt all over my skin and I shiver, hating that the feeling is back. It's happening more often now. It used to be just once or twice a month, but it's nearly daily now. A noise comes from the trees to the right of me, and I slow my steps further so I can hear easier. I try to calm my breathing, but whatever had made the noise is gone now. There aren't even the rustles from the trees because the air is still.

I turn in full circles, watching the darkness around me but I'm almost blind in here. The trees are taking away any light the night sky might be giving off, and it's leaving me in shadows that are starting to freak me out. The noise was probably an animal moving in the under-growth, but I can't get my mind to grab onto that idea. No, my mind is squarely in the panicking because I'm being followed mode. I start to back up, keeping my feet light on the ground so I become almost invisible. My eyes still scan the area, and I manage to remain calm for about a minute before my body takes over completely, and I turn and run, putting all the energy I have left into getting to the gate at the end of the walk.

Reaching the gate, I don't even bother to spend the few seconds needed to undo the latch. I just jump, my feet barely clearing the top as I land on the other side. I don't look back as I run again, putting as much distance between the trees and me as I can. It's not until I reach the well-lit street that I slow down to a walk. I struggle to get my panicked breathing under control as my heart tries to exit my body through my throat, and the longer I think about what just happened, the more stupid I feel. I'm a grown man, and I've just about given myself a heart attack, and over what? A noise in a wooded area after midnight. Of course there are going to be noises in the woods. There are hundreds of wild animals living there and most of them probably come out at night. Standing under the bright street-lights, I would put my money on the noise a fox or a badger looking for food in the fallen leaves. Something simple and what did I do? I took off like the devil himself was behind me.

Fuck. I need to get a grip on this paranoia thing. All because I'm getting a strange feeling that I can't explain. Of course that means someone is out there watching me. I'm acting as though my life is so exciting and I'm that gorgeous that someone would spend their time focusing on what I'm doing. I make myself laugh out loud at my crazy mind, and the noise echoes through the silent street. I cover my mouth with my hand to try and block the sound, but it just makes me laugh harder. Oh god, I'm finally losing my mind. I start running again because I need to get home before I get picked up by the police for being a crazy man loose on the streets.

***

BY THE TIME THE HOT WATER HITS MY MUSCLES, I'VE MANAGED to forget about my embarrassing reaction from earlier. My mind is now entirely on James and how fantastic the date was tonight. It'd seemed such a silly thing to do when he asked me to go to the cinema, but I'm so glad we did it. It was like taking a step back in time, apart from I never got to date like that in my teens. I was out by the time I was fifteen, but that didn't mean there was anyone else in my group that I was able to date. What it did mean was my teenage years were spent lusting over hot friends who were only interested in girls. It wasn't until I went to University that I finally got the chance to finally explore.

That means tonight was unique and something that I'll never forget. It also means that I need to make tomorrow night, or that should be tonight now since it's well after midnight, as memorable as I can. I said that it would be a meal, but I want it to stand out from all his other dates. I haven't had anything to compare it to for several years now, but I'm under no illusion that a guy like James has been on a lot of dates. He must be in so much demand with men, so I need to stand out in the crowd.

The smile on my face happens without any real thought. Just having James in my head makes me happy, and when I picture how he looked tonight as he was licking the ice cream from my spoon, it's not just a smile that happens. God, he's so fucking sexy. His eyes were on mine as his tongue slipped out, touching the tip of the spoon before he wrapped those perfect pouty lips around the ice cream. I wasn't sure I would be able to get my brain to work as he moaned while savouring the mouthful of ice-cream, because every spare ounce of blood in my body was heading straight to my dick. That's the state I spent most of the evening in. I don't know if James was being a tease or if he genuinely doesn't know how sexual he is when he does things like that, but I'm happy either way as long as I'm the one that is there to enjoy the sight. And enjoy it I did.

Even now it's the only thing I can picture while I pretend that my dick needs an extra long wash with all the soap I have in my hand. I don't want to be that sleazy guy who jacks off to inappropriate thoughts of someone, so instead, I'm just going to make sure I clean my dick well. Even as my hand slaps against the wet tiles so I don't fall to the floor, or when my eyes pinch shut as my orgasm slams through my body, I still won't admit I just came with visions of James on his knees in my head.

CHAPTER SIX

NICOLAI

I'M SO FUCKING LATE FOR MY DATE WITH JAMES. I SEEM TO HAVE spent the day running behind even though this is the only thing I had planned. I knew that agreeing to help Gareth would be a bad idea, but he begged me to help him out of a bind, so I went over. Little did I know what he actually wanted was for me to look after Libby while he took Clara to the doctor. It wasn't what I had planned for my afternoon, and I was close to telling him that I couldn't do it, but when he looked at me with that sad pathetic face, I just couldn't say no.

So I spent the afternoon looking after Libby and to be fair it wasn't too bad, well apart from when she decided she'd spend an hour styling my hair. I wasn't aware that my short hair could have so many hair bands put in it, but as I stand in front of the mirror trying to get the last of them out, I know it can take at least a dozen. None of that matters though, all that's important right this second is to get these out so I can get ready for James coming over. The last thing I need is for him to see me with my hair sticking up all over the place.

As soon as the last band hits the sink, I'm in the shower and rushing through getting washed. I spent an extra few moments cleaning my body a second time, because if tonight goes the way I want it to, then I'll be naked before the night is out. I turn off the water and grab a towel, wrapping it around my waist as I rush to my room. I'm suddenly thrilled I set out my clothes earlier, so it's now just a case of putting them on and styling my hair. I'm pulling my boxers up my legs when the doorbell goes.

"Fuck." I look at my jeans contemplating whether or not I have time to put them on, but the bell ringing through the house again tells me I don't. I rush down the hall not wanting James to think I've stood him up. As soon as I reach the door, I look through the peephole just to confirm that it is in fact James. I don't want to scare some random human being with my nakedness, but when I see him on the other side of the door looking at his watch, I quickly open it and grab the front of his shirt. I pull him into the house and slam the door behind him.

James' eyes are wide with shock, but when he registers that I'm standing there in just my boxers, they go even wider.

"I'm sorry. I'll be five minutes, and we can leave." I don't wait for a response before I turn and rush back to my room. I wonder if James will be upset at the way I greeted him. Oh well, there's nothing I can do about that now. I just need to get dressed and get out to my abandoned date.

Nearly precisely five minutes later I walk back into the living room and find James looking at the pictures on my main living room wall. He turns in my direction, and the smile he gives me makes my stomach tremble with butterflies. God, I'm in my thirties and I'm standing here with stupid butterflies like this is my first love.

"Glad to see that you've decided to get dressed." The side of his mouth quirks up, and it makes him look younger than he usually does. Not that he ever looks old, he looks at least five years younger than me, but tonight he seems playful.

"Ouch. If you prefer me with clothes on, then I'm doing something wrong."

James moves to stand in front of me and puts his hands on my waist. The heat from his palms sears into my skin, and I have a sudden urge to remove my t-shirt so I can feel him properly. "Oh I didn't say I prefer it, but if we're planning on leaving the house at any point, then I think clothes are a good option." He leans forward and kisses me for the first time tonight.

My arms find their way around James' neck, and I lean into his body. I open to him and savour the feeling of his tongue exploring my mouth. All too soon he pulls back, and even though he doesn't stop holding me, his lips aren't on mine, and I miss them.

"Running late were you?"

"Yeah, but blame Gareth." I've mentioned Gareth to James before because it's hard to tell him about my life without talking about Gareth.

"Did he distract you with something shiny?" The smile on his lips takes any possible sting out of his words. I know he's just kidding, and I should answer him, but all I can do is stare at his still wet lips. "Nicolai, did I lose you?"

"Sorry. I was babysitting while he took one of the kids to the doctor." I lean forward to kiss James, but he only lets me brush my lips against his briefly before he pulls away.

"Is everything okay?" There's concern in James' voice, and it shows what a great guy he is. He doesn't even know Gareth or his family, but he's worried about them.

"Everything's fine. Clara has an ear infection because of her teething. Some antibiotics, and probably even less sleep for Gareth, but she'll be back to her normal self in a few days." My answer is apparently enough to ease his mind because when I kiss him again, he lets me have my way.

Unfortunately, the universe is against me kissing James because just as my tongue tangles with his, there's a knock on the door. I groan at the interruption, and James laughs against my lips.

"Popular tonight, aren't you?"

I roll my eyes at his comment. "Two minutes and I promise we leave."

I leave James standing in the middle of the room and head to the door. I don't know what I expect when I open it but what I'm met with is the last thing imaginable. "Dillon?"

Dillon looks up at me just as the first tear rolls down his cheek. "I'm sorry, Mr Morgan. My dad isn't home, and I didn't know where else to go."

My mind goes a little blank as I take in his bloodied face. He has a cut on his head and one under his eye, high up on his cheek. There's blood dripping from both of them, and it's joining with the blood coming from his burst lip. The redness on his cheek looks like it's been caused by a punch and I know that it's going to become a bruise. "Shit, Dillon." I take him gently by the arm and pull him into the house.

James is over as soon as he sees the state that Dillon's in. James tries to offer Dillon help, but when his hand touches Dillon, I feel him flinch in my hold. James must sense it too because he pulls back instantly. He looks at me over Dillon's head, and I can see the concern in his eyes. When we reach the couch I carefully lower Dillon to the seat, his face wincing when he connects with the cushions. My heart aches as I wonder what other injuries he has that I can't see. I kneel in front of Dillon and take a good look at him now he's at eye level. He is a complete mess, and my heart aches for him. He is such a young, lonely guy but tonight he also looks broken and sad, and like he needs someone to help him.

"Can you get the first aid box from the bathroom. It's the second door on the left down the hall. You'll find it under the sink."

James nods as he does as I ask, vanishing quickly down the hall where I directed him.

"What happened, Dillon?"

He looks up at me, and I can see more tears building in his eyes. "They just came out of nowhere." He goes quiet again when James returns with the first aid box and passes it to me.

I place it on the couch next to Dillon's leg and open it up, taking out one of the small gauze pads that are in there. I place it gently against the cut on his forehead since it's the worst, and press down to stop the bleeding. "Who came out of nowhere? Who did this?"

Dillon doesn't speak, and his eyes flicker towards James before he looks down at his hands. James must see him because he puts a hand on my shoulder.

"I think I'll go and leave you to it."

I reluctantly stand as James heads to the door. I don't want him to go, but I think we both know that tonight isn't going to happen. I follow him onto the front step before pulling him close, needing to hold him one last time. "I'm sorry."

James cups my face and pulls me into a gentle kiss. "It's fine. Today is just your day to play the hero." He turns to look at Dillon. "Do you think he'll be okay?"

"I don't know. I better go, and thank you for understanding."

James kisses me deeply, and I rise on my toes to get closer to him. I love the fact that he's slightly taller than me. It makes me feel like he could take control of me any time he wished, and I really want that.

I pull back because he's making me hard and the last thing I need is an erection when I'm going back to deal with Dillon. "I'll call you later."

James' lips brush mine one last time before he's disappearing down the steps to his car. I watch him go, and all I want to do is rush after him, but a noise from behind me makes me remember that Dillon needs me right now.

I close the door and return to my position on the floor in front of Dillon. I use more gauze and wipes to clean up his face as we speak. "Okay, it's just us now. Want to tell me what happened?"

"I was out, and this group of guys were just there. They shouted at me, but I ignored them and walked away. They wouldn't leave me alone ... and they ... they..." He starts crying, and I put my hand on his shoulder to comfort him. I can only imagine what he went through. He's such a young guy, and I have a feeling that his dad is away more than he lets on. He must be lonely, and I never see him with anyone. There's never any friends or family.

"I think we should call the police and maybe go to the hospital." I clean the blood from his cheek but stop when his eyes open in panic.

"Not the police."

His response confuses me. He was attacked so you would think he would want the people that did it caught. I know I would. "Why?"

"I just don't want the police." He goes to stand, and I use my hand to keep him where he is.

"Fine, no police. But how about the hospital?" I'm hoping that he'll go for getting treatment. His cuts don't look too bad, and I could probably deal with them myself, but if a doctor sees him, they might report his injuries to the police. I don't know if his attack embarrassed him or something, but I would like it reported to someone.

"I'm fine. I just ... didn't want to be alone." He looks at his hands again, and I shake my head. I want him to be seen by a professional, but I can't force him, he is an adult after all. No matter what, there's also no way I will ask him to leave. He might be an adult, but he's young and alone. I couldn't live with myself if I told him to go home alone.

I stare at his face as I apply two small butterfly strips to the cut on his eyebrow. He stares at me as I work slowly and my eyes keep flickering to his. "Is this okay?"

"Yeah."

I take another strip and start working on the cut on his cheek, trying to focus on that and not his eyes that feel like they're burning into my skin. This is probably the closest I've been to Dillon at any time, and it's strange.

"Thank you, Mr Morgan."

I look at him once I put the last strip on his cheek. I cleaned up his lip before I started with the strips and since there's no new blood, I leave the cut alone. "You're welcome, but I'm not happy with you not seeing someone like a doctor." I press my fingers against his cheek, and he flinches slightly. "I don't think anything's broken, but I'm not an expert."

"I'll be fine. I don't like hospitals so I'd rather not go."

"How's the pain?"

He touches his cheek, and he sucks in a little breath. "It's not too bad. It hurts, but it isn't unbearable."

I get up from the floor and pick up all the used materials. I close over the first aid kit and add it to the stuff in my hand. "I'm just going to put this in the bin, sit back and relax and I'll be back." I head to the bathroom to return the first aid kit and put the used stuff in the bin. I wash my hands and dry them before grabbing my mobile from my back pocket. Now that I know Dillon's not seriously injured I wish James had stayed. We could have probably still made dinner, but even as I think it, I know there'd be no way I would leave Dillon alone now. I take a minute to type out a message to James before I grab some ibuprofen and head to the kitchen to get some water.

Sorry again for tonight. I will make it up to you very soon. Call soon x

I smile as I put the kiss at the end of the message. It's a small thing but means a lot. The first time James replied with the kiss I felt like I was walking on air the rest of the day. I think that I'm connecting with James in a different way than usual, something deeper, and I love it. I've known him about two weeks, but it feels like months. The easiness between us makes me think that I knew him in a previous life, like I was meant to meet him in this one. I'm trying not to act like an impulsive person, to not fall for him in an inappropriately short amount of time, but James makes it hard to keep that resolution. Gorgeous, smart, funny, and kind, he's everything I'm looking for in a guy. Part of me wishes we had met when I was a lot younger so that we could have spent years together already.

I laugh as I grab a bottle of water from the fridge so Dillon can take the painkillers. I'm trying to talk myself out of falling further into lust with James, and here I am, wishing we'd been together for years. I would like to say I had my emotions and hormones under control, but I think it's clear even to myself that I don't. I hope I don't fuck this thing up because it's going to hurt if James leaves.

Walking into the living room, I take a seat next to Dillon on the couch. I hand him the water and ibuprofen, and he swallows them without any complaint.

"I'm sorry I ruined your night."

"You didn't ruin, just delayed. It's not like you planned on being hurt." I feel my mobile vibrate in my pocket and I take it out, smiling as I read James' words.

You owe me big time, and I will hold you to that. I hope everything's okay and your neighbour isn't too hurt. Missing you x

Oh god. Goosebumps explode over my arms as I read that he misses me. How is it possible to have this reaction when he isn't here? It shouldn't be possible, but it's something I can't ignore.

"I miss you too. It's only been one night, but it feels too long. Dillon is fine, refuses to go to the hospital or call the police, but going to let him sleep here the night to make sure he's okay. Xx

"Is he your boyfriend?"

I look up at Dillon and realise I've been ignoring him. I put my phone on the table in front of me and give him my full attention. "I'm not sure of the official title, but I like him."

Dillon bites the uninjured side of his mouth and looks at his hands. The silence feels strained, but I don't know what to say to him. I don't know him, but he's no longer my student so maybe I should. I know Mrs Corbis, who lives in the house on the other side of me, so being friends with Dillon wouldn't be strange. I haven't taught him in over two years, and I don't think people would frown at a friendship now.

"When does your dad get home?"

"Isn't that the million dollar question? I don't know. He isn't home much these days, and any time I see him, it's a shock."

That has to be so lonely for someone as young as Dillon. Truthfully, it would be lonely for anyone. I always remember thinking that he was home alone far too much for a kid, and apparently, nothing has changed on that front. "Why do you stay at home then? Couldn't you get a dorm room or share with a friend?"

"I don't have many friends, and staying at home saves money."

I suddenly wish I'd picked up a beer when I was in the kitchen, not so much to drink, but to give me something to do with my hands as we speak. I'm a natural fidget and having nothing to do with my hands is making me feel awkward. "A young guy like you should have tons of friends. Isn't college the time when you should be out there and sleeping with all the ladies?" Oh god, I just sounded like my dad, and that's not a good thing. Actually, I'm pretty sure that is something he said to me.

"I ... uh..." He takes a deep breath, and I worry a little about what he's about to say. "You do know I'm gay, Mr Morgan?"

CHAPTER SEVEN

NICOLAI

I KNOW MY MOUTH HAS TO BE HANGING OPEN AT HIS confession. Never once had I thought about Dillon being anything other than straight, in fact, I never thought of him being straight either. Gareth and James have mentioned him having a crush on me, but I never thought past them being crazy. "Nicolai." It's stupid to correct him about my name, but I don't know what else to say to him.

"Sorry, Nicolai."

I nod but still don't comment on him telling me he's gay. I don't know what to say. It doesn't feel like its something I should talk about, even if we do become sort of friends. "Are you enjoying college?" I inwardly cringe at my lame attempt at a subject change.

"It's okay."

"Wow, that good?"

He laughs, and he flinches when his cut re-opens a little. "It's college I suppose, not exactly anything to write home about. I just want to be done with it so I can get on with life. I want to be done with this part."

"What part?"

"The being talked down to part. People seem to think that I don't know anything because I'm young, but I know what I want. I want to get to the place where people stop seeing me as a young kid. I want people to see me for who I really am." His eyes never leave mine as he speaks.

"It'll happen one day." I don't know what else to say to him, but I'm saved from thinking of something when my phone beeps. I pick it up and open the message from James, a smile on my lips before I even read his words.

Make sure you lock your bedroom door, you don't want to wake up beside him ;) Don't mind me, I'm just jealous of him. You better call before you go to sleep, I need to make sure your virtue is still intact. X

"Thank you again for tonight."

I turn my attention back to Dillon who's now getting up from the couch. Standing, I get in front of him before he has a chance to move any more. "Stay here the night." It comes out more like a statement. "I mean, I would be worried about you all night if you went home. Your dad isn't there so you won't have anyone to keep an eye on you."

Dillon's cheeks go red even though it's difficult to see under the darkening bruise on his face. "Are you sure? I don't want to overstay my welcome."

"It's fine. Come on, and I'll show you to the spare room." I lead the way, pointing out the kitchen and bathroom on the way to my second bedroom. Thankfully the sofa bed in there is easy to pull out and make up, and in five minutes I'm standing at the door to the room saying goodnight to Dillon. "My room is just over there if you need anything. Hope you sleep well." I smile before closing the door and heading to my room.

Even though I usually sleep with my door open, James' message comes back to me, and I quietly close my door behind me. I tell myself it's to give Dillon a bit more privacy, but I have a feeling that it's not. I strip off my t-shirt as I walk to the ensuite and close that door behind me as well. I get my phone from my pocket and press James' number. It rings twice before he answers.

"Hey, sexy."

I lean my back against the door and slip down until I'm sitting on the tiled floor. "Hey."

"How's everything?"

I lean my head back and close my eyes, suddenly feeling very tired. "I'm tired. I set Dillon up in the spare room because his dad isn't home and I don't want him alone. I swear that kid spends about eighty percent of his life alone."

"That's sad. Luckily he has a kind and sexy neighbour to help him."

I laugh, but the memory of Dillon's gaze comes back to me. I wouldn't say he looked in love with me, but I wouldn't say the look was completely platonic. "Well, this sexy neighbour wishes that he wasn't alone tonight. I miss you."

"You'll see me soon enough. I had a feeling that maybe Dillon didn't want me there, that he would be more relaxed if I left."

He's right. Dillon had relaxed as soon as James left and I don't blame him. Dillon doesn't know James, so to trust him after he was hurt would be asking a lot of him.

"I think he was a little in shock."

"Did he tell you what happened?"

"He only said that a group of guys jumped him and he didn't want to go to the police. I was worried he would take off if I pushed him too hard, so I left it."

There's a silence between us, and I enjoy knowing that he's on the other end of the telephone. It's not quite as good as having him here, but it's better than having no contact at all. I've come to rely on these nightly chats, and I use them as a way to get through some tedious days.

"Sooooo ... whatcha wearing?"

Laughter bursts out of me before I get a chance to stop it. "My jeans, so slightly more than earlier."

He groans, and I feel the vibrations of it over my skin like he's right next to me. "I never got a chance to tell you earlier how much I like you in just your underwear."

"It's not really how I'd planned on getting almost naked with you."

There's that groan again, and this time it spreads over my skin and ends in my balls. "God, I want to get you naked."

He's killing me. "Why are you doing this to me? The one night I can't have you over you decide to get frisky. Why do you hate me so much?"

"I don't hate you. I like you a lot in fact. I like you enough to tell you that the next time I see you I want to get you naked and see how good your body tastes."

My dick pushes painfully against the front of my jeans, and I have to straighten my legs to try and ease some of the discomfort. "James, why are you doing this to me?" I know my voice sounds breathy, but I don't care. He's making me feel like my body is heating to the point of combustion, and I want him to know it.

"Because I'd hoped tonight would be the night I would come in when I dropped you off. Seeing you in those tight little boxer shorts just confirmed how much I wanted you. You're really fucking sexy, Nicolai."

I'm practically panting as I listen to him. It's been far too long since I slept with someone, especially someone I wanted as much as James. The last guy I was with was after a drunken night out, and I can't remember much about it. "James."

"I wanted to strip those boxers off you and see what you looked like completely naked."

I slip my free hand down to my jeans and undo the top button and zip, pulling the edges of the denim apart and down slightly over my hips. It eases the ache in my dick slightly, but what really helps is when I press my hand against the front of it.

"Did you just touch yourself?"

I'm past the point of caring, and even though I know I'll be embarrassed about it later, I'm honest with him. "Yes."

"I wish I was there to see you do it, to see how you look when you are so turned on."

I'm about to answer when a knock comes through the bathroom door. I jump at the sudden noise and drop my phone.

"Nicolai?"

Shit, shit, shit. I grab my phone, and I hear James laughing. "I need to go."

"It's becoming a bit of a habit you getting caught with your dick in your hand."

"Fuck off. I'll speak to you tomorrow."

"Yes you will. Have pleasant dreams, sexy."

I groan at the huskiness in his voice, but I'm smiling by the time I hang up, James' laugh still in my ear. I take a deep breath and do up my zip and button. I tuck my still very present erection into my waistband and hope it's enough to hide it since I left my t-shirt in my room. Opening the door slightly I use it to hide as much of my body as I can without being obvious. "Everything alright, Dillon?"

"I was just wondering if you had any paracetamol. My head still aches a bit, and I can't get to sleep."

"Yeah, of course." I go to the medicine cabinet on the bathroom wall behind me and search through the contents until I find the tablets. I turn and squeak when I find Dillon standing right behind me. I hold out the bottle, and he takes it, his fingers brushing against mine as he does.

"Thanks." He doesn't move, and I can't get past him without us touching far too much.

"You're welcome. I'm going to go to bed now."

He stares at me for a few moments, and my hands twitch to move him out of the way. I feel awkward around Dillon sometimes, and the last few times I've been around him, I've noticed that he isn't exactly the boy I thought I knew. He was always the quiet kid who got pushed around a lot, but now I can see something else in his eyes. I'm not sure how to explain it, but sometimes he looks ... different. "Goodnight, Nicolai."

I nod at him as he leaves the bathroom and then my room. I continue to stand in the same spot once he's gone, wondering what the hell just happened. It was strange, almost like he was waiting for permission for something, I just don't know what that something was. Shaking my head, I go through to my bedroom, closing the door before taking off my jeans and collapsing on my bed. On second thought I get out of bed and put on a pair of shorts and a vest, deciding that I should be more covered up since I have a guest staying.

I FEEL LIKE I'VE JUST FALLEN ASLEEP WHEN THE SOUND OF movement has me stirring. I don't fully wake up to begin with, but a thud makes my eyes open. I blink a few times to try and clear my vision, and I find myself facing my bedroom window. The window is open, and the curtains are blowing in the warm breeze, but there's no way it was that that woke me. Rolling onto my back, I stretch my arms above my head, scanning the room while I do, but I can't see the source of the noise and nothing looks out of place. I sit up and twist until my legs are over the side of the bed. I run my hand over my stubble, groaning when I think about shaving for work tomorrow. That's a problem for later. Right now I want coffee and a shower, but first I need to brush my teeth.

Leaving my en-suite after getting rid of my morning breath, I'm just entering my room again when the bedroom door catches my attention. I know I closed it last night, but now it's standing wide open. I wonder if Dillon needed something while I was asleep? *Shit, Dillon.* I completely forgot he was here. I'm about halfway to the door, so I can check on him when I kick something, and it rolls under my bed. I curse up a storm as pain radiates through my toes. When the pain eases a little I get down on my knees to try and find what I kicked, but whatever it was has rolled right to the back corner, and it's sitting in the darkness. I reach my hand under to try and grab the item, but the doorbell goes, and I give up so I can answer it.

I take a second to pop my head into the spare room to see if Dillon is there, but the room is empty. Voices catch my attention, and I head towards them to see what's happening. When I walk around the corner into the living room, I see Dillon standing with his arms crossed over his chest, and he's scowling at James. In that second, the whole world fades away and all I can see is James' bright smile as he looks at me.

"Good morning, sexy." His eyes move slowly over my body, and I'm now very aware of how little clothes I'm wearing. It's enough to hide my modesty, but it's revealing enough that I know James will be getting a good view of what could be his.

"I'm going to head home, unless you need me to stay."

My eyes barely flicker to Dillon as he stands there. "Are you feeling well enough to be on your own?" I finally look in his direction and see that his face is a lot more bruised than it was last night. I really should ask him to stay, but truthfully, there's nothing I can do for him now. His paper stitches are holding his cuts together, and there are no broken bones, or he would know about it.

"Yeah, I'm good." He looks like he wants to say something else, but he stays quiet. "Thanks for last night."

"You're welcome. If you need anything, you know where I am."

He nods and leaves, closing the front door behind him.

"And finally we're alone." James walks towards me, and it takes everything in me not to run to him. When he stands in front of me, I give in to my need to touch him and place my hands on his chest. I rub my thumb back and forward, moving them over his muscles so I can feel them under my fingertips.

"Finally."

It's James that kisses me, but I only let him have control for a few moments before I take over. We kiss for what feels like hours, my tongue enjoying its exploration of James' mouth, and when we pull apart, I'm struggling to breathe. "Fucking perfect."

"What do you want?" I'm hoping James is on the same page as me about what he wants, but there is no way that I'm about to take it for granted that he wants to take the next step. Nothing happens until he makes it clear to me that we are moving on.

"I want you."

"I need more than that."

James' hand slips under the waistband of my shorts and grips my hard on. The moan that slips from my mouth is loud and full of need, and thankfully James is there to catch me as I melt into his arms. "I want you, Nicolai."

"Yeah, okay." His touch is making my brain misfire, and I'm struggling to find my words.

"Show me your bedroom or I'm gonna fuck you against this wall."

The words are whispered into my ear on a growl, and they don't help me to function. I'm torn between actually showing him my room or just letting him take me where we stand. It's only when he lets me go that I decide my bedroom is the better option. My bed is in there, and I want to see James in it.

Grabbing his hand, I practically drag him down the hall behind me. As soon as we reach my room, he pulls me back and spins us until my back hits the wall just inside the door. I grunt when my back connects with the wall, but James swallows the noise with his lips as he takes whatever he wants. His mouth falls from mine and works its way down my neck and out over my collarbone, his tongue coming out to taste me as he moves my top out of the way. "I want you naked."

I have no problem with that, and as he steps back, I start working on my clothes. Thankfully I don't have to tell him to strip, and since he has more clothes on than me, I get to watch him finish the job. My mouth waters as more and more flesh comes into view. He's always worried about his appearance, continually telling me not to expect too much from his body, but holy shit he's beautiful. His chest and arms are toned and sexy, his stomach slightly softer looking but not any less perfect. His chest has a fine coating of hair, and my fingers twitch with the need to touch him. I want to caress every single part of him, and not just with my hands. I want to run my tongue over his skin and see if he shivers like my imagination wants.

All thought flies from my head as he drops his underwear to the ground. *Holy shit.* James might not be the largest guy I've ever seen, but damn, his dick is as gorgeous as the rest of him. Hard and thick, and pointing straight at me. I can't wait to have it in me.

I don't notice at first that James has moved, my focus fully on his dick, and it's only when his fingers brush against my cheek that I finally look up at him. "Do you still want me?" He seems worried, like I might turn him away at any second. Is he insane?

"Of course I still want you. Fuck me, James. You're stunning."

His cheeks get red, and I lean forward to kiss him. I don't know who in his past told him he was anything less than perfect, but it's time for me to show him just how much he turns me on.

CHAPTER EIGHT

NICOLAI

"Morning." I let the staff room door close behind me as I make my way to the coffee machine on the back table. There are a few teachers putting stuff in their assigned lockers, but it's Gareth that I'm talking to. I pour coffee into my travel mug before heading to the table where Gareth is and sitting down. As soon as my arse hits the seat, I wish I'd just left and gone to my classroom.

"You got laid."

I can feel my cheeks burn with embarrassment as a few heads turn in my direction. "Shut up, Gareth."

He laughs, and I want to punch him in the mouth. Instead, I get up and leave the staffroom, heading straight to my classroom like I should have done in the first place.

I'm barely inside for a minute before the door opens behind me. I don't look away from my task of writing today's assignment on the whiteboard.

"So are you gonna spill?"

I cap the pen and put it on my desk before taking a seat behind it. I pick up my cup and take a long drink while keeping eye contact with Gareth.

"Oh for fuck's sake, just tell me you got laid."

"Who said I did?" I have no idea how he managed to guess, especially since he managed it after looking at me for roughly three seconds.

"I know you did, I can tell. You look ... satisfied. So tell me, how was your man?"

I swear Gareth is nosier than anyone else I know. He always wants far too many details on anything that happens, even my sex life. "Let's just say I'm smiling today for a reason."

"So is he *the one*?"

"I don't know, but I know that I want him to be the one for now." I lean back in my chair and know I have to be smiling like a crazy person. I can't help it when my mind goes back to yesterday and all I can think is how amazing it was.

Gareth holds up his hands in front of himself and shakes his head at me. "No, stop with all the details. It's just too much."

I pick up the whiteboard eraser and throw it at Gareth, hoping to hit him in the head, but he catches it out of the air and grins at me. "I'm not giving you details on the sex, but we spent the whole day together just chilling, and it was the best Sunday I've had in a very long time." Thinking back to lounging all afternoon in bed with James makes me want to go back in time and do it all over again. Sex had left my body completely used and drained in the best possible way, so we ordered in Chinese and lay in bed eating it.

I thought the first time with James was earth-shattering, but he proved that it could only get better. Every time he touches me, it's like my body responds quicker than before. The last time we made love it was slow and drawn out, James only taking me over the edge into orgasm when he was ready. I honestly thought I might never recover from that last one, because I came with such an intensity, that I was sure I wouldn't be able to get hard again. I was wrong in that assumption though because thinking about James this morning in the shower showed me I could get hard again very easily.

"Sunday? He stayed all night and day?"

"Oh, Saturday night never happened."

Gareth looks confused so I sit up so I can tell him all about Dillon.

"Dillon turned up at my door covered in cuts and bruises. He'd been attacked and didn't have anyone else to help him."

I thought Gareth would be utterly sympathetic to Dillon and I'm a little shocked when he looks suspicious. "And you just happened to be the only person who could help him?"

"Um ... his dad is out of town again."

He nods his head, but the suspicious air never leaves him.

"What?"

"I just think that it's convenient that he gets hurt and none of his friends could help, or maybe the police."

I'm still trying to work out why he looks the way he does, and the more he talks, the more confused I get. "He says he doesn't have many friends."

"I'm sure he doesn't. And what about the police? The hospital?"

"He didn't want to go to the police and hospitals scare him. What do you mean about him having no friends?"

Gareth bites his lip and stares at me, almost like he's trying to decide what to say. When he chooses to speak, I almost wish he hadn't. "Haven't you noticed he's a little strange? I mean he's always polite and smiling when you're around, but when I had him in his final year, he barely said two words the entire time."

"So he's shy. It's not like there's anything wrong with that." I'm being defensive, but it's not because I am defending Dillon. The reason is I don't want to listen to Gareth because part of what he's saying makes sense.

"You know it has nothing to do with him being shy. I've told you before he has this weird thing for you, and this will encourage him."

"What was I meant to do, send him home alone while he was bleeding? I had to put his face back together, and I didn't think he should be alone." My agitation gets enough that I get up from my seat and go back to the whiteboard. I start to write out more of today's tasks but turn back to face Gareth abruptly. "He might have a little thing for me, but that doesn't mean anything. He's half my age, and I wasn't willing to overlook the fact that he was alone. Should there have been someone else to help him? Yes. But his dad wasn't there, and I refused to send him away."

"I hear what you're saying, and I completely agree, but I also think you shouldn't get too close to your friendly little neighbour. Be honest here, have you seen him be friendly to anyone other than you?"

I think back to all the times I've seen Dillon while I've had company. There was the day at the pool with Gareth. Dillon had seemed to be unhappy with Gareth being there, but I put it down to the shock of them seeing each other after so long. Then with James on Saturday, I think it was more that he was shaken up after what had happened. A group of guys attacked him so being wary around strangers is understandable. "He's just shy." My words don't come out as confident as they should. I want to tell Gareth that he sees something that isn't there, but I'm not so sure.

Gareth gets up from the desk he was leaning against and comes to stand in front of me. With his hands on my shoulders, he looks me square in the eye. "Be careful, that's all I'm saying. Just be careful."

"Hey, sexy. I was calling to say goodnight. I haven't heard from you all day, so I hope you're okay. I miss you. Call me back when you get this, it doesn't matter what time."

I hang up my phone and throw it onto my bed beside me. It's the third time I've tried to call James tonight but there's no answer, and since I haven't spoken to him since he left yesterday, I have a heavy feeling in my stomach. I don't know how long I should keep calling before I get too worried, or give up so I don't look desperate. We spent such a great day together yesterday, and when he left we made arrangements to speak, but his phone just rang out the whole night. I put it down to him being tired and probably falling asleep, but I've also text him today and got nothing in return.

I pick up my phone again and press redial. My stomach churns with butterflies, but it's not the fun kind I usually have when I think about James. Tonight they're caused by nerves and nothing else. As the ringing sounds in my ear, my mind drifts, and it doesn't go anywhere good. I can see James' face, but it isn't how I'm used to seeing it. This time he's laughing at me, a smug smile on his face because he knows he got what he wanted. Is that what this was, was he just playing me to get me into bed? It can't be that because I was willing to sleep with him on the second date and he was the one who resisted.

James' answering machine clicks on again and I listen to his voice for a moment before hanging up. I've left three messages now, and I won't leave any more. I'm not going to be that guy who annoys him if he isn't interested any longer. God, I must have experienced something very different than he did yesterday if he's decided he doesn't want to speak to me again.

Rubbing my hand down my face, I throw my phone down and get off my bed. I'm being dramatic, and I don't like it. It has been barely twenty-four hours since I heard from James and here I am making up shit in my head. He's probably busy at work today, it's happened before, and hasn't had a chance to call yet. I need to do something other than sit here and phone watch. I change my clothes into running gear and grab my running earphones from my charger. I need to get out of the house before I go insane. If I miss James' call, then I'll return it when I get home.

I STARE AT MY PHONE AND WILL IT TO RING. I'VE ALREADY showered after my run, but still, James hasn't returned my call. I refuse to give in to my urge to call again because I don't want to seem desperate, especially if he's busy today. If he looks at his phone and sees thirty-two missed calls, I'm going to come off a little stalkerish. So no, if James wants to call, he's going to have to make the next move. Doesn't mean I won't spend the next few days obsessing over where he is. Shit. I hope it isn't a few days.

Grabbing my satchel, I take out the test papers I should be marking and spread them out over the kitchen table. I need to hand these back to my students in two days, and I haven't even started the corrections. I couldn't face them earlier, but maybe they're exactly what I need to distract myself from the very silent phone that's mocking me from the table.

I'm about to start on my third paper when my front door opens.

"Hey, butt face."

I roll my eyes but feel relief through my body. A visit from Andrei is just what I need tonight. "Hey, fuck nut." I cap my red pen and put it on the table as I turn to face my brother. "What's up?"

He holds up a six-pack of beer and shakes it as he sits across from me. He rips open the box and hands me a bottle. "I know it's a school night, but I'm here to celebrate."

I take the bottle and open it, not mentioning that I don't care if I have work tomorrow, I need a drink. "What are we celebrating?"

"I got a new contract. You're looking at the lead contractor for the High West Shopping Centre."

"Holy shit. That's huge, Andrei." I can't stop smiling at my little brother because he's just landed the most sought-after contract in the area. Building the new ninety million pound shopping centre in the city next to ours is a career-making job. After he's done, the whole country will know the name of his company.

"It's bigger than huge and seriously fucking scary. I can already feel the ulcer starting to grow."

I don't blame him. I feel nervous enough when I go back to school for a new year, and it's the same thing again and again. To have such a huge responsibility on my head would scare the shit out of me. "You'll do great. I will say, you might need a few more men if you are going to build something that size."

"A few more? Shit, I'm going to have to at least triple my workforce."

Andrei's company isn't tiny, but it isn't exactly the size of some of the other companies that put in a tender for the project. "Not that I don't think you're the best man for the job, but how exactly did you get the contract over everyone else?"

"I've worked for one of the project managers before, and he influenced the board a little. I promised I could finish the job on time and within budget, that's all they cared about."

I hold up my bottle and smile when Andrei clinks his against it. "I'm so fucking proud of you, little brother."

He's beaming, and I like to see him like that. The last few months have been worse than crappy for him, and this is hopefully the turning point for him. I won't bring that up because any mention of his ex-fiancé Samantha still makes him flinch in pain. No, it's better to focus on the great news of this new contract and not the cheating bitch that left him for his best friend.

"God, it still feels a little unreal. Nic, I'm building a shopping centre. *Shit, I'm building a shopping centre.*" The colour drains entirely from Andrei's face leaving him looking a little green.

I'm up instantly and rushing around to kneel in front of Andrei, mimicking my position from Saturday night. I shake my head to clear that thought and look at my baby brother. "Not just any shopping centre, the best fucking shopping centre in Britain. Don't talk yourself out of this. We know that even with the small team you have you could do this. Adding men will only speed up the build."

He takes a deep breath and lets it out slowly. It brings a little colour to his cheeks, but he still looks pale. "You think I can do this?"

"I know you can. I might be your big brother, and that means I think you're a little shit, but I think you're a talented little shit. No one could do this job half as good as you, stop stressing yourself. You've got this." It's usually Andrei that talks me off the ledge, so it feels unusual for it to be this way around. His smile lets me know that I've managed to do the job he's an expert at.

"Okay, but I might need you to talk me out of that ulcer at a later date."

"On it. Have you told mum and dad?"

"Yeah. Mum did her usual hyper screaming thing, and dad grunted and told me good job. Was strange getting that much praise from dad."

We both laugh because that's about as much pride dad ever shows. You can tell he supports us in our lives completely, just not in an obvious way. God forbid he should show some emotion. Dad is very old school, and he loves us, he just doesn't show it.

"And while we're talking about the 'rents, mum says if you don't call her soon she's coming to your work to see you."

I don't take that as an empty threat because the last time I didn't call her for a few weeks, she turned up in the middle of my class one day with a Tupperware of spaghetti and shouted at me in front of all my students. That was the last time I left it so long between calls. "Noted, I'll call her tomorrow night."

"I would. I'm still trying to live down her coming to the building site on Northside."

I remember the video that one of Andrei's employees put on his Facebook page. It was of my mum shouting at Andrei while he was standing there in the middle of a building site looking like a five-year-old being scolded by his mum. "But that was so funny."

"Fuck you, Nic. God, can't she be normal?"

"You know it'd be weird if she was. No one ever had a mother like ours. I still think we made her this way, having us so close together would make any sane person snap." I'm only kidding about my mum. I wouldn't change her for anything in this universe. She's one of a kind, but she's ours, and I love her.

"Speak for yourself. I was the model child, especially after the hell you put them through. So if anyone made her crazy, it was you."

"Me? I clearly remember it was you that came home when you were fourteen and told our parents that you'd gotten your girlfriend pregnant."

Andrei's cheeks go bright red, and he opens another bottle of beer. I'm planning on sticking to one, so I can drive Andrei home when he needs it. It's his celebration so he can make the most of it. "In my defence, I didn't know you needed to have sex to get someone pregnant. I didn't exactly pay attention in those classes."

"I still remember mum's face as she tried to process what you were telling her."

"I swear I thought you could get pregnant from oral sex. Donna told me that she'd missed her period and was pregnant. I just didn't know that it wasn't me that got her into that situation."

I have tears building in my eyes as I remember that day. It was so funny, and even now thinking about it still makes me laugh uncontrollably. "Mum's face ... oh god, it was priceless."

Andrei is laughing right along with me, tears running down his cheeks as the memory hits him. "It was dad that finally had to sit me down and explain things to me. Fuck, having him tell me about sex afterwards was mortifying."

I can only imagine how that went because thankfully I had come out by that point, so I never had to hear about the birds and the bees. My sex talk with my dad had been him patting me on the shoulder and nodding. That was it, talk done. That was the day that I decided that being gay had one benefit.

CHAPTER NINE

NICOLAI

"Heard anything yet?"

I glower at Gareth over the top of my pasta bowl and contemplate locking him out of my class. He closes my classroom door and puts his lunch on my desk before pulling a seat to the opposite side so he's sitting across from me. I've been avoiding the staff room because my company sucks this week. I've been growling at anyone who dares speak to me, but I can't seem to stop.

"Still nothing then. Have you called him?" He undoes his sandwich and takes a large bite.

"I'm not calling him again. I think it's time to chalk this up to being used for sex. If he wanted anything to do with me, he would have been in contact before now." I try to make my words come out like I'm joking, but I can hear how pissed off I sound. Who could blame me though? I was used in the worst of ways, even if I enjoyed it at the time.

"I get you're pissed, but part of me thinks that maybe something happened, like a misunderstanding or something. You were so sure about him, and you aren't usually off like that. You can usually tell when someone is spinning you a line."

He's right, but it doesn't make me feel any better. I'm an excellent judge of character and James came over as such a nice guy. I wouldn't have expected this of him, but three days of no contact makes me realise how wrong I've been. "Doesn't matter now, does it? He won't answer his phone, and I don't know where he lives. We've only ever been to my house. That should have been a clue that something was off, maybe he has a boyfriend or wife at home?" God, it's the first time I've thought of that, but now it makes perfect sense.

"Did he give you that vibe, that maybe he was cheating on someone with you?"

I think back to our time together to see if there were any clues but I didn't pick up on anything. James always replied to my texts, answered when I called, and he never seemed to hurry our conversation like someone else was there. No, that conclusion doesn't seem to fit with James. "Never. So he obviously didn't like my sex."

Laughter is not the reply that I was expecting from my best friend but it's what I get. And not just a little snigger, it's a full-on belly laugh with tears in his eyes. "Oh god, Nic. You're so fucking funny. Didn't like your sex." He laughs again, and I throw my fork at him.

"Fuck you. I was being serious."

He takes a moment to compose himself as he picks my fork up off the floor and passes it back to me. "If he has done a runner, Nic, it's on him, not you. I've told you before that you're a catch and I didn't lie. Stop acting like all this is your fault, maybe James was just a cockwaffle?"

Against my better judgement, I laugh at Gareth. He has this way of being deadly serious as he speaks and it just makes what he says funny. "Cockwaffle?"

"Yeah, cockwaffle. Don't try and defend him. I might not have met him, but I know his type. Hit it and quit it. Hump it and dump it. Ejaculate and evacuate."

"Holy fuck, please stop talking." I lean my elbows on my desk and drop my head into my hands. Gareth may give me a headache some days, but at least he's managed to get rid of my sour mood for a little while. I'm about to speak when I hear a voice in the hall, a thunderous voice and the panic starts up inside. Shit, this cannot be happening. Gareth's face lights up when he hears it and I know I'm not going to live this down.

"Nicolai Arthur Morgan, this is your mother. I don't know what room you're in this year, but I suggest you get out here now."

"This can't be happening." I want the ground to open up and swallow me, but my luck isn't that good.

"Oh, it's happening my friend, and I'm so glad I'm here to witness it."

I don't know why she does this to me. Normal parents don't do this to their children. I'm just glad I have a boss who finds the whole thing as hilarious as everyone else does or I would be fired.

****

IT'S BEEN FIVE DAYS SINCE I HEARD FROM JAMES AND SITTING alone on my couch on a Friday night tells me that I've been ghosted. I've tried calling him again and even texted a few times, but there has been no response, so I gave up. He apparently wants nothing to do with me, and I need to come to terms with that. I fell far too fast for someone I didn't know, and that's on me, I can't even blame James for that.

I take a huge drink from the glass of vodka in my hand and enjoy the burn deep in my chest. It's not how I planned on spending my Friday night, but since the guy I thought liked me has vanished with no trace, my only option is to feel sorry for myself and drink myself to sleep. I've spent every night going over what happened on Sunday to see if I could see the moment I did something wrong but I don't remember anything. We smiled and laughed together, and when James said he was looking forward to seeing me this weekend, I believed him. Fuck, I'm stupid and apparently only good for fucking.

A knock on my door has my treacherous heart beating faster in my chest. I've resigned myself to not seeing James again, but here I am, hoping it's him on the other side of the door. As I said, pathetic. I'm tempted to leave whoever it is on the other side of the door, but I get up from the couch and head to it, opening it without looking to see who it is.

"Hey, Nicolai." Dillon is standing on the top step with a bottle of wine in his hand. Gareth's words of warning echo in my head but the vodka in my blood makes me not listen to them.

"Hey, Dillon. You look better than the last time I saw you."

He laughs, and his cheeks get red. I've noticed he blushes a lot, just like Andrei, and I wonder if he hates it as much as my brother does. "Yeah, been keeping myself out of trouble. I brought this as a little thank you." He holds out the bottle of wine, and I take it from his hand.

"You didn't need to do that, but thank you. Do you want to come in and have a drink?"

He follows me inside and closes the door. "I'll have whatever you're having."

I spend a few minutes making him a vodka and sprite, before collapsing onto the couch next to him with a huff.

"Is everything okay?"

I look carefully at Dillon, wondering how much to tell him. I should keep my life away from him if what Gareth thinks is accurate, but since I've already let him in, would it do any harm to talk to him? "Man trouble, you must know what that's like?"

He looks down at his glass as he twirls it in his hands. "Yeah, I know."

"I'll tell you mine if you tell me yours?" I quirk up the corner of my lip, and it's in that moment that I realise how numb my nose is. When did that happen?

"There's nothing much to tell. I like someone who's a lot older, and that keeps us apart. I know that he likes me, but he feels that it's inappropriate."

"Oh." There was part of me that thought that Dillon was talking about me, but apparently, it's just me being big headed. Relief spreads through me as I realise that everything Gareth thought was wrong, it's someone else that Dillon wants. "James did a vanishing act after we had sex and I haven't seen him since." I cringe as the verbal diarrhoea stops, and Dillon is left staring at me. I can't work out the look that's on his face because it's somewhere between happiness and anger. I take another large mouthful of Vodka, hoping that it starts to make me numb soon.

"I'm gonna go home and get something. Mind if I just let myself in when I come back?"

He doesn't wait for an answer before getting up and leaving. I should go after him and say thank you for the wine, but explain that I should spend the night alone. Maybe Gareth would come over and have a drink with me. It's the least I could do to make up for being like a bear with a sore head all week. I think he was close to bashing my skull in with a coffee mug at one point, but since he's a good friend, he just bought me more coffee creamer and told me to get the fuck over it.

The front door opens, and Dillon comes in carrying a bottle of tequila and two glasses. He uses his foot to close the door behind him and takes his seat next to me on the couch again. He sits closer to me this time, his leg brushing mine as he leans forward and fills the two glasses. He passes one to me and holds his own up in front of himself. "To the men who don't know what they're missing."

I clink his glass and down the tequila in one go. It burns on its way down, and I hiss when I remember how much I hate this drink. The last time I had some shots, it led to some dodgy decisions. Dillon picks up the bottle to refill my glass, but I put it down on the table. "No more for me. Tequila tends to lead me to nasty places, and I could do without any more shit in my life right now. " I pinch my eyes shut as they get a little fuzzy.

"That sounds like there might be some stories there."

"Stories that your ears are far too young to hear." I laugh, but it sounds hollow. My head is fuzzy, and I feel a little like I'm floating. I blink a few more times trying to focus on Dillon who's moving in and out of my vision.

"I keep telling you, Nicolai, I'm not as young as people think. I'm a grown man with needs and wants. I'm sure anything you say wouldn't shock me."

"I ... I'm sorry, Dillon." I try to stand but my head spins, and I sit back down quickly so I don't fall.

"Are you okay?" Dillon's voice sounds like he's talking from above a pool and I'm underwater and sinking fast.

I grab onto the table and pull myself up, swaying as I finally get upright. That tequila must have been stronger than I thought but it's never hit me this fast. I've only had two vodkas and the shot. It usually takes a lot more than that to have any effect on me. "I need ..." I don't know what I need, and my voice fades off as I head towards my bedroom. My bed, that's what I need. I should lie down before I fall over. I'm hoping Dillon can find his way out, but as I stagger into the wall, I forget about him.

Using the wall to slide along the hall I make it to my bedroom without falling on my face. I try to find the light switch inside the door, but I can't get my body to do anything I want it to. My head spins, and the only thing that stops me from hitting the floor is a set of arms that grab me from behind and wrap around my waist.

"Come on, let's get you lying down." I grip onto the arms that are holding me and allow Dillon to move me towards my bed.

As soon as I feel the mattress against my legs, I fall forward, not even putting my hands out to catch myself. I feel like I've got no control over my body and I'm finding it difficult to think. My head feels like it's full of cotton wool and all I want to do it sleep.

My body moves, and it takes me by surprise. It's only when I feel Dillon's hands against my waistband that I realise that I didn't move myself, it was him that did it. My jeans slide down over my hips, and I want to fight his hands off, but it's as though my body weighs the same as a small bus. Fear grips me hard when I feel Dillon's hands brush under my t-shirt now that my jeans are off my body. His touch is wrong on my skin, and it makes me want to shudder, but I can't even get my body to do that.

"Dillon, stop." The words are weak and barely make it past my lips, but I hope he hears them. I need him to stop whatever it is he's doing. I don't want him to touch me. I want him to leave.

He doesn't heed my words, and my worst fear comes to life as I feel Dillon's lips against my stomach. My stomach churns, and I want to get off the bed, to push him away and put a stop to this, but I can barely raise my hand higher than my waist. I've never felt this wasted on such little alcohol and I'm starting to think something is very, very wrong. My panic increases when my boxers are pulled down my thighs and over my bare feet. I'm now naked in front of Dillon, and it's the last thing I want. "Dillon, please."

"It's okay, baby. Everything will be fine. I'll take care of you."

I don't think he understands what I'm trying to say but I can't get my mouth to work. Words have vanished. My eyes flicker closed, and I use all the energy I have left to open them, blinking rapidly to try and focus. The act makes tears build in my eyes, but I know it's the fear that's causing them. I don't want this to happen, but I can't do anything to stop it. My eyes roll into my head, and I struggle to open them again, but it doesn't last long. I can't keep my eyes open to see anything, but I can still feel.

I can feel as Dillon pushes my legs apart and kneels in between them.

I can feel as his hands cup my balls, and he slips a finger lower.

I can feel as his lips brush over my chest and his finger pushes inside me.

I can feel as my legs are pushed up to my chest, and something much larger replaces his finger.

I can feel as the tears fall unstopped down my cheeks.

****

I GROAN AS I ROLL OVER IN BED, BURYING DEEPER INTO MY pillow as I try to hide from the sun that's beating through my window. I don't remember coming to bed last night, and going by my aching head, I must have drunk a lot more than I had planned to. It feels like there's a marching band practising in my skull, and they brought some friends along with them. I try to think back to what happened last night, but even that hurts far too much.

I battle with my full bladder for about ten minutes before I finally have to leave the comfort of my warm duvet. I take a deep breath and slowly sit up until my legs are over the edge of the bed. With my feet flat on the floor, I take a few seconds to take stock of my body. My stomach is protesting at my movements, but I think that's as bad as it's going to get. I slide forward on the mattress, and the ache in my arse surprises me. I barely have time to think about that when the mattress dips behind me as someone moves.

I sit still and try harder to remember what the fuck happened last night. It's now evident that I'm not alone, which explains why I feel like I bottomed last night, but it doesn't tell me who's in my bed. I'm pretty sure I didn't leave my house so that rules out a random hook-up, but then who else could it be? My heart starts to race a bit faster as I think about the obvious answer to that question. *James.* Did he finally get in touch last night to explain why he had vanished? The side of my mouth quirks up as I turn my head expecting to see James' smiling face. That's not what I find though, and suddenly my stomach rethinks the whole not vomiting thing.

I get up from the bed as quickly as I can and scramble to my bathroom. I barely get to my knees in front of my toilet before everything I ate and drank yesterday makes an appearance. Even after my stomach is empty, I dry heave for a good few minutes before I get myself under control. I reach my hand up and press the button to flush before dropping onto my arse and leaning back against the cold tiled wall. I close my eyes to block out the world around me. I want to hide from what's waiting for me in the other room, or at least remember a little bit of what happened last night. I want to pretend to myself that I didn't have sex, but the dull ache in my body tells me that I did.

God, I'm so fucking stupid. How did I let this happen? The most worrying fact is that I don't remember any of it. I don't remember drinking that much, I don't remember getting any visitors, and I certainly don't remember inviting anyone into my bed. I bang my head gently against the wall behind me and pray to anyone who will listen that I imagined what I saw in there.

"Morning."

Just as I was finishing up my silent prayer the hopeful figment of my imagination makes himself known. "What happened last night?" I don't even open my eyes as I speak to him. I can't look at him without feeling disgusted with myself, so it's better to keep hiding.

"You don't remember anything?"

I shake my head and hope he's looking at me. My mouth has suddenly come very dry, and I don't think I could get words out if I wanted to.

"You kissed me and then ... well, then you asked me to fuck you."

Oh god. I can feel the bile rising in my throat again. I slept with my neighbour and not just my neighbour. My extremely young neighbour who I taught at school up to just a few years ago. I move quickly when I feel myself heave again. I'm going to be sick, and I'm not sure if I'll ever stop.

CHAPTER TEN

NICOLAI

I TAKE MY TIME GETTING DRESSED, NOT WANTING TO FACE what's waiting for me in the living room. After puking for far too long earlier, I asked Dillon to leave so I could shower. I needed a minute to breathe without his presence. I needed a minute to think about what I'd done. I should have listened to what Gareth told me and stayed very far away from Dillon. But no, I had to go and have sex with him. *How the fuck did I let this happen?*

The worst thing is I still can't remember anything past having the shot of tequila. Everything is clear up until that point, and then it's just gone. So now I have to go out and face Dillon with absolutely no information at all. He said I asked him to fuck me and that doesn't sound like something I would do. I've never looked at Dillon as anything other than my old student and neighbour, so why would a few drinks change all that? I've slept with people when I've been drunk, but it's because I've found them attractive and the drink made me confident enough to make a move. It's never made me attracted to someone I had absolutely no interest in.

Deciding to man the fuck up, I make my way out of my room where I've been hiding and walk quietly down the hall. I need to get this over and done with so I can go back to being on my own and hating myself. Telling Dillon that last night was a mistake is going to be difficult, and I'm hoping I won't have to say to him that I don't remember any of it. This is going to be a clusterfuck, and there's no way around it. I made a huge mistake last night, and now I need to deal with the fallout. Maybe it will be okay. He might already realise that last night was a one-night thing that shouldn't have happened, and we can go about our life without mentioning it again?

That thought vanishes from my head when I turn the final corner and come face to face with Dillon. He looks so fucking happy, a huge smile on his face as he steps in front of me. He bites his lip, and his eyes flicker down to my mouth. He doesn't look like someone who realises what I'm about to do and that makes me feel even shittier.

I take a step back to make sure there is some distance between us and cross my arms over my chest. I'm trying to put up as many barriers as I can, which is also why I'm wearing jogging bottoms and a hoodie top. "We need to talk about last night, Dillon."

He gets a little look of confusion on his face, but he covers it quickly with another smile. "Last night was everything I imagined it would be. I've dreamt of it so many times, so when you kissed me, I thought I was dreaming again."

I kissed him? Shit, I need to stop drinking so much – well after tonight since I'm planning on drinking this day away. "I'm sorry, I shouldn't have done that."

"No, it's fine, better than fine. I swear I wanted it. Making love to you has been the highlight of my life. Nicolai, I've wanted you for years."

I swallow deeply to try and clear my throat that's suddenly filled with bile again. This can't be happening. It has to be a joke. "Dillon, last night shouldn't have happened. It was wrong on so many levels."

Dillon laughs and steps closer to me. I try not to flinch because I don't want him to feel worse than he's about to. "I swear, Nicolai, I wanted everything that happened. The way you whispered in my ear while I was inside you, the things you said made me realise you've wanted me too."

Oh shit, no, this has to stop. "I don't remember anything I said. I don't remember what we did. Dillon, you need to know that I don't want you like that. There's nothing between us."

I expect him to fall apart in front of me, to break down in tears while begging me to take that back, but what he does disturbs me more than any of that. He smiles at me, his eyes glittering with happiness as he speaks. "I know you think that, Nicolai, but I know different. Last night was only the start, you'll see soon enough. We will be together. It's meant to be." He winks at me as he turns and leaves my house.

I'm left standing in the middle of the room with my mouth open in shock. He didn't listen to a word I just said to him, or he did and chose to ignore me. *What the hell have I gotten myself in to?*

I SMILE WHEN MY MUM OPENS THE DOOR AND DRAGS ME INTO her arms.

"Nicolai, my baby boy. You're here."

I laugh when she makes it sound like such a surprise that I'm here. She had ordered me to turn up when she embarrassed me at school last week. "Mum, I didn't have a choice. You threatened to come back to school if I didn't."

She pushes me on my chest in a dismissive way. "You know I was only kidding." She giggles as she walks away, leaving me standing at the front door with my mouth open.

There was no part of her visit that made me feel like she was kidding. I'm pretty sure my students thought that they might have to turn up today with how serious she was. This is typical mum though, making it sound like you're making such a big thing out of everything. I smile as I follow her into the house.

I find her in the kitchen stirring a pot of what smells like lettuce soup. "Good crop this year?"

My dad, who is sitting at the dinner table reading a paper, doesn't even look at me as he answers. "Enough that I'm now on my second week of soup. Might plant less next year."

Mum turns and ruffles my dad's hair the way she always does when he gets grumpy about something. "You love my soup, Gregor, you just like to pretend you don't."

Dad grumbles in his usual way, but I can see the edge of his lips turn up into a gentle smile. This is the way we grew up. Dad growled and acted like he wasn't affected by anything, but he has a heart of gold and would bend over backwards to help anyone. I asked him once why he never showed anyone how kind he was and he explained that he grew up in a different time, a time when men didn't show their emotions. I suppose I understand that to a certain extent. When I came out the world was very different. I couldn't be as open as I can be now because it wasn't talked about. I've seen a lot of changes in my years, ones that I'm proud that happened.

I take a seat at the table and bash the back of dad's paper. It's an old habit that I still do, annoying him until he pays attention to me. When I don't get him to lower his paper with the first hit I make the second one harder, and this one has his sighing and lowering the paper, a scowl on his face. "Hey, dad."

"You are a pest. I thought maybe we left that behind when you left puberty and got some common sense."

It's the same argument as always, so I play my role and give him my sweet answer. "Love you, dad."

He scoffs and gets up from the table to get me a drink of mum's homemade lemonade. Today feels normal, and it's something that I've craved since the shit storm with Dillon. It happened two nights ago, and I've pretty much not left my house since I made the biggest mistake of my life. I can't believe that it's been just over twenty-four hours since I told him that what happened between us was a mistake, but time has moved so slowly. It's like the clock is mocking me by making sure I live each second twice, and the hours are dragging because of it. I couldn't wait for this afternoon to come so I could put some distance between Dillon's house and me. Just knowing that he was a short distance away made me hide out and avoid going outside for anything.

I didn't realise what a coward I was until I found myself closing all my curtains so that Dillon couldn't see me. I'm not proud of my actions this weekend, not the sleeping with Dillon or the hiding, but I need some time to sort out my head. I'm hoping spending the day with my family will reset something inside and help me make some sense of what I've done recently. The fact is I did the unthinkable on Friday night, but I have to get past it, and since I refuse to move, it means just sucking it up and acting normally.

Just as dad places my glass in front of me, the front door bangs closed. Heavy footsteps sound in the hall, getting closer to the kitchen as my dad grabs another lemonade.

"Hello, family." Andrei's cheery voice brings a smile to my face, and I feel some of the tension draining from shoulders.

"Hey, baby boy. How is my handsome favourite today?" My mum looks happy as she speaks, her eyes clearly on my brother.

"Uh-oh. What did you do to piss off mum?"

"Language, Andrei."

He walks over and kisses mum on the cheek before sitting across from me. "What did you do?" He nods his head in mum's direction as dad puts the glass in front of him.

"I didn't call."

Andrei bursts out laughing because he knows what that means. "And?"

"And she turned up at school and let everyone know she was unhappy with me."

"Shit. I did try to warn you." And he had, but I'd had a lot on my mind, so I forgot.

"You did. You're a good brother."

Dad joins us at the table and smiles. I can see that he's trying not to say something, something important, but both Andrei and I learned his tell a long time ago. There's a secret that dad has, and I would like to know what it is.

"What?"

Dad shakes his head like he is completely innocent, but I'm not buying it for a second. "Nothing. Just good to have you boys home. It's nice that we can all be here."

"Okay, you're seriously freaking me out now. Why are you being nice?" Andrei is right, dad being nice is a little freaky, but it also confirms my suspicion that something is happening.

Dad reaches out and slaps Andrei across the back of the head. "I can be nice you cheeky shit."

As Andrei rubs the back of his head, he smirks at me. That was more like dad, not that sweet guy from before.

"Soups up, come and get it." Mum starts dishing out large bowls of lettuce soup, and we all crowd around the small dining table to eat it with the homemade bread that's sitting in baskets.

I'm tucking into my soup, the taste as good as I remember it, when mum lets us in on what is going on.

"So, boys, your dad and I have some news."

I pause with the spoon halfway to my mouth, and I almost laugh when I see Andrei doing the same thing. I've always been told that we are doubles of each other, but I don't see it. My brother has less grey hair and a lot more muscles. I've always felt like the much less attractive older brother, not that I've ever admitted that to Andrei.

The silence draws out until my dad takes over the conversation, my mum holding his hand as he speaks. "We've decided that it's time for a change."

A change? There are a thousand things that could mean.

"What kind of change?" Apparently Andrei has his brain switched on a bit more than I do. After the last week, I'm surprised I'm still able to think.

"Well, you see, we've decided to sell this place and move."

The statement is met with complete silence. I don't even know how to respond.

"Move?" Andrei's voice comes out quietly, and for just a moment he sounds like he did when he was twelve.

"Honey, this house is far too big for us now. We don't need all this space, and it's becoming tiring to keep it clean. Since your dad retired, we've wanted something else, something smaller."

I can understand what my mum is trying to say. They moved into this house before me and my brother was born. They had bought the five-bedroom house with the money my great grandmother left my dad in her will, and they thought that maybe they would have a much larger family, but that never happened. I don't think they noticed how large the house was when we were both here, we both take up the same amount of space as three people, but now that we're gone it must feel massive. That doesn't mean I have to be happy about it though, this was my childhood home, and I thought I would always be able to come back to visit it.

"Smaller? How much smaller?" That's what Andrei is focusing on, the fact that they want a smaller house?

"Are you still staying local?" This is the most important thing to me because I don't care what house they're in as long as they're still close by. The silence I'm met with doesn't fill me with much confidence though.

"Depends on what you class as local." My dad answers while he takes my mum's hand. "We are thinking of moving to Cornwall, buying a little cottage near the sea."

"Cornwall?"

"Yes, Andrei, Cornwall. It isn't that far away, only about ninety minutes."

"But you won't be here." I know exactly how my little brother is feeling, but I also understand my mum and dad's decision. Neither Andrei or I are young children anymore, and we both have lives that don't allow us to visit our parents very often. Why shouldn't they do something for themselves? They spent their entire lives providing for us, and they don't have much time left to have the life they want.

"I know, baby boy, but you can come and visit any time." Mum takes Andrei's hand like she does when we're upset. The act is soothing, and as I watch her with Andrei, I want her to take my hand, but I let her calm my brother instead.

"We need to do something before we die. You boys are grown and have your own lives, and we want to have something that is ours." Dad's comment seems harsh, but it's true. I'm hoping to one day be married and have a house full of dogs, and I'm pretty sure that Andrei will meet the love of his life at some point and he will have kids. That will leave mum and dad seeing us even less than they do already. Yeah, they need to do this, and I will support them.

"I think it'll be good. We can come to the seaside for holidays."

Andrei looks at me as though I've lost my mind and I glare at him in return. If he doesn't get on board, I'm going to smack some sense into him. He must finally understand what I'm trying to get across to him because he smiles, even if it's the fakest smile I think I've seen, and goes back to eating his soup. "Yeah, a holiday on the beach sounds good." I know that he'll have a complete bitch fest at me later, but at least for now he's keeping his thoughts to himself.

Mum smiles, and you can see relief spread through her entire body as she grips dad's hand harder. "I'm glad you're both okay with it. It won't happen overnight anyway. We still need to get the house on the market and see if it will sell. We can't buy until we sell this one but we have an estate agent coming over next week. So, saying that, it means we need you to have a look through your old rooms and see if there's anything you want to keep."

I've been out of the house for nearly fifteen years, and even though my old room has been re-decorated to a certain degree, you can still tell it belonged to me. Mum told me there was no point changing things when they didn't need the room, but I've always wondered if she secretly thought I might come back. Not that she didn't believe in me or my capabilities of making it alone, but she loved having us here, and the day I moved out she cried harder than I imagined she would.

"Oh, I wonder if my old magazines are still in my room?"

Mum reaches out and slaps Andrei on the back of the head. "No, they aren't you dirty boy. Those were found and binned within the first month of you leaving. I can't believe that you had that sort of thing in my house, your brother didn't."

I smile smugly at Andrei who's now returning my earlier glare. I always love getting one over on him and mum thinking I was a good boy is one of those things. I won't bother to tell them that they didn't have dirty magazines for gay men when I was young and that I didn't buy the gym magazines for the articles. No, I will allow them all to see my halo for a while longer.

CHAPTER ELEVEN

NICOLAI

I walk down the bread aisle, taking my time to look on the shelves to see what I want. I always come shopping on a Sunday night so I can buy everything I need for my lunches for the rest of the week. I choose to do it on a Sunday night being there are a lot fewer people here to get annoyed with. I came to the supermarket once on a Saturday afternoon when I first moved into my house. It was a mistake I only made once. There were so many screaming children that I abandoned my trolley in the middle of an aisle and walked out. I might work with kids, but it doesn't mean I need to like them.

Thankfully tonight I've only seen one other person, and that's an older lady who smiled before returning to her shopping. This is the grocery shopping I love. I pick up a box of pecan brownies and put them in my trolley. Monday is always lunch with Gareth, okay every day is lunch with Gareth, but on a Monday we eat in one of our classes so we can catch up after having the weekend off. I'm not looking forward to telling Gareth about my Friday night adventures, and that's why I bought him his favourite cake. Maybe it will sweeten him up enough that he won't shout at my stupidity. He's going to lose his shit at me, especially after his warning, but I'm just going to suck it up and deal with what he's going to say.

I find myself wandering down the alcohol aisle, staring at the bottles of vodka on the shelves. My mind goes back to Friday night and my problematic amnesia. I've never forgotten a whole night before, no matter how drunk I got. There have been nights where I wish I would lose my memory, but it's always there in bright multi-colour clarity. Friday night is gone. There's nothing, nada, not a fraction of a memory. It's like someone took the whole night and removed it from my head. Sleeping with Dillon should never have happened, and I will regret it the rest of my life, but not remembering a second of it worries me more.

I shake my head to try and clear my spiralling thoughts and head towards the freezer aisle. I refused to spend the rest of my life drunk to try and outrun what I did at the weekend, but that doesn't mean I can't eat my body weight in ice cream. I stand in front of the six-foot fridge and eye up all my choices. I'm trying to decide if I want lots of my favourite or one of each different kind when the back of my neck tingles. My head turns instantly, and I look both ways along the aisle. It's the feeling I've been having for the last few months, the one where it's like someone is watching me, but there's no one there. The hairs on my arm stand up on end and I shudder, a paranoid feeling spreading through my body.

I take a deep breath and give myself an internal talking to, telling myself that I'm losing my mind, and look back into the fridge. Opening the door, I grab a few tubs of cookie dough ice cream and a few salted caramel. The tingle builds, but I try to ignore it, to move on and pretend that nothing is making me feel anxious. When I get to the end of the aisle, I let my eyes drift back to where I was standing but there still isn't anyone there. Shaking my head at my craziness, I decide that I'm done. I don't have my usual full trolley, but I can come back another night if I need anything. I'm not in the right frame of mind for this tonight so I should just go home and sleep. I want to finally kiss this week goodbye and start fresh tomorrow.

As I turn towards the checkout, the lady that smiled at me earlier seems to come out of nowhere. I jump when she says hello, her voice quite loud over the gentle music playing from the shop speakers.

"I'm sorry, sweetheart. I didn't mean to scare you." Her smile is sweet, and even though I still have my heart racing in my chest, I smile back at her.

"Don't worry. I just get into a little world of my own sometimes. I forget I'm not the only person who shops at this time of night."

She reaches out and pats me on the arm, and where I'm not much into strangers touching me, the move is so motherly it doesn't bother me. "I know that feeling. I was shocked when I saw you and that other person here tonight."

I look around and see no one else in the shop. I've only seen this lady in here tonight, if you don't count the staff, and even though common sense tells me that it's natural to miss someone in a shop this size, my souring stomach makes me ask the question I don't think I want the answer to.

"What other person?" I don't know why I suddenly have a sick feeling in the pit of my stomach, but I have this feeling that this stranger might be able to help me with something that's been plaguing me.

"The other gentleman, the one with the camera."

My skin erupts with sweat, and I can feel it running down my spine. I have the sudden memory of the SD card that I found in my garden, the one that looked like it'd come from a camera. Her information points to me being right about someone watching me, but instead of making me feel better about not going crazy, it adds to the fear of knowing that someone is out there.

"GOOD AFTERNOON, SWEET CHEEKS." I LOOK UP WHEN GARETH walks into my classroom and dumps his lunch on my desk.

My lunch is already sitting on the desk but my stomach has been a mess since last night so I have no appetite. I don't even know where to start with all the stuff I need to tell Gareth, but when there's a knock on my door, I think I might have lost my chance. I relax a little when I see a deliveryman and not another teacher. He's carrying a huge bunch of flowers so I think he's got the wrong room, that is until he speaks.

"Mr Morgan?"

"Um, yeah."

He walks over and puts the flowers on my desk, producing a clipboard from under his arm so I can sign for them. As I'm signing, my ever nosey best friend grabs the card and opens it before I get a chance to grab it from his hand. I thank the delivery guy, and he leaves just as Gareth starts to read out loud what's written on the card.

"Thank you for an amazing time on Friday. Being with you was a dream come true. Until next time, Dillon." He laughs, and I know he hasn't fully registered what he's just read.

My heart is racing as I wait for the words to catch up with him and I can spot the second that they do. His eyes go wide, and I fear that they might pop out of his head, and I'm waiting for the outburst that I know I can't avoid. I don't want to avoid it though, I need to be held accountable for what I did, and Gareth has always been that guy for me. He's the devil and angel on my shoulder, giving me whatever I need at any given time.

"I don't understand what I'm reading here. I thought it was a thank you for a booty call but it's signed from Dillon. I only know one Dillon." He looks up at me like he wants me to deny everything. "Do you know another Dillon?"

I shake my head.

"Did you have sex this weekend?"

I nod my head, and Gareth nods his head in response. He bites his lips, and I brace myself. It's coming and soon.

Less than thirty seconds later Gareth gives in to his needs. "You fucked Dillon?! Seriously, Nic, please tell me I'm reading this wrong, and you put curtains up for him or something? God, who am I kidding? You had sex with him. *Shit, you had sex with Dillon.* What the fuck is wrong with you? He's like twelve years old! Have you lost your ever-loving mind? Not only is he far too young, but he's also not right in the head! Didn't you listen when I told you to stay away from him? He's weird."

Gareth finally finishes his rant and stares at me. It's like he's waiting for me to give him answers but I'm stuck with what to say. There were so many questions in there, and I'm not sure how many were rhetorical.

"Well?"

"I don't know what to say to you. I slept with Dillon, but I don't remember it."

This gets Gareth's attention, and he settles back into his chair slightly. He throws the card onto the desk like it disgusts him. "What do you mean you don't remember? Were you drunk?"

"No. Yes. I don't know." My voice comes out low because this is the hardest thing I've had to admit. I'm a grown man and have had my share of one-night stands gone wrong, but nothing like this. I've never been left with such a feeling of disgust and worry.

Gareth sits forward and leans his forearms on my desk. He glowers at the flowers for a second before he picks them up and puts them on the floor where I can't see them. I love my best friend, and he always seems to know what I need. When the desk is clear, he goes back to his original position, leaning over so he doesn't have to speak too loudly. "You have to know if you were drunk."

"I don't think I was drunk, I mean I'd only had two vodkas. I didn't feel any effects of the alcohol until Dillon brought over the tequila."

"Tequila, really? That's like asking for trouble. No good story ever started with tequila."

He's completely right, and if I'd had more than one shot then the amnesia wouldn't surprise me in the slightest, but I'm sure I only had one. There's no way I would have had more than that with Dillon there. "I swear I only had one shot. I didn't even want that one but with the whole James thing I wanted to forget. I suppose I got my wish."

Gareth screws up his face, and I can see his brain working overtime. "You only had two vodkas and a single shot? That's not enough to get you even a little tipsy, man. You have hollow legs and can drink anyone under the table."

"I know, and that's why I'm worried about the lack of memories. And I would say Dillon was lying about what happened between us but ... but I know that it happened."

"How do you ..." It's like a light bulb goes on in his head and his question freezes on his tongue. "Okay, let's move on. I don't like the fact that you can't remember anything. Even in my most drunken state, I remember something."

"Exactly. Things are strange just now, and I don't know what's in my imagination and what isn't." I put my hand into my pocket and pull out the SD card, throwing it on the desk in front of Gareth. He picks it up carefully like he's scared it's about to explode.

"What's this?"

"I don't know. For the last few months I've had this strange feeling that I'm being watched. I've never seen anyone, so I just put it down to my imagination, but then I found that. I forgot about it until a little old lady told me last night that someone was in the supermarket with a camera." I don't say anything else because I'm worried that Gareth will laugh at my suspicions.

"It's a memory card."

I roll my eyes. I might not be an expert in anything, but I know this shit. "Yeah, I know that."

"What's on it?"

I go to answer, but the end of lunch bell goes signalling that this conversation is over for now. I stand and start tidying my lunch away. "I don't know. I don't have a card reader."

Gareth mimic's my actions by cleaning away his lunch, not that either of us ate much. "I might have one at home. I'm sure that Claire has one for her camera but let me check. Are you busy on Wednesday?"

I give him a look that I hope relays the question is a stupid one, but just in case he doesn't catch it with the full distain I'm trying to fill it with, I use words. "I'm trying to avoid my neighbour who I slept with, who isn't twelve by the way, so I'll be hiding out in my house on Wednesday."

"Fine. I'll come over, and we'll try to get to the bottom of all this."

I'm about to tell him to bring food with him when my mobile buzzes. I open the message, and my stomach drops when I read the message.

Hey, babe. I hope you liked the flowers. We need to get together soon. I miss you! D x

Gareth must see the colour draining from my face because he guesses straight away who the message is from. "We'll also work out a plan to get him to back off."

I nod but don't say anything as he leaves me alone in my class. I just hope that we can get Dillon to back off, but there's a huge part of me that says it won't be that easy.

WHEN I GOT HOME FROM WORK TONIGHT, I FOUND A BOTTLE OF wine just outside my front door. There was no tag or anything on it, but my gut told me there was only one person who would have left it there. It made me lock my front door quickly before closing all my curtains and taking up refuge in the back of my house, hoping my enclosed back garden will keep me away from Dillon's prying eyes. His car missing from his driveway also helped me relax, so I got changed into my shorts and t-shirt before heading out the back to start the barbecue. I love the better weather because it means I can cook outside and that's where I love to be. The winter months suck so much, and I make the most of every beautiful day we get in this country ... which isn't many.

I'm now sitting on my deck out back while my steak cooks on the barbecue. There's also salad in the bowl on the table, and my crockery is all ready and waiting. I love nights like this, I just wish I didn't have the constant fear of Dillon appearing. Every time I hear a car approaching the front of my house I hold my breath, wondering if it's him coming home. The knowledge of my garden being fully fenced with large gates still doesn't help me relax, and I keep waiting for him to appear from the shadows. God. I've never had this sort of regret after sleeping with a guy, but maybe that's why ordinary people don't fuck their neighbours. This is my penance for not keeping it in my pants. What I should do is march over to Dillon and tell him that he was the biggest mistake of my life and he needs to get the hell over it. Pity I'm not brave enough to do that.

I turn on my iPod when I go to check on my steak. Music will stop me from stressing over every noise I hear from the front street. I hum along to The Script as I spend a few minutes moving my steak around so it can rest. It will make sure that it's perfect when I want to eat, which isn't right now. I'd been hungry when I first came out, but now that I'm more relaxed, I'm happy with my glass of lemonade. I turn the music up and move to the lounger that isn't sitting in the shade. I close my eyes as I feel the early evening sun coat my skin. Being stuck in the cool, air-conditioned school all day meant that I missed most of today's nice weather. Thankfully it isn't too long until the summer holidays, and I can't fucking wait. The last few weeks are always chaotic but those first few weeks of holidays are a dream. I'd hoped to have someone to share them with, but since that doesn't seem to be on the cards, I will make plans with Gareth and the girls.

My mobile sounds a new text, and my hand automatically grabs it from my shorts pocket. I hesitate when I realise what I've done. I don't want to look because I'm scared that it's another message from Dillon. He's messaged me several times since this afternoon, and it's making me nervous to check my phone. I give in and read the name on the message, struggling to place the name Len. A few seconds later and the memory of a guy with shoulder length hair and electric blue eyes comes to me. I'd met him on the app I'd joined, but we hadn't spoken since I met James. His message comes as a surprise and for the first time in what feels like weeks I smile.

His message says he wants to meet for drinks sometime and my initial response is to say no, but I spend a few moments rethinking my answer. Maybe the best way to get over James is to get right back on the horse, or in this case, the guy? I had fun talking to Len the few times we had chatted before my date with James, so hopefully, in person, we'll have a connection. I thought I had one with James, but I was wrong. I can't let that one experience ruin everything for me. One bad apple doesn't tarnish the whole barrel. I reply to Len before I let anything change my mind, telling him I would love to go out with him at the weekend if he's free. I put my phone back in my pocket before going back to enjoying the sun.

Maybe this is the start of good things happening in my life. Could it be that I've repaid Karma enough that she will pick on someone else for a change? I relax even more, the smile still on my lips, but it leaves instantly at the sound of rustling from the bushes at the side of my garden. My eyes open instantly, and I look to the area between Mrs Corbin's house and mine. I watch because I expect one of her five cats to come walking out of the greenery, but there's nothing. The bush itself moves but it's not from the bottom, it's more like something large is moving in the middle of it. I get up slowly and approach the area. The bush is located in the back corner, so it takes me a moment to get to it especially since I'm taking my sweet time getting there.

I take a deep breath before pulling a few of the leaf filled branches to the side and Tom, Mrs Corbin's ginger cat jumps out on me. I scream in the most undignified way and then burst out laughing. I can't believe that I just about died because a cat jumped out on me. I shout after the cat, telling him that I will kick his arse if I catch him, knowing I won't lay a finger, or foot, on the gentle old guy. My good humour fades instantly when I look at the back fence and see the section that connects with the waste ground behind my property.

I can put a lot of strange things down to my imagination, but this is very real, and it has my nerves spiking. I back away slowly, watching the area like I expect the devil himself to race from the corner. Maybe not the devil, but someone has been here, and the considerable area of wood that's been cut away is proof of that.

CHAPTER TWELVE

NICOLAI

I HAMMER THE LAST NAIL INTO THE NOW CLOSED SECTION OF fence. I went straight to the local building merchants after I got off work this afternoon because there was no way I was going to be able to sleep knowing that the hole was still there. As it was, I barely slept an hour last night, and that hour was spent on the couch because my imagination had made up some scary scenarios. I'd sat on the couch all night with the curtains closed and all the lights off. I might want to pretend that nothing much rattles me, but the thought of someone being out there watching me is freaking me out.

I step back and admire my handy work. I'm not exactly known for being the best at DIY, my brother is the one I call for that, but no one is getting through that hole now. It's not pretty, but it's going to do the job that it's meant to do. As long as I do a nightly walk around the fence, then I might be able to sleep. Throwing the hammer into the small toolbox that Andrei bought me last Christmas, I grab the box and turn to head towards the house. A loud scream escapes me when I bump into a large body, and the toolbox falls to the ground.

"What the fuck, Nic?" Gareth stands there with wide eyes and his hands up in front of him like he was about to grab my fist that is up in front of me. I would laugh at the way he looks but with my blood pressure now somewhere in the clouds, I'm finding it hard to see the humour.

I bend down to pick up everything I dropped. "Sorry, I'm a little jumpy today."

"You don't say."

When I have everything off the ground, I stand to see him staring at the fence behind me. He points even though there's no mistaking what he's talking about.

"What happened?"

"Long story and I need a drink before I tell you." I start back towards my house, and Gareth falls into step beside me. We stay quiet until we're both sitting on my couch with a beer in our hands.

"Spill it."

I take a large drink to give me a little bit of confidence. "How long can you stay?"

"Shit is it that bad?"

I nod.

"Claire's at her mum's with the girls so as long as I make it to work tomorrow, I'm all yours."

Thank god. I didn't get a chance to see Gareth at work today, and I rushed away as soon as the bell rang, so I need to get everything off my chest and let him fix this shit for me. "For the last few months, I've had this weird feeling that someone's watching me. I've not seen anyone, but I can feel it."

I look towards Gareth to see if he's looking at me like I'm insane but he seems more concerned than anything. "Feel it?"

"Yeah, you must know what I'm talking about? That prickle on the back of your neck and the shivers it gives you. Please don't say you've never had that."

"No, I totally get what you're saying. So you've been having this for months?"

I nod and take another drink. I haven't had a drink since the weekend with Dillon, but I need it tonight to settle my nerves. Talking about this with Gareth is making it feel so much more real, like now I've put the suspicion out in the universe it makes it possible. "I didn't think anything of it at first, just that I was being paranoid over nothing. But there've been other things that are making me think that maybe it's not all in my head."

"Like what?"

"That hole in the fence you caught me fixing, well I didn't make it."

Gareth's eyes go wide in shock, and it's a familiar look on his face recently while I talk. My life never used to be this interesting, or should that be fucking awful, so there was never anything that shocked Gareth. A night in while marking school assignments never brought this level of surprise. "Someone cut through your six-foot wooden fence?"

"And I think someone was watching me at the supermarket. This old lady told me that someone had been taking pictures of me, but then left." Okay, it's not exactly what she said, but I know with complete certainty that's what had happened that night.

"Oh shit." Gareth gets up from the couch instantly and grabs his jacket. I'm starting to think he's about to leave but he takes something from his pocket and comes back over. "Claire's SD card reader."

I get a tumble of nerves in my stomach as I reach down the side of the sofa and grab my laptop. As it turns on, I take the SD card from my jeans pocket, which is where I have started to keep it because I've been worried about losing it. I'm at the stage where I need to see what's on it, even if I have a feeling that I won't like it. It might not be pictures of me, it might be that some random person lost their memory card from their camera, but I doubt that with every part of me.

We're both silent as my computer finally boots up, and I click the card reader into the USB port. I can feel my muscles tighten with tension as the little spinning wheel appears on my screen.

"Holy shit, we're acting as though the computer is about to explode."

Gareth's outburst scares the shit out of me, and it takes everything in me not to reach over and slap him. Apparently he finds himself very funny because he's chuckling away as he drinks the last of his beer. "You're a dick, just so you know."

He shrugs his shoulders like it's not new information but his attention is drawn to the computer screen, and the colour drains from his cheeks.

This isn't going to be good.

I force myself to look at the screen, and the instant I see what's loading on the screen, bile rises up my throat. I swallow hard to clear the lump of fear from my throat, but it doesn't work. As picture after picture appears on the screen, I can feel dread building up inside. I knew this is what I would find, but seeing it is scary as fuck.

"You might want to start closing your curtains."

Laughter gurgles up into my throat, and it escapes, leaving my body on a slightly crazed, high-pitched sound. Gareth is trying to lighten the mood like he always does when I'm panicking, and usually he does a great job, but it's not going to work tonight. No, tonight I'm scared, and nothing can take away from that.

I scroll through the pictures, my eyes taking in my life like it's been documented for some strange photo album. There are shots of me in my work out room at the back of the house, my body on show as I strain to lift weights or run. Others show me cooking and cleaning, or sitting on my decking reading a book. Those pictures invade the privacy that I thought I had, but they don't make me want to scream like the next batch of photos.

"Shit man, this is bad."

I hear Gareth's voice, but it's faint through the ringing in my ears. I feel like the world around me closing down, and all I can focus on is the pictures of me naked, getting dried after a shower or changing my clothes in my room. These photos are intimate and shouldn't exist, but here they are in living colour.

"You need to report this to the police, Nic. This isn't right."

I finally turn to look at Gareth and see him sitting close to me, a worried look on his face. I don't know what to say to him about this because I don't know how to feel. So much is going through my head, and I don't know what to focus on first. I look back at the screen and stare at the pictures. Most of them were taken at the back of the house where I don't close the curtains, the place I thought was private because it was closed in and away from prying eyes. But I was wrong. All this time someone has been watching me, invading on my private moments and I didn't know about it. Actually, that's a lie, I did know, or at least I thought I knew. All those feelings suddenly make perfect sense, but it doesn't make me feel any better knowing I was right. I wish to god that I had imagined the whole thing and Gareth was now laughing at my overactive imagination. Instead, I have him looking at me with pity, and I hate that.

"You need to go to the police, man. This isn't right. This is ... I don't know. Creepy as fuck? Scary? Whatever, but you need to report it."

I think about what he's saying, and most of me knows he's right, but there is a part of me that is fighting against his advice. "What am I meant to tell them? I found this memory card, and it's full of nude pictures of me. No, I don't know who took them, and I don't know why. I'm sure they would get right onto that."

"You can't just ignore this. I'm being serious, Nicolai, this is some fucked up shit. Make a statement, and maybe they can investigate."

My mind goes back to when I was in college, and someone spray painted the word homo on my car. I went to the police and reported the vandalism, but when they asked if I was gay, and I told them I was, the police officers had looked at me as though I had just crawled out of the gutter. Apparently, because I was gay meant that they didn't have to take the incident seriously. They did all the right things like taking a statement, but they acted like there was no real crime, telling me not to expect them to catch who did. I thought there had been a crime, and the evidence of it was there for weeks every time I had to get into my car. I don't want to live through that humiliation again, and having to show them the pictures will be just that. Humiliating. "They won't be able to do anything. It was dropped weeks ago so there will be no evidence or anything."

"Jesus Christ, Nic. Someone cut through your back fence to take pictures of you. That's a little more than just making the most of an opportunity, that's breaking in." He looks at me as though I'm insane and I don't blame him. Gareth has thankfully never had to live with someone looking at him like he's less because of his sexuality. I'm glad for that, but it also makes him naïve to some of the things that go on in this world. I know years have passed, and opinions have changed, but that moment has lived me for years, and I can't forget it.

"There's no point. And now that he knows I've found his entry-way, he will probably stop. He'll probably be too freaked out about getting caught to come back." I try to keep my voice light to pretend I believe what I'm saying, but I'm not even convincing myself.

If I thought Gareth was looking at me before like I was insane, I was wrong. Now he's looking at me like I've lost the plot. I think he's trying to find something to say, but he's got nothing, so just sits and stares at me. All too soon he finds his voice. "What the actual fuck? How can you be so fucking calm about this? Nic, someone was watching you while you were dressing. You had your dick out! What else has he seen that isn't on this SD card, how many more of them does he have?"

Well fuck, I hadn't thought about that. I think of what he might have seen, and I slam my computer closed and get off the couch. My skin feels like ants are crawling all over it and I rub my arms to try and ease the goosebumps. "I could have gone a lifetime without thinking about that. Thanks for pointing that out to me."

"I'm not going to hold your hand and tell you everything will be okay. This is serious. You need to call the police."

My stomach churns again at the thought. Everything he says is true, and I know the police would help me, but would they? Shit, I don't even know what to think. I have spent my life trying not to do anything that would need police involvement, and now this.

I'm about to give in to his requests when the doorbell goes, and I stop pacing instantly. I stare at the door like someone's going to burst in through it and attack me. My move has an exasperated noise coming from Gareth, and he walks towards the door mumbling something about crazy friends and their stalkers.

He pulls open the door, and I see Dillon on the top step. Well, this isn't going to end well. Gareth leans against the doorframe so he's blocking Dillon from seeing me, and I think the move is on purpose. The move makes me worried about what Gareth is going to do. I should step in and stop Gareth's plan, but I don't want to face Dillon, and maybe this will stop him coming around. Yeah, like I said. I'm a fucking wimp.

"Good evening, Dillon. Can I help you?" Gareth crosses his arms over his chest, and I take a few steps back. I want to see everything that's happening, but I want to stay out of any action.

"Hey, Mr Downes. I was just wondering if Nicolai is in." Dillon's voice sounds like he's smiling and I can't help but cringe. Our night together has given him ideas about what is happening between us, and I feel bad even though I've tried to tell him there's nothing there.

"I'm afraid he isn't, he went out on a date."

"A date?" The happiness is instantly replaced with hurt, and I close my eyes to try and rid myself of the urge to go to the door. It wouldn't make things any easier, but it might make Dillon less hurt.

I press my feet into the floor to stop myself from moving. Going to Dillon won't improve the situation, in fact, it would probably make the whole thing worse. Maybe he needs to be hurt a little to get him to move on because no matter what he thinks, the other night shouldn't have happened.

"Yeah, a date. You know those things you go on when you're into someone." Ouch. Gareth isn't pulling his punches, and I hate to admit, I'm happy he isn't.

"I don't understand, I thought..."

"You thought what? That after one night together that you were important?"

"No ... yes... I thought that he liked me?"

I should stop listening, walk away and let Gareth deal with this because the pain in Dillon's voice is seriously making my chest ache. I never meant to do this to him, but he needs to hear it. He needs to learn that I don't like him like that. I wish I was brave enough to tell him myself, but I'm not, so I need to rely on Gareth. I just pray he isn't going to be a complete arsehole about it.

"Dillon, you need to listen to me. The other night was a mistake. One that Nic doesn't even remember, so I would say it's better if you get on with your life and forget it ever happened."

"It wasn't like that. I know he felt it too, the connection."

"He didn't feel anything, like at all. He blacked out, and I have to tell you that it's shitty you took advantage of a drunk guy." Oh god, Gareth is making it sound like Dillon is the bad guy in all this, and even though he's telling the truth about me blacking out, it's still is a shitty angle to take. I'm about to approach the door when Dillon speaks, and the hurt now comes out as anger.

"You know nothing, Gareth. Fucking nothing."

"And there he is. I knew he was in there somewhere. You might have Nic fooled but not me, Dillon. I know shit about you that he doesn't know, and I will never forget."

I'm getting confused trying to follow the conversation. What the hell is Gareth talking about? He's never told me anything about Dillon, not anything that would make me think of him as anything other than a sweet guy.

"As I said before, you know nothing. Now tell me where Nicolai is."

"I told you he's out."

"I don't believe you. There's something between us, and he knows it. He would never go out with someone else."

I cringe at Dillon's words. His voice is loud, and it's clear to hear that he believes every single word he says. Again I asked myself, *how the fuck did I get myself into this situation?*

"Dillon, do yourself a favour. Go home and leave Nic alone before you embarrass yourself."

I can hear movement, but I can't see Dillon from my new position. What I do see is Gareth standing to his full height and putting his hands on his hips. It's an aggressive pose and one he always takes when he wants to make someone feel intimidated.

"Don't do anything stupid, Dillon. I'm not someone you want to fuck with. Now take my advice and fucking go home. I've tried to do this the nice way, but you won't hear what I'm saying. Listen closely. *I don't trust you.* There's something really fucking dodgy about Nic not remembering anything the other night, and after talking to an old friend of yours, I think I know why."

My breathing hitches as Gareth continues to talk. My memory loss was strange, but I didn't think anything suspicious about it. Now I'm not so sure. What has Gareth found out and why hasn't he told me?

"So I want you to take a walk and leave Nic alone. Your crazy arse is not something he needs in his life right now."

His statement is met with silence, and I'm hoping that Dillon took the hint and left. The silence stretches out, but I realise that Gareth isn't coming back in so he isn't alone. It's confirmed when Dillon's voice rings through my house, rage in his voice as he spits his words at Gareth. I've never heard him like this before, and it makes my body shiver with fear.

"You will regret this, Gareth. Nothing will come between Nicolai and me, do you hear me ... nothing!" I can hear the sound of retreating footsteps before Gareth comes back inside and closes the door.

"Well, isn't he a little fucking ray of sunshine?"

I would laugh, but my mind is still firmly stuck on the fact that Gareth knows something and hasn't told me. "What did you find out from his friend?"

Gareth sighs and puts his arm around my shoulder. "Come on. You are going to need more alcohol for this."

CHAPTER THIRTEEN

NICOLAI

"Do you remember a kid called Timothy Mann? He transferred from the school the year before Dillon graduated."

I remember the name but not much else. "Was he a quiet kid with dark hair? Kept to himself a lot?"

"That's the one. What do you remember about the transfer?"

I shake my head. "Nothing. Wasn't it because he moved house or something?" I wrack my brain, but I'm coming up with nothing more than that.

"That's what we were told, but that never rang true to me. I saw his family a few times after he left and it was always at their old house."

I take a long drink of the scotch I poured for myself after Gareth hinted I would need it. Gareth is funny and likes to make a story interesting, but in situations like this, he doesn't exaggerate. So when he told me I needed a drink, I believed him.

"Then with all this shit with you and Dillon I started to think, and you know how dangerous that is. I've told you before that I thought Dillon was a little weird, that there's just something off with him. Well, this whole thing just smells iffy."

I resist the urge to roll my eyes because he sounds like some conspiracy nut.

"So I searched out Timothy, and he had a fascinating story about why he left."

"I'm not going to want to hear this, am I?" Gareth wouldn't be telling me any of this if it didn't have a connection to the other night, and probably something terrible to do with Dillon too.

"Probably not, but I think you need to. It might help you work out what happened between you."

I take another gulp of Scotch and motion for Gareth to carry on. I seem to have lost my voice, and I don't want to risk squeaking out an answer.

"You were right when you said Timothy was quiet, but he did have one friend."

"Dillon." I squeak the name out past the lump of dread in my throat.

"Yeah. Dillon befriended him when he first arrived, and Timothy thought they were good friends. Until one night something changed it all."

I don't want to know what happened and I should tell Gareth to stop talking, but the sick part of me can't get the words to come out.

"Timothy doesn't know what went on. All he remembers is waking up in the morning and feeling something had happened. When he asked Dillon about it, Dillon punched him and told him to leave him alone. Timothy panicked, and that's when he asked to move schools. My thoughts on the whole thing? Sounds kinda familiar do you not think?"

It does. It sounds really fucking familiar, but I still don't know what it means. I stare at Gareth as I try to get all the little pieces of the puzzle to join together.

"I think he drugged you, Nic."

That's what my common sense was telling me but hearing Gareth saying it out loud makes it sound very real. Can I honestly believe that someone like Dillon could drug me and then have sex with me? I can't believe that he would take advantage of me like that, take something that I didn't consent to. Is it possible that Dillon raped me? I shake my head and refuse to think that Dillon could do something like that. He is a little weird, but I think it's because he's never had anyone to care for him. He's become attached to me because I was the first person to pay attention to him. "I don't think so. Look at him. He wouldn't be capable of anything like that."

Gareth looks exasperated, but he keeps his voice level as he talks to me, almost like he's talking to a kid. "He isn't the innocent kid you think he is, Nic. He's a grown man, and he's more than capable of doing something like this. I mean, what do you know about him?"

I think hard, but the truth is I know next to nothing. Other than being his teacher for two years and seeing him in class, I don't know much about Dillon as a person. I don't know his hobbies or who his friends are, he could be hanging out with a gang and I wouldn't know. "Okay, so I don't know that much about him. But he's only a kid." I'm trying to convince myself that Gareth is wrong about Dillon because the alternative is too scary to think about. The only reason that Dillon would have to drug me would be to have sex without me saying no. Bile churns up in my stomach and I down the last of my scotch to try and hide the feeling.

Gareth reaches out and puts his hand on my wrist. I look at him, and the look of sympathy on his face nearly breaks me. "I'm sorry."

I blink rapidly trying to hold back the tears that are threatening to fall. I feel violated and used. Something important was taken from me, and I don't know if I will ever get that back. Trust. I trusted Dillon after he had been through his attack and this is how he repaid me. "I helped him after his assault. I can't believe he did this." My voice comes out quiet, but I can't put any more effort into getting them out louder.

"About that, are you sure he was actually attacked?"

All I can do is stare at Gareth. He keeps throwing this shit at me, destroying everything I thought I knew.

"I just think that it's pretty convenient that he was attacked, but then he didn't want to go to the police. I don't know why he wouldn't want to go."

I want to scream at Gareth that he's wrong about everything. There was a good reason that Dillon didn't want to go to the police, I just don't know what it is. Now all I think is Dillon didn't want me to report it because he had a plan. Did he do all this to get into my house? I struggle to believe that all this is happening, and I cling to the story I'm trying to tell myself. "That doesn't mean anything. I don't want to go to the police, but that doesn't mean I'm not telling the truth about all this."

"I'm not saying he wasn't attacked, but did he tell you where it happened, or who did it, or even why it happened?"

"No, he didn't explain anything." I get up from the stool at the breakfast bar and walk to the cupboard to grab a clean glass. I fill the glass with water and take a drink. I'm not thirsty, but I need to do something before I go insane. Everything that Gareth is explaining makes sense, too much sense, and I realise how fucking stupid I've been. I've invited someone that I don't know into my house and life, and he's done the unthinkable.

A laugh escapes me when I think about the situation that I'm in, but there's no humour in it. I am thirty-five fucking years old, and I put myself in the position where another man could take advantage of me. I thought I'd gotten drunk and let the alcohol make stupid decisions for me. Now I know it's much worse. There's a small part of me that's glad I was drugged so I don't remember the moment that Dillon raped me, but that thought only lasts for a second before the weight of everything hits me. My laughter doesn't stop but along with the manic sound comes the tears. Emotions start to mix, and I'm not sure how I'm meant to feel. I was raped which rips into my heart as I stand here, but I think it shouldn't affect me since I can't remember it. Confusion and anger also fight for dominance, and it all becomes too much.

The glass of water slips from my hand as I collapse to my knees. I'm finding it a struggle to breathe now that my quiet sobs have become body wrenching wails, leaving me shaking as I kneel on the kitchen floor as I try to come to terms with what's happened. Arms wrap around me, and I'm thankful to Gareth because I feel he's the only thing holding me together.

"I'm sorry, Nic. So very sorry."

I hear Gareth whispering into my ear as I rock in his arms. I try to control my crying, but there's no stopping the tears that are soaking into the sleeve of Gareth's shirt. Minutes or hours, I don't know how long, but finally my body calms enough that I can hold my own weight. Gareth removes his arms, and I shuffle backwards until my back hits the kitchen unit. I pull my knees up close to my chest and drop my head against the wood at my back. Gareth's arm brushes against mine as he sits next to me. We sit in silence, but I can feel the thousand things he wants to say vibrating out of his body. I roll my head until I'm looking at him and it must be the permission he's been waiting for.

"I think you should go to the police. They might not be able to prove anything after this time, but I think it's important you tell them what happened."

I nod, not able to find the words to agree with him.

"I'll come with you but let's wait until tomorrow."

I nod again. I feel completely detached from reality, so I'm happy to let Gareth make all the decisions. I want to go to bed and pretend my world isn't collapsing around me. I close my eyes and try to clear everything from my mind. I don't want to think. I don't want to feel. Thankfully the few drinks I've had make it easier to let my brain slip away from reality.

Hands on my arms pull me from my happy place. I open my eyes and look up at Gareth who's trying to get me to stand. I allow him to drag me up and when I'm upright, he keeps me moving until I'm next to my bed. I watch Gareth as he walks around my room but I make no attempt to do anything other than stand there. The numbness that I craved before has come and along with it is the need to sleep. The only problem is I don't think I can actually get into bed. My limbs won't move, and I can't seem to get my brain to force them into action.

Gareth saves me again as he pushes me and I sit heavily on the edge of the mattress. He removes my shoes and socks before making me lie out flat across my bed. When I'm in a prone position, he undoes my jeans and pulls them down my legs. He doesn't say anything as he works to get enough clothes off me so I can sleep, and I have a feeling it's because he knows I'm not capable of any response.

In my head, I tell him how grateful I am that he's my friend and how sorry I am that he's having to treat me like one of his daughters. The words stay stuck but he smiles gently at me when our eyes connect, and in that second it's evident that he can tell what I'm trying to say.

He gives my jeans a final tug as they leave my body and Gareth vanishes for a few minutes. He comes back and grabs my feet, using them to spin me so I'm lying in the right direction. When my head hits the pillow, I relax into the softness. The duvet appears over me, and I suddenly feel protected, like I can hide here forever, and nothing can hurt me. I know that it's not going to happen like that, but at least for tonight, I can pretend that my whole life isn't going to implode tomorrow. I close my eyes and take a deep breath, fighting to block out the worries that are struggling to retake control.

"I'm going now, Nic. Sleep and tomorrow we'll get all this sorted."

I nod, and he ruffles my hair like I used to do to my brother before he got bigger than me.

"I'll see you at work, and when we finish, we'll go to the police. But tonight you need to rest. I'm with you the whole way, buddy. No one is going to hurt you again."

His words make my chest ache. I've never had anyone but family that was willing to go to bat for me. Family is expected, but knowing Gareth is all in, it makes me love him even more. He saw a problem when I had my head in the sand, and not once has he blamed me for any of this. Tomorrow I need to finally face what I've been hiding from, but as I slip into a surprisingly restful sleep, knowing that Gareth will be with there makes it a whole lot easier.

I SIT AND STARE AT MY PHONE, WILLING IT TO RING. I EXPECTED to hear from Gareth this morning but its now second period, and there's been nothing. My morning had been a rush, and I hadn't had time to go to the staffroom before the start of my first class so I thought he might have messaged me, or at least replied to my text.

"Mr Morgan?"

I look up to find Tilly staring at me, and it takes a few beats to realise that the whole class is staring at me. "Um, sorry. What's the problem, Tilly?"

"The video finished like five minutes ago."

I turn quickly to look at the now blank screen that was showing the life journey of an embryo. It's not part of what we're learning at the moment, but I'm so twisted up inside today that there would be no way that I could teach the kids anything. Videos seemed to be the easiest option, and this was the first one I could find. "Right, yeah."

I stand and grab the stack of books in front of me. I look at the clock as I hand one out to each kid. I'm barely halfway through the period, and I have no idea what to do for the rest of the time. I'm pulled from my task when my mobile goes off at the front of the class. I rush to my desk to see who it is. The number calling is unknown, and I'm tempted to ignore it, but my gut is screaming at me that it's important. I have been feeling off-kilter all day like something has happened and I just haven't worked out what yet. It's the reason that I left my phone on during class, which is something I never do. Deciding to answer, I press the button to connect the call and wait for a beat before speaking. "Hello?"

"Nicolai?" It takes me a confused second to recognise the voice as Claire's. I would have recognised it sooner, but she sounds like she's crying.

"Claire, what's wrong?" There's already a boulder-sized lump in my stomach, and it only gets bigger when her tears increase in volume. It takes her a minute to get words out and when she manages my world stops turning.

"It's Gareth. There was an accident. He won't wake up."

I collapse onto my chair as all feeling leaves my body. An accident? That cant be possible, I only saw him last night. "When? How?" The words barely make it out of me, but I'm using all my energy not to bring up the coffee churning in my stomach. I'm still not fully comprehending what she's trying to tell me, the only thing that has registered is that Gareth is hurt.

"I don't know everything. He had a crash, and he's hurt. It's bad, Nicolai. Really bad. Can you come?" She ends her question with a sob, and I'm packing my bag before I even answer her.

"Where are you?"

"St Helens."

I tell her that I will be there as quickly as possible and hang up, the sound of her sobs still ringing in my ears. I'm just about to rush out the door when I remember where I am. I turn to look at the shocked faces of my class. Shit, what do I do? "Everyone take out your textbook and read chapter eleven. I need to step out for a moment, but someone will be here in a minute to take the class."

I turn and leave, a small part of my brain trying to work out what I've just told them to read, but as I rush towards the Head's office to explain what's happening, I don't care. It's something to keep them occupied until another teacher can get there. I'm not meant to leave them in class on their own, but I'm hoping that Mr Johnston, the head teacher, will understand that there was a perfect reason to do it. When I reach his door, I bang on it and wait for a response, bouncing on the balls of my feet when I don't get it instantly. I need to get to the hospital, and all this is just holding me up.

I PRESS THE BUTTON FOR FLOOR SEVEN OVER AND OVER TRYING to get the lift to go faster. When it pings and stops at the fifth floor, I curse under my breath. The older woman standing in front of me turns and glowers, and I usually would feel bad, but today I don't care. I need to get to the seventh floor, to ICU, and see Gareth with my own eyes. Claire said he won't wake up and there's no way that is a good thing.

The lady finally exits the lift, and I press the close door button continually until the doors close. I start bouncing on the balls of my feet again in an attempt to relieve some of the nervous energy thrumming through my body. It's times like this that I wish I carried pens in my pockets so that I'd always have something to fidget with when needed. The doors start to move, and I'm rushing down the hall before they are fully open. I stop briefly at the reception desk to ask what room Gareth is in, listening carefully as the nurse explains the procedures for this ward. I want to tell her to hurry the fuck up, but I also know that this ward is for the sickest of people, so I take the time to make sure I understand how to keep them safe.

She finally stops speaking and points down the hall, telling me that Gareth is in the third room on the left. I make my way down the hall quickly, and when I reach the door, I grab the door handle. I stare at the metal in my hand, but I can't get my hand to press down to open the door. My stomach churns, and I can hear the beating of my heart in my ears. I want to go in and make sure Gareth is alive, but I'm scared to open the door in case he isn't. Standing here I can live with the illusion that he's okay, that he's no different than last night when he left my house. As soon as I open the door, that illusion will be gone.

Oh god, what if he dies? I let go of the handle, and without noticing that I'm moving, my back hits the wall behind me. I can't go in there. I can't see Gareth like this. He is the most energetic and vivacious person I've met, and I want to remember him like that, not lying in a bed, just a body that doesn't move. I close my eyes and take some deep breaths to try and calm my heart that's trying to beat out of my chest.

Just as I prepare myself to leave, to call Claire and tell her I couldn't make it, I hear the door in front of me open, and I know I've lost my window of time. As soon as I open my eyes, guilt hits me like a steam train. I've never seen Claire look so bad in all the time I've known her. Even just after giving birth she looked radiant, now she looks tired and scared. I can't believe that I was going to leave her to deal with this on her own. The love of her life, the father of her children, is lying in there and she's all alone. I'm only thinking of myself, and that makes me the shittiest friend in the world.

CHAPTER FOURTEEN

NICOLAI

I don't bother saying anything as I pull Claire into my arms. She looks about a minute away from falling apart, and I need to get over myself so I can help her through this. Her small arms wrap around my waist before her hands grip the back of my shirt, and I feel more than hear her sobs as I hug her tightly. My guilt builds as we stand there in the hall just holding each other.

"How is he?"

It takes a moment to get a reaction from Claire, and I think that she hasn't heard me when she pulls out of my hold and wipes her eyes. "He's alive, and that's the main thing." She takes me by the hand and drags me into Gareth's room before I have a chance to think about what's she's doing. I don't know how she knows that I'm having difficulty in entering, but like a few times in the past it's like she can read my mind. She drags me over to the edge of Gareth's bed and leans up to kiss me on the cheek. "Talk to him. I know you being here is important to him." She doesn't say anything else but I can hear the door click behind me, and I know that I'm alone with my best friend.

I stare at the wall in front of me because looking down at Gareth is too hard to do. I reach my arm out to the side of me and when my hand connects with his arm a painful sob escapes from my chest.

Finally looking down I wish I hadn't. It's a vision that I will never forget as long as I live. My usually smiling, energetic best friend is pale and lifeless. There are bandages covering his head and one eye, and the parts that aren't covered are bruised and grazed. He looks so small lying in the bed, like he's shrunk inches and lost half his body weight, even though I know that's impossible. Tubes and wires are coming from his arms and chest, but it's the tube in his mouth that has the tears falling faster.

God, what happened to him? Just a few hours ago he was his usual self, now he looks like he's gone a hundred rounds with a heavyweight boxer, and he's not come out the winner. I grip his arm harder and lean down to put my forehead to his, making sure that I'm not pressing on his bandages. I want to be able to hug him, to hold him and tell him everything will be okay, but there's just too much damage to his body. "Gareth, I'm so fucking sorry."

I know it's stupid to feel guilty for him lying here, but the only thing I can think is if it weren't for my problems then he never would have been out last night. He wouldn't have come over to my place. He would have stayed at home, and he would have been safe. Instead, my drama made him come over to support me, and he got hurt because of it.

"Oh, I'm sorry. I didn't realise that there was someone in here."

The male voice has me standing up and wiping my eyes. Making sure my tears are dried from my cheeks, I turn and come face to face with a man in scrubs. He's holding a file folder in his hand, and when I look at his face, he is looking at me with sympathy.

"I was looking for Miss Walker."

I cough to clear the lump that's threatening to choke me, and when I speak my voice sounds rough, making it obvious that I was crying. "She stepped out for a minute, can I help?"

"I had Mr Downes test results, but I can only tell his family."

"It's okay, Dr Miller. Nicolai is family."

Both Dr Miller and I turn to find Claire entering the open door.

She holds out her hand to me, and I take it, pulling her to me until our arms are touching.

"Okay then. We got the new set of scan results, and I've had a look. I'd hoped that the bleeding on Gareth's brain would have started to shrink, but it hasn't. It's not great news, but on the upside, the area of bleeding hasn't increased. This tells me that it might have stopped. We will need to keep an eye on it, but I'm taking it as a step in the right direction."

"When will he wake up?" Claire's fingers grip mine tighter, and I can tell that she's not expecting a good answer.

"I don't know. His body has been through a lot, and it's healing. This might be his brain's way of protecting itself from damage. We have to be patient and give him the time he needs. In the meantime I think you should rest, he'll need you if he wakes up."

The pained cry from Claire makes the doctor's face crumple, and I think he realises what he's said. I tuck Claire under my arm and pull her into my body where she buries her face into my chest.

"I'm sorry. Everything that I've seen points to Gareth waking up, but I don't want to give any false hope. The brain is a complex organ that differs greatly from person to person. But I have seen these injuries before, and the people have woken after a few days with no lasting effects."

"And have some died?" I know I shouldn't ask, especially with Claire in my arms, but I need to know how this might end.

The doctor nods his head, not voicing the devastating news. He looks at me with sympathy again, and I bite my cheek to try and stave off the fresh bout of tears building in my eyes. I need to stay strong for Claire. She's the one who deserves to break over this.

"I should go, but if you have any questions get the nurse to page me."

"Thank you." It feels strange to be thanking someone for delivering such bad news, but I can't blame the doctor for that. He's doing his job, and he is the one who's working to save my best friend's life.

I SIT STARING OUT OF THE WINDOW WATCHING THE SUN RISE over the top of the opposite hospital wing. It's the third sunrise I've seen, and Gareth is the same for this one as he was for the others. The bleeding on his brain has stopped, but the area isn't getting smaller as the doctors had hoped. The only thing that's stopped them stepping in surgically is that the surrounding tissue still looks healthy. He doesn't have much time left before they go in though, so I'm hoping with everything in me that he wakes up soon.

The door behind me opens, and I turn my head to see who it is. I expect to see one of Gareth's many nurses, but instead, my eyes connect with Dr Miller.

"Good morning, Nicolai. Is Claire not here?"

I stand from the chair and stretch my arms above my head. My back cracks in several places and I almost sigh in pleasure. The seats in here are so uncomfortable, but since they're the only ones here, I'll deal with the pain that comes with them. "No, I finally got her to go home. She needed to sleep, and she needed to cuddle the girls. I don't think she's ever gone that long without seeing them."

He gives me a small smile as he makes his way over to Gareth's bed. He takes his medical notes from the end and looks through them before doing something to the machines and making notes. It's the same thing that's done every few hours, and I'm pretty sure I could do it if they asked me to after watching them so often.

I lean back against the wall and cross my arms over my chest. Dr Miller looks younger than I would expect for such a senior position. I mean, I don't know much about this profession, but he looks in his late twenties at the most. This means he's either older than I think and looks great for his age, or doctors graduate a lot younger than I realised.

"Everything still looks good, no major changes which is fantastic." He's still writing as he speaks to me and it gives me a chance to look at him.

Being stuck in this room for so long without any entertainment has me going slightly crazed. I've been too stressed to read, and the television gets roughly three channels, so watching that has been limited. In a bid to stop myself from falling deep into a hole of madness, I've started constructing lives for all the staff that I've met. The nurses all have their own unique story, and it has honestly been a lot of fun. Today is Dr Miller's turn as I really look at him, taking in details I never did before. His hair is blonde but when the sun hits it there is a tinge of red through it, making me think that one of his parents must be a redhead. It's longer than I noticed before, lying loosely around his ears even though it's styled neatly back. He has a relaxed look but in a way that makes him look even more professional in his scrubs. I wonder who he has at home waiting for him? My imagination says that it a strong, muscled man. Someone who could rough up his perfect composure. I can see two dogs, big ones, that he and his husband take to the beach every weekend so they can play in the water. All this would happen in the morning before they went home and had brunch together, their laughter showing how happy they are.

A cough brings my eyes up instantly, and I see Dr Miller staring at me with his eyebrows lifted. Heat covers my cheeks, and I know I have to be blushing at being caught. I wrack my brain to find something to say, but his stare has me struggling to find anything. I can't admit that I was daydreaming about what he does at the weekend. It would sound creepy, and a lot like a come on.

"When will Claire be back?"

I could kiss the man when he gives me an out for my sudden dumbness. "This afternoon I think. She said she wanted to spend a few hours with the kids and I promised to call if there was any change."

He nods and puts Gareth's medical notes back on the end of his bed. "I'll be back in a few hours to check on him. You know where I am if you need me." He still has a smirk on his face as he leaves the room, and I dread to think what he's imagining. Did it look like I was checking him out?

The door closes behind him, and I'm left leaning against the wall with my cheeks burning. I go back to my chair and collapse back into it, pulling it forward until I'm sitting close to Gareth. "I swear when you wake up I'm gonna kick your arse. So if you could hurry up and come back to us all that would be great."

Leaning my head down on the top of his hand I let my mind wander to the past, to all the times that we have spent together. I've not had Gareth in my life long enough to lose him now. We still have so much to do together. I want him to see me find the one, to be my best man when I finally walk down the aisle to declare my love to the world. I want to grow old with him, watching him try to deal when his girls get old enough to date. I want to do it with him by my side. "I need you to wake up, Gareth. I can't do this all without you."

I turn my head until I'm lying on the mattress, Gareth's hand still in mine, and close my eyes. The pain in my chest doesn't ease as I lie there and as I slip into an uncomfortable sleep, I pray that the nightmares from the last few nights don't come back.

I STAND UNDER THE HOT STREAM OF WATER AND LET THE HEAT relax my painful muscles. After spending time sleeping in that god awful chair in Gareth's room, I feel like I'm about ninety years old. When he wakes up, I'm going to need to visit a chiropractor so they can try to put my body back the way it's meant to be. Not that I would change being there for anything in the world. There is nowhere else I could imagine being other than in that room, keeping Gareth company and giving Claire support.

I didn't even want to leave this afternoon when Claire returned from seeing the girls, but after she told me I looked and smelled like crap, I knew that I should take a few hours to get cleaned up. I know she was lying about the smelling part, but I'm sure she was accurate with the way I looked. Too many days in the clothes I was wearing, sleeping and sitting in them until they were creased like I just stepped out of a tumble drier. She'd told me to go home but made the same promise I did. If anything changed, she would let me know straight away.

The water turning cooler finally has me shutting off the shower and getting out. I dry roughly before slipping into my jeans and t-shirt before taking a look in the large mirror above the sink. My lack of shaving the last few days have turned my designer stubble into an unkempt mess, making me look a little like my great Uncle George. I grab my trimmer, deciding that the look isn't a good one, and spend some time taking the worst of the craziness off my face. It won't help with the dark circles under my eyes, but hopefully, it will make me look a little more human. If nothing else it means when Gareth wakes up he won't complain about how shit I look. That thought makes me smile. I miss the grief I get from Gareth about everything, and I can't wait for him to be able to do it again.

The doorbell catches me off guard, and I rush through my house to answer it. As my hand connects with the handle, I stop, suddenly worrying who it might be out there. I haven't seen Dillon since Gareth told him to leave me alone, but then I've also not been here to see him. My gut twists as I imagine him standing on the other side of the door. I haven't spoken to the police like I'd planned with Gareth, my problems seeming so little compared to Gareth being hurt, but that doesn't take away what I know happened to me. I haven't seen Dillon since Gareth made me realise what he did, and I don't know what I will do if it's him on the other side.

A knock on the wood in front of me has me jumping in shock. I put my hand over my chest as I try to calm my racing pulse. Leaning forward I take a look through the peephole, seeing a stranger standing outside looking around the house. This has me moving, and I open up, smiling at the man on my front doorstep. He's wearing a dark grey suit and looks like he would fit in surrounded by businessmen in a meeting. I don't think I've ever looked as comfortable in a suit as this guy, and I hate him a little at how at ease he appears.

"Mr Morgan, Mr Nicolai Morgan?"

"Yes."

"I'm Detective Peter Ramsey, and I was wondering if I could have a chat with you?"

A detective? My mind instantly goes to the Dillon situation, but I dismiss that thought. There's no way that the police know what happened because I never reported it, and I doubt Dillon handed himself in. The most obvious reason for him being here is Gareth's accident. Claire probably sent him here to talk to me about it. "Come in."

The detective gives me a polite smile before entering, his head turning as he looks around my house. I move past him into the main area of my living room as he continues to check everything out. I might not have much faith in the police, but if it helps Gareth, I'll put my feelings aside.

"What can I do for you, detective?"

If I expected to recount the night that Gareth was here, the last time anyone saw him before the accident, I would be completely wrong. Nothing would make me expect the words that come out of his mouth, leaving me standing in shock.

"I'm here in connection with the disappearance of James Kaine. I believe you knew him."

CHAPTER FIFTEEN

NICOLAI

I STAND STARING DUMBLY AT THE DETECTIVE IN FRONT OF ME. "Excuse me?"

"I believe that you met Mr Kaine on a dating website," He takes a pad from his pocket and turns over a few pages. "Called back to basics?"

"Yeah, I met him, and we went out a few times. What do you mean he's missing?"

Putting the notepad back in his pocket, the detective looks at me with intense eyes. "Mr Kaine was reported missing by a family member last Monday. He missed a lunch date with her, and no one has heard from him. It looks like you might have been the last person to see Mr Kaine." The detective's face is completely neutral as he speaks, and he looks cool and calm which is the complete opposite of what I'm feeling.

"He stayed over on Saturday night, but he left early afternoon on the Sunday to go home."

"Do you remember the exact time?"

I try to remember exactly, but I was in such a happy place that I floated aimlessly the whole day. "I can't remember, but I know it was before five because my mum called then." I'd spent the entire time talking to her thinking about my time with James, zoning out so much that she had hung up before I realised she'd gone.

Detective Ramsey nods his head at my answer. "We looked around his house, and there was no evidence that he arrived there after leaving here. Did he say anything that would make you think that he wasn't going home?"

I shake my head. He had told me he was going home to get prepared for work on Monday. We spoke about meeting up, and then he drove away. "He didn't say anything to me. Has he been missing all this time?" I take a few steps back until my calves hit the sofa and I collapse onto it with a thump. I can't believe that any of this is happening.

"Has he contacted you at all?"

I shake my head, closing my eyes when I realise that I should have worried instead of thinking he was the shallowest man in the world. I thought he'd gotten what he wanted from me and blown me off. Instead, he was missing and possibly hurt.

"You didn't think to mention to anyone that he hadn't been in contact? I find that a little strange, Mr Morgan."

I scrub my hands over my face before looking at the detective looming over me. What I'm about to admit is embarrassing, but I have to tell him. "We had sex before he left and I thought ... shit. I thought that he was blowing me off because he got what he was looking for."

If Detective Ramsey is shocked by my admission, he doesn't show it. His face is blank as he continues to stare with those assessing eyes. It's like he's trying to see inside my head to tell if I'm lying. "Did he seem like that sort of guy, one to vanish?"

"No. He was sweet, and I thought that we connected. When he didn't contact me like he said he would, I was hurt. I called and texted a few times, but when he didn't reply I wasn't going to be *that* guy. The one who harassed him and acted desperate. I didn't know that he was missing, I swear I would have contacted the police." And I would have. I would have put aside my dignity and called them so they could help James. Oh god, what's happened to him? Dread creeps through my veins as I imagine James dead in a ditch or his car wrapped around a tree somewhere.

"When he left here was he driving his car? Blue BMW 5 series?"

"Yeah, it was the only one I ever saw him driving."

Detective Ramsey nods his head again. He stares, and his jaw works like he's trying to decide if he's going to share something with me. It's the first time that he's shown anything other than indifference and it worries me. What could make a guy like this lose his confidence? He takes a breath before he speaks, his decision made. "We found his car four days ago. It was parked behind an abandoned business and had been covered by a tarp. Whoever left it there was obviously trying to hide it. We just don't know if it was Mr Kaine that did it or someone else."

"Why would he hide his car?"

"He might have wanted to leave but to make sure that no one knew where to. When people want to disappear, they do strange things. Do you know if Mr Kaine was having any problems?"

None of what this guy is saying sounds like the James I was getting to know. The James I met was confident and warm, with no noticeable stress in his life. He talked about his family and work with an air of happiness, and not once did I get the impression that he wasn't happy. "He seemed happy. I only met him a few times, but when I did, he seemed relaxed. He told me about his life, and there wasn't anything that made him seem stressed or upset. I know I don't really know him, but he didn't seem like the kind of guy who would take off on his responsibilities."

"That's what his family and boss also said. This is completely out of character for Mr Kaine, and that's why we're taking it seriously. You're probably the last person to see him before he vanished, so is there anything else you can think of that might help?"

"I wish there was. Honestly. We said goodbye and arranged to meet again. It's why I thought he was ghosting me."

Another nod from the detective and he pulls a card from his jacket pocket. "If you can think of anything else, Mr Morgan, please contact me. I will be in touch again if we have any other questions, and obviously, if you hear from Mr Kaine, please let us know."

"Of course." I take the card and show him out, closing the door and leaning my head against it. This whole week is turning into a shit show of epic proportions, and I'm close to hiding myself away. First the whole thing with Dillon, then there was Gareth's accident, now James is missing. Just when I thought Karma was finished with me.

I turn until my back is leaning against the door and slide down until I'm sitting on the floor. I drop my head back against the wood and close my eyes. How much more do I have to put up with before the universe thinks I've had enough? A few weeks ago my life was going exactly the way I wanted it. A new guy on the horizon, my best friend unhurt and causing me shit, and the whole thing with Dillon hadn't happened. It was perfect, or as close to perfect as anyone could get. Now I have more worries than I thought possible and I honestly don't know how to sort any of them.

Banging my head against the door, I try to pull myself from my pity party. I'm sitting here feeling sorry for myself when Gareth is lying in a hospital bed, his girlfriend and children missing him desperately. Then there's James' family who are missing a part of them and doesn't know if he will ever return. Yeah, my life isn't so bad when I compare it to theirs. I have everything going for me and I'm acting like my life is hard. *Get a grip Nic.* So what if Dillon did something to me that I can't change, in the long run, it's nothing when I think about Gareth. It was one little thing that I can't even remember. So what if the thought of it makes my stomach churn and my chest tighten in pain knowing that he touched me like that, took something that he had no rights to? God, the thought of him touching me makes my skin crawl. So maybe it is worse than I'm trying to make out, but I would gladly go through it again to protect Gareth.

My mobile ringing pulls me from my downward spiralling thoughts. I don't plan to answer it, but when I see Andrei's name on the screen, I do. "Hey."

"Hey, Nic." There's a moment's hesitation from Andrei, and it takes me back to the first time I spoke to him after the accident. He knows how much Gareth means to me, so he struggled with what to say. "How are things?"

I laugh because I have no fucking idea how to answer him. How do I explain that I want to give up? Tell him that I would give anything to swap places with Gareth so I could have a few minutes peace. Even sleep isn't giving me the escape I want because I started having nightmares the first night I stayed in the hospital. Most of them have been about Gareth dying, but there have been a few of Dillon thrown in for shits and giggles. "It's okay. No change."

"What's wrong?"

"Nothing."

"Don't give me that shit, Nic. I've been your brother for long enough to tell when something's wrong. Is it Gareth?"

I should have known that Andrei would be able to tell from a few simple words that I'm struggling. He's always had this way of sensing that I needed him, even without talking to me. "It's not Gareth. It's just …" Those words are all it takes for the dam inside me to break. The tears come quickly along with chest heaving sobs that I can't control.

"Nicolai, tell me what's wrong. I swear if you don't I'm getting in my car and driving over there."

I can hear Andrei talking, but I can't reply, my voice is lost under all the emotion.

"That's it. I'll be there in thirty minutes."

This finally gets me under control enough to talk. "Don't … I'm fine … don't come over."

"Bullshit, big brother. This doesn't sound like there's nothing wrong. Talk to me."

"I can't, not just now. I need to get back to the hospital. I'm fine … I promise." I take a deep breath and use my sleeve to wipe the tears from my cheeks. The sobs subside leaving only the odd stuttered intake of breath. I push the emotion deep, building the dam back up around it so I can carry on. I don't have time to break apart. I need to be there for Gareth. When he's awake and back home, I will take a moment to let it all out, until then I need to pull all my shit aside.

"Nic, stop being a fucking martyr. You always do this, take on other peoples problems as your own. You don't have to be the hero."

This garners a dry laugh from me. Little does Andrei know that I'm as far from a hero as you can get. "I should get going. I'll call you soon and let know how Gareth is."

"Don't think I'm letting this go, Nic. Be home tomorrow night. I'll be there at eight."

I know better than to think he doesn't mean his threat, he's more like our mum than he wants to admit. "I'll be here."

We say our goodbyes, and I get myself off the floor, my arse cheeks numb from sitting so long on the carpet. I check the clock and realise that I've spent longer away from the hospital than I'd intended. Shit. I grab everything I need and hurry out to my car. I know there is nothing I can do at the hospital, but I don't like leaving Claire too long on her own. Even after her visit home, she looked tired, and I want to take some of the pressure away from her.

I STOP OUTSIDE GARETH'S HOSPITAL ROOM AND WATCH CLAIRE inside as she sits next to the man she loves. She's sitting further back from the bed, close to the window where I've made my home, and she's smiling, talking to Gareth like she has been for days. It makes my heart ache to see the love that's still so obvious between them, even when Gareth isn't able to respond.

I turn away from the door to give them a few more moments of privacy and come face to face with Dr Miller. I jump a little, not expecting to see anyone standing there. "Holy shit." The words slip out without my consent, and it makes him laugh.

"I'm sorry. I didn't realise I look that bad." His eyes are alight with humour, and it makes me smile, the tension that was tightening my shoulders easing slightly.

"Oh, you don't. Um... what I mean is I was just shocked to see you there, Dr Miller." There is not one bit of Dr Miller that looks bad, but I think that I will keep that bit of information to myself. He has been smiling at me more the last few times I've seen him, ever since he caught me staring.

"Please call me Ben. Dr Miller makes me feel old."

That smirk on his face could make any man melt, and if it was another time, I might fall for it myself. "Ben."

"See, that wasn't so difficult." He's been asking me for days to call him Ben, but I've tried to keep it professional. I don't have the energy to argue with him today, not after finding out about James. My chest tightens when I picture James' face. He has the most beautiful smile and I loved putting one on his lips. Soft whispered words or a gentle kiss always made him get a twinkle in his eye and then he would grin like he knew a secret that you didn't. He was perfect, and now I don't even know where he is.

"Where did you go?"

I blink a few times, not realising that I'd zoned out on Ben. "Sorry." My voice comes out thick with emotion, and I struggle not to break down like I did with Andrei.

"Hey, is everything okay?" He reaches out and puts his hand on my shoulder. The move is meant as comforting, but all I can think about is getting away from him. He seems like a nice guy, and the last thing I need is to fuck up his life like I do to everyone else around me.

"I'm good, just tired I think. But thanks for asking."

Ben doesn't look convinced, but he squeezes my shoulder before letting go. "Don't let this drain you. The last thing that anyone wants is for you to become ill with stress. I need to go, but you know how to get me if you need me." He takes a few steps back, his eyes never leaving mine until one of the nurses calls his name. He gives me one last smile and turns away, making his way down the corridor.

I turn back to the door into Gareth's room, my pulse speeding up without permission. Ben's attention might be welcomed at another time, but with my head full of James I don't have space for anyone else. I was falling for James before he vanished, and now I know he hadn't used me. Something horrible has happened to him, and I want to help as much as possible to find out what.

I take a deep breath to try and clear my thoughts of James. I can only deal with one problem at a time, and since the police are helping James, I'm going to focus entirely on Gareth. Helping him get better is the only thing that's important at the moment, that and making sure his girls are okay. Decision clear, I open the door and walk into the room, heading straight to Claire. I lean down and kiss the top of her head before taking my usual seat at the side of the room.

"You and Dr Miller looked rather cosy out there." I can hear the humour in her voice, and it makes me sink further into the seat. The last thing I need is for Claire to make setting me up with Ben a pet project. She's the world's worst romantic and thinks that everyone needs to be in love as much as she is. In theory, it's a fantastic idea, until she sets her sights on you and doesn't stop until you and the other guy are thoroughly embarrassed.

"Uh huh. I was just chatting with Ben."

"Oh, Ben is it? Funny how I still call him Dr Miller."

I groan internally at my mistake. I should stop talking so I don't give her any more ammunition. She's like the CIA once she gets the urge to go after information, and the sooner she leaves this alone, the better. "Leave it."

"I seriously hope you're hitting that."

"I said leave it, Gareth." It takes a few heartbeats for my words to register in my brain and when they do my eyes instantly turn to Gareth's bed. I didn't even look over when I came into the room, my focus on Claire, but if I had, I would've seen the differences in my friend. The tube is gone, and the section of the bandage that was covering his head has been removed, leaving both eyes uncovered. Eyes that are now open and looking at me.

I'm out of my seat and standing over Gareth before I can take a breath. "You're awake. Oh god, you're awake." I am practically screaming as I resist the urge to pull him into my arms for a hug.

"And not deaf." His words are weak but hearing his voice is the most beautiful sound in the world.

"Sorry. Shit, when did you wake up? How do you feel? Is everything okay? Did the doctor say you were fine? And you," I turn to point at Claire. "Why the hell didn't you call me?"

She smirks at me as she continues to read her magazine. "Talk to him. Apparently, all this didn't make him lose his sense of humour."

I stand and look between Claire and Gareth. How can they both be so fucking calm about this? I want to run up and down the hall screaming in excitement, and they are just so blasé.

Claire puts her magazine down, and the look in her eyes shows me she isn't as relaxed as she wants people to think. There's less worry in her eyes now, a brightness that's been missing the last several days, but she still looks cautious. "But to answer your questions. He feels okay, sore and tired, but after everything he's been through, he's not too bad. The doctor is happy that he's awake but wants to keep an eye on him with scans for a few days more. Waking up is a huge step, but there's still a long way to go until he's healed."

I turn back to Gareth and take him in, finally seeing all his face after far too long.

"Stop it." He may be injured and his voice not working entirely, but he can still read me better than anyone.

"You could have died."

"But ... I didn't." He coughs, and his eyes close for several seconds before opening again. "Wouldn't leave my girls ... or you." The last words fade out as sleep claims him. I squeeze his hand, my chest filling with joy when he squeezes back.

"Sleep and heal. I'll be here when you wake up."

CHAPTER SIXTEEN

NICOLAI

"Do you want any coffee?"

I look up from my book to see Claire standing in front of me. "No thanks, I'll stick with water."

"Don't know how you drink that stuff." She shakes her head and mutters as she leaves the room.

I go back to reading once I'm alone. It's the first time that I've been able to concentrate on anything, and it has everything to do with hearing Gareth's voice again. The story drags me in, and within minutes I'm reading about a hot biker who is trying to win the love of his life. Maybe not the most intellectual book in the world, but shit it's good.

A cough pulls my attention to the bed where Gareth is lying. His eyes are open, but it's clear that he's in pain. I put my book down and approach the bed. "Hey."

He coughs again, his uninjured arm coming up to cover his mouth. "Thirsty." His voice is croaky and strained.

I look around and see a glass of water with a straw in it. I pick it up and put the straw to Gareth's mouth, letting him drink as much as he wants. When he's finished, I put it back where I found it. "Don't get used to this. I'm not your man slave."

"Fuck you." The words come out on laughter, and I instantly feel bad when it leads to another coughing fit. Once finished Gareth groans, discomfort evident on his face.

"Should I get a nurse for more painkillers?"

He shakes his head gently while he closes his eyes. "Nah, I'm good. Just sick of being asleep."

I can understand that, but I also hate to see him in pain. While he was, his injuries weren't such a concern because we knew he wouldn't be able to feel anything. Now his pain is front and centre in my mind, and I wish he would stop turning down painkillers. With a cracked hipbone, fractured wrist, bruised ribs, and his head injury, he needs to stop being so fucking stoic. I'm close to pinning him down and force-feeding him morphine, but I'm going to be selfish for a little bit so I can talk to him. Grabbing the chair behind me, I pull it close to the bed.

"What happened to me?"

I'm not sure how much I'm meant to tell Gareth about his accident, but as he looks at me with his pleading eyes, I know I can't keep anything from him. "No one is a hundred percent sure. What do you remember?"

He's quiet for a minute, and I would think that he'd fallen asleep again if his eyes weren't open. "I remember leaving your house but not much after that. No one will tell me anything about it. I think they're scared I will go off the deep end."

"Will you?"

"Just fucking tell me." His voice is stronger now, not like he's been asleep for days.

"They found you on Lexington Bridge, well just off it. You were hit and pushed into the ditch by another car. You don't remember that?"

Gareth reaches up with his good arm and rubs over his forehead. His bandage was removed this afternoon, leaving just a large dressing covering his injury. "Who hit me?"

"They don't know. Whoever it was left the car at the scene, taking off and leaving you there. If it wasn't for a lorry driver going past they aren't sure when they would have found you. Even when they did, there was no identification on you. No phone or wallet, that's why it took so long for them to contact Claire."

He looks really confused, but I don't know what part is doing it. "Why wouldn't I have my phone? I had it at your house, and I know I left with it. I text Claire that I was on my way home."

I remember him having the phone at my house. He checked messages on it while we had been talking. "It must have gotten lost in the crash."

He still doesn't look convinced, but tiredness catches up with him. His eyes close but there's a wince on his face, and I know that he's in more pain than he's letting on. Picking up the buzzer next to his bed, I press it to summon a nurse. When she comes in, I tell her that Gareth's in pain, making her smile when he grumbles about him being okay. Thankfully she doesn't listen to his weak arguments and injects something into his cannula.

Gareth's body visibly relaxes when the pain relief kicks in. The side of my mouth picks up as I watch him slip into a comfortable sleep. I push the chair back so I'm close to the window again just as Claire comes back into the room. She smiles at me before kissing Gareth on the lips. She whispers something to him, and I close my eyes to give them privacy, giving in to a blessedly peaceful sleep.

MY SON RUNS TOWARDS THE WAVES IN FRONT OF ME, RUNNING away from them before the water can get above his ankles. I smile at his antics, amazed that after thirty minutes he's still finding this fun. The arms around my shoulders tighten, and I snuggle back into the hard chest behind me. There have only been a few moments in life that feel as perfect as this, and they all include the two men in my life.

"Daddy, Papa, did you see me?" Darren runs up, and I grab a towel, wrapping it around his tiny body.

"We did, little guy. You having fun?"

He nods his head before pulling out of my hold and rushing back into the water. A small laugh breezes past my ear making the hairs on the back of my neck stand on end. God, I really am the luckiest guy alive.

"Daddy!"

I focus on Darren as he runs towards me, his legs moving quickly but he doesn't get any closer. I sit up and hold my arms out to him, but the sand creeps up his ankles and slows him even more. I try to stand, but the sand sucks me down, keeping me in place as Darren gets further away.

His mouth moves, but the only sound that comes out is a loud screaming, like an alarm sounding through the air. I cry out to him, shouting his name but it gets lost in the deafening sound.

I sit upright in the chair I fell asleep in, my dream taking far too long to clear from my mind. It takes me several moments to realise that I can still hear the alarm from my dream. I blink a few times, and that's when the chaos around me comes into focus. Gareth is in his bed, the screaming I heard in my dreams coming from him. The sound is loud and echoes through the room. Claire is standing at his side, her hair in her hands as panic freezes her to the spot.

I'm moving before I realise it, gripping Gareth by the shoulders as I struggle not to shake him. I need to get his attention without hurting him, but his wide dazed eyes tell me he isn't seeing what's in front of him. "Gareth! Gareth, wake up."

His eyes are frantic as he looks around, finally focusing on mine with some clarity. "Dillon."

"What?"

"Dillon."

I have no idea what he's talking about. Dillon was a big part of our last night together. Is that what he's remembering? "I don't understand, Gareth."

"Dillon did this. He ran me off the road." I want to say that he's confusing what happened, but this is the most alert he's been since he woke up. "I remember. After the crash he opened my door, he told me that I wouldn't ever come between you both. He left me there."

Commotion around me makes me take a step back as nurses surround Gareth but his eyes stay connected with mine. I can almost hear the words that he's still trying to say to me. He's telling me that Dillon hurt him and I need to be careful because he might do something to me. I can feel sweat drip down my back as everything hits me all at once, but it's not fear I feel. This time I am full of pure, raging anger. I clench my hands at my sides with the need to hit something, my blood boiling with a fury I've never felt before.

The alarm that's been sounding through the room finally goes quiet, bringing my attention back to what's happening around me. Ben is standing over Gareth trying to get him to calm down. I didn't even notice him enter the room but his eyes flickering over to me periodically lets me know that he's seen me. I can't stay here. I need to get out and let this angry energy out before I explode. I take one last look at Gareth, seeing that he's finally starting to calm down. Claire's holding his hand and crying, but since there's nothing I can do to help either of them, I slip out of the door and down the corridor towards the lift. I only have one goal in mind.

I'm going to find Dillon and kill him.

I SLAM ON MY BRAKES IN MY DRIVEWAY, BARELY STOPPING before hitting my garage door. I'm out the car and racing towards Dillon's house in seconds, my rage fuelling my need to find him. There are no lights on, but I don't let it deter me. I look through the windows, but there is no movement from inside. I keep moving towards his front door, and as soon as I'm in front of it, I start banging my fists against the wood, the noise echoing deep into the house. I don't stop for a full thirty seconds, the pain radiating through my hand only adding to my fury. "Dillon, open this fucking door." I bang a few more times before rushing back to the living room window. I cup my hands over my eyes and look through the glass, checking every square inch of the room. No one is in there, and there's an aura of emptiness to the place. I move around to the next window and continue my search but come up empty again. "Fuck!"

Racing around the back of the house I check the doors but find them all locked. I bang on the glass door there, venting my frustration on it. I don't know if I expected to find him here, especially after what Gareth remembers him doing, but I'm so fucking frustrated that I can't take my anger out on him. Maybe it's a good thing that he isn't here because I'm not sure I would be able to control myself if I saw him. I need to go home and think this through properly. If Dillon did have something to do with Gareth's accident, then I need to let the police know. My mind instantly goes to Detective Ramsey, and I'm tempted to call him. Would he help me though or is this more a matter for the local police? He's obviously further up the chain of command, and a road accident might not be anything he would deal with.

Fuck.

I drop my head back and stare at the sky. I want to scream out my frustrations, but I'm worried about neighbour's seeing me. Granted, the pounding and shouting at Dillon's door must have garnered some attention already. I should go home before I end up on the wrong side of a police officer's questioning. That would be the final straw for this week, being arrested for trespassing. As I turn to leave I let my eyes survey the back garden, and when they reach the fence that separates our gardens, I stop. It takes me a moment to work out what I'm looking at but when I do I can feel my stomach drop to my feet.

I approach the ... I don't even know what to call it ... structure? Whatever it's name, it's leaning against the fence between our gardens. It looks like one of those wooden houses for kids but it's on top of legs which raises the height, and it's placed behind several large bushes, so it's partially hidden from the surrounding area. I take the steps up slowly, worried what I might find when I get to the top. My brain is screaming at me to turn around, that it's better not to know why this is here even though a horrible thought is starting to form.

As soon as I reach the top of the steps my breath is stolen from my lungs. Every single piece of a puzzle that I didn't realise I was trying to fit together finally clicks into place, and I can see it all so clearly. I back out slowly, taking my time so my legs don't give out on me. I concentrate hard to put one foot in front of the other as I walk back to my own property. Pictures flash in my head, and no matter how much I try to force them out, I keep getting glances of what was in there. A camera with several zoom lenses, a video camera set up on a tripod so it was facing into my garden, and stacks of pictures that I refused to look at because my gut was telling me what they would show. It would be like the pictures on the SD card I found, the ones that invaded my privacy without me even knowing. All this time I've felt like there's someone out there watching me, following me through my life but I put it down to my imagination. Not once would I have dreamt that the quiet kid next door was to blame.

I unlock my front door and make sure I chain it behind me as soon as I'm inside. I clench my hands as I look around my house, no longer feeling safe in here. All this time it's been Dillon that's been following me, taking my pictures without me knowing, and I've had him in here. I asked him to stay the night, in my safe place because I thought he needed my help. A laugh escapes me when I realise how back to front that was. It was me that needed help. I just didn't know it at the time.

My skin erupts in goosebumps when I think about all the times that I've left Dillon alone in my home, and not just even that. The times that I've been in the shower or naked when he's been in here. Did he look? Did he sneak around and look at me when I didn't know? A memory of kicking something under my bed flickers through my mind, and I'm instantly running down the hall to my room, grabbing the bed frame and dragging it from the wall. I climb over the mattress until I can see into the back corner where the item landed. My vision flickers when I see the camera lens lying on the carpet. He was in my room.

Holy shit.

I back slowly off the bed and keep going until my back hits the hall wall. I can't take my eyes off the corner like I'm worried that Dillon is going to appear any second. My chest starts to tighten and I rub a hand over the area to try and loosen the muscles. Panic is screaming inside me that I should run, but I stay in place, wondering what the fuck I should do. Normally I would go to Gareth and get his advice, but he's stuck in a hospital bed because of me. I brought all this shit to his door, and he's the one suffering because I didn't see what was right in front of my nose. I walk down the hall to my living room, the movement making it easier for me to control my breathing. I need to keep a level head and do what's right. Even if I don't get justice for myself, I need to get it for Gareth. It's the least he deserves after what happened to him. He could have died and it would have all been my fault.

"You will regret this, Gareth. Nothing will come between Nicolai and me. Do you hear me ... nothing!"

I hear Dillon's screamed words echo through my head from the night that Gareth had his accident, and they make me stop in place. I'd completely forgotten about them after everything that happened afterwards. He threatened Gareth in front of me, pretty much telling him that he was going to be hurt. How could I have forgotten such frightening words? I shouldn't have let Gareth leave that night. Everything that happened is squarely on me, and I could have stopped all this so many times, but I was blind to it all.

Turmoil burns through my veins along with guilt and anger. So much has happened in the last few hours and I'm having a hard time processing it all. I can feel my nerves start to tingle as everything pummels me at one time. Gareth's accident, James going missing, learning my stalker is the same guy who raped me. It's all too much. My mind twists and turns, and I struggle down the hall to my kitchen. I need something to drink, something to dull this ache inside me. My life has gone from simple to a cluster fuck within a few weeks. I've always prided myself on being able to deal with what was thrown at me, but I'm a fucking fool. My life has been full of roses and fluffy fucking unicorns up until now.

I reach into the cupboard above my fridge and grab the bottle of Scotch that I keep up there. I slam it onto the worktop and stare at it. The last time I had a proper drink was the night that Dillon was here. He poured me tequila before the world vanished. I push the bottle away, the memories churning the contents of my stomach until I need to take a deep breath to keep them from coming up. Turning my back on the Scotch, I go to the fridge and grab my water filter. I fill a glass to the top and chug the thing in one go. The coolness in my stomach seems to help my nerves a little, so I quickly drink a second glass.

I should call Andrei and ask him to come over early. If I can't speak to Gareth, then he's my guy. It will take a while to explain everything that's been happening, but he'll believe me no matter how crazy it sounds.

My head goes a little woozy, and I grab the side of the cabinet as I blink rapidly. Shaking my head to clear it, I reach into my back pocket and grab my phone, pressing speed dial for Andrei. Another dizzy spell hits me, and I stagger slightly.

"Hello?"

I hear Andrei's voice, but it takes a minute for it to register through my fuzzy thoughts. "Hey, it's me."

"Hey, big brother. Don't tell me you're cancelling for tonight because I'm coming anyway."

Darkness starts to creep into my vision. "No, it's ..." Thinking is becoming hard, and the words I need won't form.

"Nic, are you okay?"

Am I okay? I want to answer, but the darkness is swallowing my whole world. I hear a bang and look down to see my mobile lying on the floor. I stare at it not understanding why it's on the ground. I don't remember dropping it.

"Nic!"

My world tilts under my feet and I know I should reach out to grab hold of something but I can't get my body to do what I want. My back connecting with the floor knocks the breath out of me, and I stare at the ceiling, watching as everything vanishes into the shadows. I try to move especially as I hear my brother still shouting over the phone, but I can't get my body to do what I want it to. The darkness spreads, and my eyes close on their own, the sudden tiredness hitting me hard. I struggle to open my eyes one last time, and I wish I hadn't. The face that is etched into my mind as I escape into the blackness is Dillon's.

CHAPTER SEVENTEEN

NICOLAI

THE RADIO PLAYING AROUND ME PULLS ME FROM THE DEEP sleep I'm having. I don't remember leaving music on, but it wouldn't be the first time I've fallen asleep with it playing. I roll onto my side, my eyes flickering open when something tugs at my neck. My eyes flutter open, and when I get them to focus, I'm met with a brick wall and a chair I don't recognise. Confusion sneaks in as I sit up and look around, the weight on my neck tugging more. I absent-mindedly put my hand up to relieve the pressure, expecting to find my t-shirt tangled around my neck. When my hands meet cold hard metal, everything rushes back.

What I found in Dillon's garden. Connecting the pictures and Gareth's accident to Dillon. Calling my brother before everything going dark. I look around trying to get my bearings, but nothing I see is familiar. I'm in a large room with brick walls. The rest of the room is pretty bare with only a few tool chests, a table and chair, and the bed I'm sitting on. The main thing that I can see, or more accurately, can't see, is any windows. The room is completely enclosed with only two doors and a set of stairs at the far side. The light in the room is coming from a simple overhead bulb.

I move to the edge of the bed and put my feet on the ground, the weight around my neck grabbing my attention again. This time I give it my full focus, reaching up and running my hand along it. My blood goes cold in my veins as I feel the heavy metal collar hanging around my neck. I follow the smoothness, hoping to find something that will release it from my body, but there's nothing. Just as I think things can't get any worse, my fingers brush against something, and I follow it until I'm turning in place and I see the metal chain that connects me to the wall.

Instantly I'm standing, pulling the chain to try and get it free from either the bricks or my neck, but all that I achieve is the metal digging into my skin. Panic makes me pull harder, leaning my whole body into the action, and not even stopping when I feel dribbles of blood wetting my neck. I have to get out of here. I don't know what's going on, but my fight or flight response is telling me if I don't get away something horrible is going to happen. A scream bubbles up my throat, but I manage to stop it before it comes out and possibly alerts whoever has me here. The longer I'm alone, the longer I have to try and get away.

I drop the chain and frantically look around the room. There must be something I can use to get this thing off my neck, or if needed, as a weapon. There's nothing within reach no matter how much I try to stretch my body, so I collapse to the floor to check under the bed I was lying on. Frustration wells up when I lift the side of the blanket to find that the mattress is sitting on top of some wooden structure. Not only does it mean there's nothing to see under there, it means that I can't use it as a hiding space if I need to. I get back on my feet and continue to look around even though I know it's pointless. Whoever put me in here planned everything down to the last detail. A little manic laugh comes out, and it echoes through the nearly empty room. I'm acting like I don't know who did this but I do. I can remember the face I saw before I blacked out, and there would be only one reason he was there. I haven't seen him since the night he argued with Gareth, but I distinctly remember him being in my home tonight.

There's a noise from the set of stairs I saw, and I still in place when I see Dillon coming down into the room.

"You're awake." His smile is broad as he approaches me, but I notice that he stays far enough away that I won't be able to reach him.

"What are you doing, Dillon?" I'd hoped my voice would come out strong and commanding, but I fail completely. Instead, I sound frightened and unsure.

"I'm so glad you're here. I have so much planned, and I didn't think that the day would ever come that I would finally get you here."

My stomach tumbles at his words. He's been planning this all along, and that knowledge scares the shit out of me. "Dillon, seriously. You need to stop this and let me go."

"I think you'll enjoy being here, away from everyone else. People keep trying to get in between us, but they can't do that here."

It's clear that Dillon isn't listening to a word I say and that's going to make it difficult to get him to see what a mistake this is. I step closer to him, smiling like I don't want to grab him and knock him the fuck out. "I think it's great that we'll have some time, but maybe you could unlock this," I tap my finger against the collar on my neck. "And we could go somewhere and chat?" He stares at me, and I try to relax my body. If he's going to believe anything I say, I need to seem like none of this is strange, that I'm anything but freaked out by being kidnapped from my home and chained to a wall. Relaxing is hard, but I finally get my body to cooperate with my plan.

"You're lying. You didn't want anything to do with me before."

"That's because I didn't know that you liked me. If I had known..." I don't know how to finish the sentence and make it sound believable. If I try to convince him too much, there's a good chance he'll see straight through me. Better to keep everything as vague as possible.

"I tried to tell you."

"I'm sorry." He takes a step closer, and my heart leaps with joy. I don't know if he realises he's doing it, but the space between us is closing, and soon he'll be within grabbing distance. I'm not sure what

I'll do once I get him but I need to find the key to this thing around my neck.

"I've spent my life speaking, and people don't hear me. You, my dad, that's why I needed to get your attention. I needed you to see me."

At least he achieved his goal. I've seen him, and there will be no way that I will ever forget him. "I see you, Dillon."

"Not yet you don't. Not really. But you will ... soon." He gets a slightly evil grin on his face before he backs away, putting more and more distance between us before leaving me alone in the room again.

"Fuck!" I try to rush after him, but pain lancing through my neck stops me from moving far. Escaping isn't going to be easy, and I need to put some thought into it. I take a few steps back and collapse onto the bed. My brain is telling me to give up, to curl into a ball, and hide from the whole shitty situation, but I can't. If I give in to the fear and hopelessness that's trying to engulf me, then I might never get out of here and see my family or friends again. "Oh god." That thought's the one that nearly pushes me over into a pit of despair that's trying to claim me, and I drop back onto the bed, staring at the ceiling.

I DON'T KNOW HOW LONG I'VE BEEN LYING ON THE BED WHEN I hear Dillon coming down the stairs, but it's been long enough that my fear has left me, leaving in its place nothing but anger. I've spent my time alone plotting my escape. I know I can't get the chain from around my neck without a key, but overpowering Dillon will be easy enough to do. He isn't a large guy, so I need to choose my moment and attack. It's a simple plan, but it will work if I time it correctly.

"I hope you're hungry." Dillon's voice sounds happy, like he doesn't quite get what he's done.

I think back to the years I've known him and try to pinpoint anything that felt off about him. He was always quiet, someone who kept to himself and didn't have many friends. It didn't strike me as odd though, but maybe I was missing the obvious because Gareth seemed to be able to see something in him that I couldn't. My heart aches again at the thought of what Gareth has suffered because of me, but before I can let myself brood on it too long, Dillon appears at the side of the bed with a tray in his hands. I sit up, and he takes a step back, always making sure there are a few feet between us. I should rush him now and get it over and done with, but I need to be sensible. I will only get one chance at it, and I need to make sure it works.

"I brought you some food. You must be hungry after sleeping so long."

I try to keep my face neutral, but it's fucking hard when he says shit like that. He's making all this seem so reasonable, like I simply took a nap and missed lunch. "I'm fine."

He ignores me and puts the tray down on the small table across from the bed. Taking a glass of water, he turns and holds it out to me. I stare at it for a few seconds, the smile on his face irritating me more than I thought possible. When I don't make any attempt to take it, the smile slips from his lips, his eyes taking on a sad look that shouldn't have any effect on me but it does. *What the actual fuck?* How can he still make me feel bad for him after everything he's done?

When he realises I'm not going to take the glass, he turns and puts it on the tray, spending a few moments moving around the other dishes. I use his distraction to my advantage, jumping from the bed and grabbing him by the back of his t-shirt. I pull with all the strength I have, and a thrill of satisfaction goes through me as I watch him fall backwards. He reaches out to try and find something to stop his fall, but there's nothing, leaving him to connect with the floor with a loud thump as he hits the ground. His eyes bulge, and I know he's struggling to catch his breath when his face reddens. That's when I realise I'm losing my upper hand by just staring at him, letting him recover before I make my next move. I drop down onto him and sit across his waist, tightening my thighs when he struggles to throw me off. I ignore his bucking and reach down to wrap my hands around his throat, tightening my grip as he reaches up and wrestles with my arms. His nails scratch my skin leaving blood trails, but I refuse to let go. I do ease up slightly when his eyes start to bulge from his head. He won't be able to get me out if he's dead.

Dillon gasps a few times when I finally let air into his lungs, but he keeps trying to pry my hands off him.

"Where's the key?" My question is met with silence, and I want to shake him until he answers, but I stay calm. "The key, Dillon!"

His lips move, and I regret strangling him so hard. Maybe he can't speak because I pressed too hard. Fuck. I lean down slightly so I can hear any whisper that he might manage.

"Fuck you." The words come out very clearly, and I barely have a second to register what he's said before something hard hits me on the side of the head.

I slump to the side, sliding off Dillon's body and collapsing onto the floor. Stars float in my vision as I lie and stare at the ceiling, blinking to try and get some sense back. My head is screaming at me to move, to get up and find Dillon because this is my only chance. The only problem is I can't get my body to do what I want. When I hear a noise next to me, I force my body to move until I'm on my knees. I won't get another attempt to escape, so I need to finish this before Dillon gets away. I don't know what will happen if he does and I don't think I want to find out.

I lift my head to find that Dillon hasn't moved as far as I thought he had. My heart jumps again at the knowledge that I might still have a chance to get free, and I reach out, grabbing him by the foot and dragging him back towards me. I crawl behind him as he gets to his knees and I try to grab his hair, but he turns on me, moving quicker than I anticipated. His eyes connect with mine for a fraction of a second before his elbow connects with my jaw, splitting my lip instantly. If I thought I'd seen stars before I was wrong. I shake my head in an attempt to clear my vision, but I know that it's already too late. I've lost the upper hand.

A punch to the side of my face knocks me backwards, and I land with a thud on the floor. I groan as I roll, my face feeling like it's on fire. The ache in my cheek is worse than anything I've felt, and I just want to lie here and feel sorry for myself.

"You ruined everything! Why couldn't you be nice? I did all this for you ... why can't you be honest about your feelings?"

Dillon's voice is filled with rage as he screams at me and I mentally prepare myself for another attack. When it doesn't happen, I open my eyes, squinting as the tightness in the side of my face pulls at my skin. I see Dillon's retreating form as he storms through a door at the end of the room. I've wondered what was in there, but my chain didn't let me reach it to find out.

A minute later I find out what's inside and I wish I hadn't.

I don't know the guy Dillon's wheeling out on a chair, but I feel sick while I watch everything unfold in front of me. Dillon pushes the guy until he's in front of me, still out of reach but easy for me to see what's happening. His face is a mess of bruises, one eye almost closed with the swelling, and his mouth is covered by a piece of tape. My heart goes out to the guy because the ache in the side of my face is bad enough, and it's clear to see that this man's been through a lot more than that.

"Aren't you going to say hello?"

Dillon pulls my attention, and I stare at him, not sure what he's talking about.

"Oh come on. You seemed friendly enough before."

I struggle to stand, but I finally manage, using the end of the bed for balance. My eyes never leave Dillon though, so when his smile changes I see it instantly. There's an edge to the way his lips are pulled up like he has a secret that he can't wait to share. "Dillon, I don't understand." My voice comes out weaker than I would like but I'm struggling now like my body has had enough and wants to just shut down. I wipe the blood from my chin as he walks over to the guy and I cringe, worried that he is about to hurt the stranger again.

When he gets to him, Dillon grabs his hair and pulls his head back, earning a grunt from the man. It's a little bit of a relief knowing that the guy is alive, but that relief fades instantly when Dillon speaks. "Look at that, James, he's forgotten about you already."

My stomach drops and I turn to look at the guy that Dillon's talking to. Silvery, grey eyes connect with mine, and I know instantly that it's him. *James.* A sob breaks free as the facts fully register in my mind. The fact that no one has seen him since the night he left my house. I was the last person to see him, except I wasn't. Dillon must have been watching and taken James after we said goodnight. *Oh god.* First Gareth's accident and now James. Both of these are my fault. I was falling for James, and now Dillon is using him as a pawn against me.

"James, I'm sorry. Dillon, what did you do?" I can't get my eyes to leave James, registering all the injuries that mar his body. He's wearing a shirt, but most of the buttons are missing, showing several bruises and cuts that litter his chest. The more I look, the more damage I see, and it makes the tears fall faster.

"Oh look, he finally remembers you. You must have been a shitty fuck, James. Sorry, dude." Dillon still has an evil glint in his eye as he stands straight, grabbing something from behind the chair. My focus is entirely on Dillon now, my heart hurting too much to look at James. He takes a step forward until he's level with James' legs but his eyes never leave mine. He has blood dripping down his neck where his nails scratched at his skin when I was choking him, and his eyes look bloodshot. It's the only obvious injuries of the fight we just had but compared to the man sitting next to him he looks like he's barely been touched.

I feel the despair from earlier seeping into my bones again as I realise that all my chances to escape are now gone. Even if I could get the better of Dillon again, which I doubt now that he knows I'll attack given a chance, there's no way I can leave here without James. He's here because of me, and I'll do anything in my power to make sure he walks away from this.

"You need to behave, Nicolai. I can't have you stepping out of line, look at the mess of your face." He looks over my face, and a genuinely sad look falls over him. He looks like he regrets making a mark on me. "I need to punish you, but I refuse to hurt you. So, James will take your punishment." He pulls something out from behind his leg and my eyes open wide in horror.

Holy shit, he can't be serious? I try to rush him, but pain lances through my neck as the metal collar digs into my skin. I watch as Dillon bends James' little finger to a strange angle, the garden secateurs digging into the skin until it changes colour.

James' eyes are wild with fear, his body shaking against his restraints and his breathing raspy as panic sets in.

"Dillon, don't! Please don't hurt him."

He doesn't move the secateurs from James' finger, but I can see the pressure ease. "Why shouldn't I?"

"Because I'm begging. Please don't hurt him. I'm sorry, I'll be good." Vomit nearly joins the words as I speak them, but I will do or say anything to get his attention away from James.

My eyes flicker to James who is no longer shaking violently. His stare is clearly on me, and he's shaking his head frantically at me. I look away not wanting to see his face as I do this. I turn my attention back to Dillon who's finally moved away from James. I give a silent sigh of relief before looking at the ground.

"That was a very stupid move."

"I'm sorry." My minds screaming at me to attack again, to take him out while his attention isn't on James, but if I do and fail again, I'm scared he'll kill James without a second thought. A shadow falls over my body, but I don't look up, knowing that it can only be one thing. He might not be as tall as me but in this situation Dillon feels ten foot taller, holding all the power against me, and it's scary.

"Get on your knees." It's the words I was expecting but hearing them still hits me straight in the gut. This whole thing was leading here, he didn't do all this so he could chat to me, but now that the time is here I want to cry.

Slowly I collapse to my knees, my head still dropped towards the floor so I don't have to see either man. I want to forget that James is sitting watching this. I need to pretend that I'm alone with Dillon and not living this nightmare with an audience.

"You know what to do." Dillon's voice sounds gravely, and when he steps right in front of me, his erection is pressing against the front of his jogging bottoms.

I fight against the bile rising in my throat as I reach up with shaky hands, gripping Dillon's waistband and pulling it down over his hips. His dick is thick and angry looking as it sways in front of my face. I can smell how turned on he is, and I struggle not to gag. I need to get on with this. It's going to happen no matter what so I just need to do it, pretend I'm somewhere far away.

Licking my lips, I move forward but before I connect with his body, Dillon grabs me by the hair and pulls my head back until I'm looking at him. His grip is punishing, and the pain in my head brings tears to my eyes. "Don't think of doing anything stupid. Be nice, or he will suffer."

CHAPTER EIGHTEEN

NICOLAI

I STARE AT THE CEILING AND TRY TO FORGET EVERYTHING THAT'S happened the last few hours. My body still aches from my fight with Dillon, but more than that my heart aches for what James has gone through. He's had no part in any of this, and I hate that Dillon is now using him to get what he wants. My stomach sours as I picture James' face and the damage there. He's been here for so long, and I don't know exactly what Dillon has done to him, but the torture is clear to see in the bruises and cuts. I'm completely to blame for every second of pain that he's endured, and I don't know if I will ever be able to get past that.

Every part of me wants to talk to James, but after Dillon was done with me, he moved James back into the room where he'd been hiding him. My plan had been simple before, get away from Dillon by doing anything that was needed. Now, knowing James is locked in that room, I'm willing to give Dillon anything he wants if it keeps James alive. That's where my head is at the moment. I want to promise Dillon that I will stay with him forever if he lets James walk away. James has nothing to do with all this so he shouldn't be here.

I don't look at Dillon as I hear him approach the bed. I don't have the energy to fight again, so I'll lie here and do what I'm told. If I'm honest, I want to fall asleep and never wake up again. It might be cowardly, but ignoring all my problems seems like a fantastic idea.

"Are you okay?"

That's an interesting question and one I don't even know how to answer? Am I okay? I'm numb. I'm scared. I'm tired. I'm a lot of different things, but I don't know if I'm okay.

"Mr Morgan."

"Don't call me that." There's more anger in my voice than I had anticipated. "Don't ever call me that."

The mattress moves next to me, and it pulls my eyes in that direction. Dillon's sitting next to me on the bed, and if I had any energy, I would go for him. Instead, I lie here, staring at his sad looking face.

"You shouldn't have attacked me."

"I'm sorry." And I am sorry. I'm sorry for James being hurt. I'm sorry that I'm probably going to end up dying in this room. I'm not sorry for attacking him, but I am sorry for not finishing the job.

"It's okay. We need to work on this, get to know each other better."

"Please let James go."

Mentioning James changes Dillon's face instantly. He no longer looks sad and distressed. He now seems angry and ready to fight again. "I can't do that."

"Why?"

"Because if I let him go then you won't be with me. I need him to make you want me."

I want to explain to Dillon that James being here will never make me want him, but it will make me behave and that's almost the same thing. "I will stay. Just let him go, and I'll do whatever you want."

"I want to be with you. I love you."

My stomach churns at his declaration, and I wonder if he's ever really loved anyone in his life. What he's doing now has nothing to do with love and everything to do with control.

"See, you can't say that to me."

"Dillon, you've had longer to get used to this than me. Give me a chance to catch up." The words make me want to vomit but it's the only way to possibly get what I want, and the only thing I want is James to be safe.

"I can do that."

"So, you will let James go?"

"No, but I'll give him a meal and let him shower."

It's a small step in the right direction, and I force a gentle smile on my face to show Dillon I appreciate it. Hopefully, if I keep Dillon happy, he'll allow James more freedom, and then he can escape from here. "Thank you, Dillon."

He rubs my arm, and I struggle not to flinch back from his touch. "I would do anything to make you happy, Nicolai." He gets up and heads straight to the room where he's keeping James. I sit up and watch, hoping he will let me see James again but he slips inside and closes the door behind him.

GENTLE MUSIC WAKES ME AGAIN, AND I STRUGGLE TO STAY asleep. I didn't dream the night before, and the darkness was amazing. If I open my eyes, I'll have to admit where I am and who I'm with. When I'm asleep, I can pretend I'm at home in my own bed. The sound of dishes being moved has me finally opening my eyes. The overhead light never went off so at least it doesn't blind me when I sit up and watch Dillon setting out breakfast on the small table I noticed yesterday. I ease myself to the edge of the bed before standing and stretching out my back. The weight of the metal around my neck threatens to drag me back into despair, but I made a few decisions last night while I waited for sleep to claim me, and that's when my plan was decided.

My plan is. Keep Dillon happy no matter what. If he wants me to be sweet, then I do it. If he wants me to get on my knees and blow him again, then I do it. If he wants me to bathe with him in a tub of honey, then I fucking do it. Keeping him happy and sane is the only thing that's important, and I plan to do it to the best of my ability. My dignity and safety don't come into play now that I know James is here. I'm merely a way to get him out of that door.

"Morning." Dillon sounds happy today, and if it weren't for the marks on his skin, you wouldn't know that anything had happened yesterday.

"Morning. I'm starving." I make sure I smile as I take a few steps towards the table where breakfast is laid out.

"I made bagels and peanut butter. I know you like them." When Dillon acts like this, it makes it difficult to remember what he's done. I could probably look at him like my old student if there weren't a cold, hard reminder chained around my neck. He seems so young and innocent, but I can't forget that he isn't.

"My favourite breakfast. I'm surprised you remember that."

"I remember everything."

I struggle to keep the smile plastered on my face, so I pick up a bagel and take a bite. There are two chairs next to the small table, and I take a seat on one of them, moving it slightly so the chain doesn't pull too much. Dillon sits across from me and pushes a large coffee mug in my direction. I take it and struggle with the idea of throwing the hot liquid in his face.

Keep Dillon happy. Play nice.

I repeat my new mantra in my head and take a drink. We eat in uncomfortable silence for a few minutes, and it's a relief when Dillon starts speaking.

"Do you enjoy being a teacher?"

"I do. I love knowing that I'm helping kids to reach their dreams and goals. I know not every kid loves science, but if I can help a few out of each class, it's worth it."

"I loved your class."

"Can I ask you a personal question?"

Dillon eyes me warily before nodding his head at me.

"Why didn't you go to medical school? You were one of the

smartest kids I ever taught and I thought your dream was to be a doctor."

"It was, but when I went to apply it meant leaving, and I just couldn't do that." His cheeks tinge red, and I have an awful feeling that he's only telling me half the story.

"Leaving couldn't have been that bad. Didn't your dad go over everything with you?" I haven't seen much of Dillon's dad over the years we've been neighbours but since Dillon was such a good student, I never really thought anything about it.

"My dad didn't care what I did. He just didn't want me to interrupt his life. You were the only one who cared." The last statement is said quietly, and I know that he believes what he's saying. I'll admit that I did care for Dillon, but no more than I cared for the rest of my students. For the few years that they're part of my class, they become like my family, and I only want what's best for them.

I keep all that to myself so I don't piss him off. *Keep Dillon happy. Play nice.* "You've never really told me about your dad."

The relaxed look on Dillon's face vanishes and is replaced by anger that I didn't think was possible on him. He was always such a happy kid at school. Even when he was being bullied, he seemed more resigned to it than angry. This look is new, and I make a mental note not to mention his dad again. "My dad was an arsehole. All he was ever interested in was women and money. The only reason he kept me around was he thought he would get more pussy being the nice single dad."

I should feel sorry for the story that he's telling me, but the words I'm stuck on is that his dad *used* to be an arsehole. Dillon either means his dad has suddenly changed his ways to become dad of the year, or it means he's dead. Neither option seems like the right one. I'm sure that I would've heard if his dad had died. Wouldn't there have been a funeral? I want to ask him what he means, but I'm genuinely scared for him to clarify his statement. Finally, the not knowing gets too much, and I give in to my need to ask. "Used to be?"

I FEEL HIM WATCHING

"Do you want another bagel? If not I'll tidy all this away so you can get cleaned up." He stands and picks up the plate of bagels, holding it out to me. I shake my head because I'm not sure I could swallow anything without choking. He gives me a sweet smile and tidies up the stuff from the table. The whole thing feels so domesticated, if you don't take into account the metal chain that I'm wearing. Dillon picks up the tray and leaves the room, his footsteps fading as he reaches the top of the stairs, and I'm left sitting on my own wondering what the day will bring. One thing this morning has proven to me, Dillon has problems that I never imagined, and one of them is seeing things as they are. He doesn't seem to think what's happening is wrong and I'm scared what will happen if I try to show him that it is.

I'm not left on my own for long, and I watch with my heart in my throat as Dillon approaches the door where James is being held. I start to get a little light headed as I take in what's occurring in front of me and I force myself to breathe.

"Out." Dillon's voice is rougher than the one he uses with me, and I realise that he's trying to sound in control. This is the side of Dillon that I hadn't seen before that night with the tequila. That's when this Dillon started creeping into the one I'd always known. At the time I didn't notice it, but now I can see it so clearly.

James hobbles out of the door, making sure that he's keeping a small distance between him and Dillon. He looks scared, and I can't blame him. He's limping and holding his ribs, but at least now he's wearing clean clothes, and he looks like he's had a shower.

"Go sit on the bed."

It takes James much longer than it should to make it to the bed I've not long left, and I have to hold onto the side of my chair not to rush to him. I want to turn away from James, to look at Dillon so he thinks he has my full attention, but I can't force myself to move my focus. Finally, James sits, taking his time to position himself carefully on the edge of the bed.

"I'm going upstairs to get your food. This whole place is rigged with cameras so don't try anything." Dillon moves close to James who flinches back. "You know what will happen if you disobey."

James stays perfectly still while Dillon heads up the stairs. His shoulders slump when we hear the door at the top bang closed.

I want to go to James, to check he's okay, but I don't want to risk him coming to any more harm. The silence grows between us like a living thing, and it becomes too much for me to cope with. "James?" I keep my voice low in case Dillon has microphones set up in the room as well as cameras.

"I'm okay." James doesn't lift his head, but I can hear him clearly. "Has he hurt you?"

I laugh at his question, and it comes out on a quiet sob. James is sitting in front of me broken, and he's worried about me? My reaction finally has James looking up and the sob increases as I get a good look at his face. The bruising is older going by the colour of it, but his eye is still swollen and painful looking. "I'm fine. God, James. I'm so fucking sorry."

"You didn't do this to me. He did. That little fucker."

"But you wouldn't be here if it wasn't for me. I'm the reason he's doing this to you."

James shakes his head but flinches in obvious pain.

"I hate that he hurt you."

He looks like he's going to reply to me, but the door opening at the top of the stairs silences us both. Dillon appears a few moments later with a bottle of water and a few slices of bread. I want to complain, tell him that James needs more than that to eat, but the way that James grabs the food and eats it makes me wonder how long he's gone without food.

I turn away to try and hide the tears in my eyes, blinking rapidly to try and stop them falling. I refuse to let Dillon see that I'm affected by anything he's doing. *Keep Dillon happy. Play nice.*

Hands on my shoulders make my body tense, and I force myself to relax, but I barely manage to let the tension out of my muscles.

"I brought you something." Dillon wraps his arm around my

shoulder until I can see his closed hand in front of my face. He waits a few moments before turning his hand over and opening his fingers. I'm left looking at what looks like a memory stick. I have no idea why he's brought me something like this, but he continues talking and explains. "I thought you might like some music to keep you entertained. I know how much you love music." His hand disappears, and he walks over to a section of the wall I hadn't paid attention to before.

I take a small step closer and see that there's a small hole in the wall. It becomes clear it's a USB jack when Dillon pushes the memory stick into it. He smiles as he approaches the tool shelves that I can't reach and takes a remote control from the drawer. He presses a few buttons and soon the sound of Imagine Dragons, my favourite band, comes through the hidden speakers. It's not the first time there's been music, but it's the first time I've seen the source.

"Here, you can change it whenever you want. I want you to be happy here." He hands me the remote and looks expectantly at me. I don't know what he wants so I smile as sweetly as I can manage.

"Thank you."

Dillon takes a step forward, and I force my feet to stay stuck to the floor. The last thing I need is for him to think I'm scared of him, even if I am. "Can I kiss you?"

No. No. No.

The words scream inside my head, but I go against them and nod my head. Closing my eyes, I hold my breath until I feel Dillon's lips against mine. He's gentle as he leads the kiss, and I try and relax into it. It goes against every part of me to kiss him back, but self-preservation and protecting James has me moving my tongue against Dillon's. I want to vomit, to rush to the closest bathroom so I can empty my stomach and then wash my mouth out, but instead, I reach out and grab Dillon's hips. The moment I connect with him, his body relaxes into mine. I need Dillon to believe that I want to be here so I can get James out, and to do that I need him to forget that I attacked him.

Dillon finally puts some distance between us, and he rests his head against my forehead. "I've wanted to do that for so long."

A memory at the back of my mind flares up, and I'm sure I can remember Dillon kissing me before. Maybe it was the night he drugged me and raped me. I take a deep breath and push the memory away. If I think too hard about that night, I won't be able to let him touch me, no matter what's at stake. I just have to keep my eye on the goal.

"Thank you." Dillon takes a step back, and I see the massive smile on his face. He reminds me of a kid who got the exact gift he wanted for Christmas. His expression makes him look younger than he is, and it makes my stomach churn.

Everything about this situation is a mind fuck, but knowing how young he is, that I used to teach him in high school, is one of the worst things. I would be shocked if a grown man could put this plan together and pull it off, so Dillon being able to do it shows me how little I know about him. He lived next door, and not once did I see anything disturbing about him. Gareth did, and I wish I could get one last chance to tell him he was right.

CHAPTER NINETEEN

JAMES

I SIT QUIETLY IN THE CORNER AND WATCH NICOLAI AND DILLON eating pizza. I've discovered that if I stay as quiet as possible, Dillon leaves me out of that fucking room and I like to keep an eye on Nicolai. He's been here for about four days now, and I can see him starting to fade away in front of my eyes. He seemed to have fight in him that first day I saw him, but the fire is fading quickly.

I still can't believe he's here. When I was dragged out of the room I thought I'd die in, and I saw Nicolai standing there, the sense of defeat nearly took over. I didn't know why Dillon had taken me, but it never occurred to me that Nic might be next. Everything seemed to click into place as Nicolai looked at me with panicked eyes, and it seemed so bloody obvious. I was there to make sure he behaved. I knew Nicolai didn't recognise me and that was the first time I realised how damaged my face was. I don't know how long it'd been since Dillon had drugged me and brought me here, all the days blurred into one another alone in the dark, but the beatings had left me wanting to die.

Since the moment I'd been attacked on the way to my front door, life had been one big nightmare. I thought I was being mugged, that if I gave over my wallet and car keys without a fight I would be okay,

169

but then the world vanished into a haze of darkness before I had a chance to do anything to fight back. Waking up on cold concrete made me think that I'd been knocked out and left outside my house, but I couldn't have been more wrong. The darkness had worried me at first thinking I'd gone blind but after blinking a few times, I worked out that it wasn't completely dark. There had been a strip of light coming from underneath what was probably a door. I planned on trying to find a handle on the door, but when I sat up my stomach revolted and I vomited all over the floor. When I heard the footsteps outside the door, I wanted to do it all over again. I thought things couldn't get worse but I had been wrong, my nightmare had only just been starting.

Dillon's laugh pulls me back to what's happening in front of me, and I shiver as the memories try to keep a hold on my attention. I dig my nails into the palm of my hand as I watch Dillon touching Nicolai, and I wonder if it was better when I couldn't see clearly out of both eyes. At least that way I wouldn't have the constant feeling of bile as I watch Dillon try to romance Nicolai. God, he really is oblivious to everything he's done. It's like he has two different personalities inside him. One of them is this sweet guy that's in front of me just now. The other is a scary fucker, and he can appear at the drop of a hat. He does damage that you couldn't imagine, and I don't want to get on the wrong side of him. Thankfully, it's the sweet Dillon that Nicolai seems to bring out, well apart from the very first day.

God. I don't know what had happened before I was wheeled out of that room, but when Dillon had dug those secateurs into my finger, I honestly thought he was going to cut it off. Only Nicolai stopped him from doing it, but when I saw what he had to do to save me, I wish he'd just let me lose the finger. My heart shattered in my chest when I saw Nicolai drop to his knees and I silently begged him to run even though it was clear he couldn't. For days I'd suffered at Dillon's hands. I was sitting in my own filth, and my body ached from the beatings and dehydration, but I would have done every single second of it all over again to get Nicolai out safely.

The day that Dillon came into the room and untied me, freeing me for the first time since I had arrived here, I thought my time was up. Instead, I was led to a bathroom to be cleaned up. Ever since I've wondered what Nicolai had to do to get Dillon to agree to my partial freedom. I try to shut my imagination down before I fall too far down that rabbit hole because sometimes it's better not to know. I may not want to know what he did, but it doesn't stop me from knowing that he did something. The simple fact is he changed the way Dillon treats me, and for that I will be forever thankful.

I drop my head back against the wall behind me and let my mind wander. I've been trying to find a way to escape since I had my binds removed but Dillon has planned this whole fucking mess out perfectly. There's only one way in and out of the room, and even though I haven't checked, I'm convinced that the door will be locked. I think we might be in a basement because there are no windows and the stairs lead down from somewhere above. I don't know if the room is soundproof, but I do know that when the music goes off, there's no noise from anywhere else. There's nothing that would hint to where we are or if there is anyone close around us. I just need an opportunity to subdue Dillon, but I've never seen a chance to do it.

"I said no!" Dillon's raised voice has my eyes flashing open, and I quickly take in what's happening. He's standing, towering over Nicolai who's staring at the floor. I missed what was said to get Dillon to lose his temper, but apparently, we have crazy Dillon with us now. Thankfully he doesn't say anything else before he storms up the stairs and out of the room, the door slamming behind him.

Nicolai sits still staring at the floor, and I struggle not to go to him.

"Nicolai." I keep my voice low as I try to get his attention, but he doesn't make any sign that he hears me. I raise my voice a little, still making sure that Dillon won't hear it and come down. "Nicolai." When his hand comes up and wipes at his cheek, I forget about keeping away and rush to where he's sitting. I keep my eyes on his face as I get closer and I see the fresh tears falling.

"I'm sorry."

I don't understand what he's sorry for, but it doesn't take away from the fact that I don't want his apology. "You have nothing to be sorry for." I reach out and grip his hand, my heart racing at the simple touch after so long. It's like my body has missed the feel of Nicolai's skin and I didn't realise it how much until now. Meeting Nicolai was like a stroke of luck, one I'm thankful for. That dating app had haunted me with all the random men looking just for a hookup, but when Nic had flagged me and I'd checked out his profile, something about him had just spoken to me. He'd seemed genuine and sweet and when we met, it was like fireworks were going off in my stomach. I'd only felt that once before, but my judgement hadn't been that good that time.

"I asked him to let you go. I got him angry. I need to behave to keep you safe."

I try to work out what he's saying, and it takes me a few minutes for the words to make sense to me. When they do, bile threatens to drown the whimper I feel in my throat. He can't be saying what I think he is. "Nicolai, look at me."

It takes a moment, but he finally looks up. The despair in his eyes makes me want to hold him, but I need him to listen.

"Don't do this. You can't give up to try and protect me. You need to fight. We both need to fight. Promise me that you won't do what he asks. Please."

The tears in his eyes build again, and I know he's struggling. He thinks this whole mess is because of him, but he needs to get angry at Dillon. To fight against anything he has planned.

"James."

The way Nicolai says my name is like a plea and I forget about the cameras and Dillon as I lean forward and kiss him. As my lips connect with his, the whole world slips away. It's been the same way every time we kiss, and I love it. My entire focus is on Nicolai, and even though it takes him a few moments to kiss me back, he finally does. I use my hands to grip his face to keep him close to me as I kiss him like it's the last time I'll be able to. I ignore my common sense that's screaming in my head, telling me I shouldn't give in to my need to kiss Nicolai, because the only important thing in the world is kissing him.

Burning starts in my shoulder and spreads through my body quickly. I feel my muscles tense up and I jerk back from Nicolai with a scream. The fire spreads through my whole body, and I collapse to the floor, my head connecting with the concrete with a thud. The pain dissipates quickly, but my muscles refuse to work correctly.

"Don't fucking touch him." The voice screams from above me, but it's taking a lot of energy to try and focus.

"Dillon, no. I'm sorry, please leave him."

I hear a thud, but I can't work out what it is. Thankfully my muscles start to relax, allowing me to turn towards the noise. I blink a few times to clear my fuzzy head, and when I do, I see Dillon standing over Nicolai who's lying on the floor with a bleeding mouth. Panic now spreads through me, replacing the pain that was there a few minutes before. Struggling to get up off the floor, I push myself to my knees before needing to take a second to breathe. I watch the scene in front of me as I force myself to move faster. I've experienced this feeling before, it's the way he kept me in control when I first arrived, and I know that Dillon tasered me in the back.

"I thought you knew you were mine?"

"I do... I am. I'm sorry." Nicolai is trying to edge backwards away from the looming man in front of him, but Dillon has a hold of the chain connected to that fucking collar on Nicolai's neck. It's stopping Nic from putting distance between them, and the fear is apparent in Nicolai's eyes.

"You kissed him." The pain is evident in Dillon's voice and from anyone else at any other time, I would feel sorry for him. The only thing in my mind just now is to kill him before he can hurt Nic.

"I was confused. I didn't mean it." I know that Nicolai's trying to calm Dillon down but his words hurt. I push that aside as nonsense before finally getting to my feet.

I sway a few times before I finally get my balance, and then I lunge for Dillon. I connect with his back, and he finally drops the chain. I grip tightly around Dillon's shoulders as I pull him backwards. What I don't anticipate is Dillon moving with me. I over balance but keep moving as Dillon uses my surprise to propel me into the wall behind us. The wind is knocked out of me as we connect, but I keep my hold, determined to win. He moves forward and turns before forcing me back into the small table where he was eating with Nicolai. It collapses under our combined weight, and I can no longer hold on to Dillon, who gets to his feet quickly while I lie there and struggle to breathe.

I scream inside my head to get up, to fight him while I can, but my body is aching and stopping me from moving at any speed. I keep waiting for his attack, and when it doesn't come, I chance a look up. The sight in front of me confuses me for a second, but when I finally work out what's happening, I get to my feet quickly. I look around trying to look for a weapon, and I see the leg that came from the table we just destroyed. I pick it up, fully planning to use it on Dillon and ending this whole thing, but he must see my movement behind him, and he turns to face me, dragging Nicolai with him.

Blood drips down Dillon's face, but I barely register that. What I focus on is Nicolai's bleeding face. He looks like he's gone a full round with a world champion boxer and it makes me wonder how long it took me to get off the floor. His cheek is red with the first signs of a bruise starting, and his lip is split in several places. The blood from his injured eyebrow is running down his face and mixing with the blood from his mouth. This is all my fault. I shouldn't have kissed him. There's no way for me to use my weapon against Dillon while he has Nicolai in front of him, and the way that Dillon has his arm wrapped around Nic's neck, I know he isn't letting him go until he's safe.

Nicolai tries to shake his head at me like he knows that I've given up, but I still drop the table leg at my feet. The smirk on Dillon's face makes me want to pick it up again, but I can't risk Nicolai. I refuse to get him hurt more than he already is. What I didn't anticipate was

Dillon raising his hand to put a little black device against Nicolai's neck and pressing a button. Nic's body shudders and Dillon lets him drop to the ground. I try to go to him, but Dillon holds the taser out in front of his body. I try to work out my chances of getting the taser from Dillon's hand if I rush him again. *Could I knock it away before he has a chance to use it against me?* I decide the risk is worth a shot, especially if it pulls his attention from Nicolai.

Taking a deep breath, I force my body to relax to give the illusion that I'm giving up. I wait a heartbeat before using all the energy I have left to rush Dillon. What I hadn't realised was that I'm running on pretty much zero energy. My mistake becomes apparent quickly, but it's too late to stop my attack. It doesn't take much for Dillon to step to the side and I prepare for the feeling of the taser before it happens. I collapse on the floor, the familiar feeling of being shocked spreading through my muscles. Dillon doesn't leave me this time though, and before I have a chance to move, his foot connects with my ribs. I double over, wrapping my arms around myself to try and ease the exploding pain.

"He's fucking mine." He punctuates the end of his sentence with another kick, this one connecting with folded arms. I curl into myself to protect myself, but it doesn't stop his attack. "You have no fucking right to touch him." Another kick.

"Dillon, please stop." I hear Nicolai crying, and I want to tell him it's okay. I don't want him to feel guilty about this, but I can't form any words.

I roll onto my back and gasp for breath. The pain is radiating out like fire from my chest, and it's making it hard not to cry. Dillon's hurt me since I was brought here, but not once has he made such a prolonged attack. He would generally use the taser and then leave me, but then I'd never fought back and hurt him like I had today. That's not what's causing this though. No, all his anger is from the fact that I kissed Nicolai.

There's a lull in the attack, and I manage to turn my face cautiously, expecting another kick any second. I'm alone on the floor because Dillon is kneeling next to Nicolai. Dillon is holding Nicolai's face in his hands speaking to him. I can't hear any of the words, but they don't appear to be said with anger, and the gentle smile on Dillon's face is in harsh contrast to the beating he just gave me. Nicolai nods his head, and it makes Dillon's smile grow before he leans in to kiss Nic. I want to close my eyes to hide what's in front of me, but it's like my mind is a masochist and refuses to make me miss what's happening.

The tension is Nicolai's body is clear, but he doesn't do anything to stop Dillon from taking what he wants. When it all becomes too much for me, I roll my body until I'm lying on my side. I don't know what my plan is, I just know I need to move before I lose my mind. Maybe I could make it to the stairs before anyone notices, and if I can, then perhaps I can get out of here. I need to alert someone to the fact that we're here so they can get us help. I bring my knees up and twist to try to get them below me, but the pressure on my middle makes me groan in pain. The noise catches Dillon's attention, and his head snaps towards me. The sweet smile drops instantly from his lips, and I can see anger darken his eyes.

Nicolai grabs at Dillon's arm as Dillon stands, but it doesn't slow him in the slightest. I try my hardest to move, but it's useless. I can see it coming, but there's no way to escape what's about to happen. Even as Dillon pulls his foot back, I struggle to stop it, but the darkness takes me the second his foot connects with my face.

CHAPTER TWENTY

NICOLAI

I keep my hands over my ears, and my eyes closed in the attempt to keep out what's happening. It's a pathetic reaction, but it's the only thing I can do with this fucking chain around my neck. What I want to do is kill Dillon, but I'm stuck here on the floor with no other option than to hide.

I might not be able to see what's happening but the memory of watching Dillon kick James in the head and James falling to the ground is still clean in my mind. He dropped like a stone and the scream I let out echoed throughout the room. My ears were still ringing when the first sob escaped me because James wasn't moving and I thought he was dead. It was only when Dillon kicked James onto his back that I saw that his chest was rising and falling. The relief brought me to my knees, but when Dillon grabbed James by the hair and dragged him towards the room he keeps him in, that's when I tried to hide.

The hands on my ears don't stop me from hearing Dillon approach me, but I keep my eyes screwed shut so I can't see him. When a hand lands on my cheek, I flinch away, but the wall behind me hinders my escape.

"I'm sorry."

I open my eyes when his gentle voice reaches my ears. A whimper leaves me when I see the blood spatters on his face. I can't be sure he didn't have the blood on him before he went into the room with James, but I would put money on the spatters not being his own blood. Dillon's bleeding, but most of the damage is around his nose and mouth. The spray is on his cheeks and forehead, and for the life of me, I can't get the image of a bleeding James out of my mind. *Did he hurt him more when he got him into the room?*

"He attacked me. You saw that."

I want to scream at him that he was the one who attacked James, but I keep my mouth firmly closed. As I've been sitting here, I've realised that my plan to get James out of here won't work. Things have progressed with James being allowed to sit in the same room as me, but every time I mention to Dillon to let James go, he lets his fury out. I'd decided early on to keep Dillon happy, but it's like I can't resist pushing him when it comes to James. Every time I felt I'd gained a little bit of Dillon's trust, I would ask him to give James more freedom. He would refuse, and it would make the doubt build even more.

A simple act had taken away that doubt, and for a few moments, I felt at peace. Kissing James had cleared my head more than any pep talk I'd tried to give myself since I arrived. The past four days had faded away when his lips met mine. I hadn't realised how much I'd missed him until we touched. I thought that he had ghosted me after having sex but he hadn't, and now it was okay to admit that I still wanted to be with him. I was shocked when he bit my lip, his teeth digging deep enough that I could taste blood, and it wasn't until he collapsed to the floor that I realised that something was very wrong.

I'd watched in shock as Dillon screamed at James, but as he moved closer to James instinct took over, and I tried to grab Dillon. Dillon must have anticipated my move because as soon as I was close enough to finally reach him, he elbowed me in the jaw. From that moment until Dillon dragged James back into the room, the time had gone past in a flash.

"I know." The words feel like bile in my mouth, but the lie is needed. It's clear I've done the right thing when Dillon's eyes soften. He looks completely different to the guy who'd attacked James, and that guy had scared me more than I thought possible. His eyes looked dead, like there was nothing inside him to make him stop. The Dillon I'd gotten to know as I taught him was completely missing from the man standing in front of me, and it made me realise I was maybe in more danger than I'd initially thought. I think there was always a part inside me that thought Dillon would come to his senses and let me go, that the good side of him would make him see that what he's doing is wrong. Now I know that that side of him is the fake side. The darkness inside him is the real face of Dillon, and that face isn't letting me go.

"Good." His smile grows, but then a frown appears on his face when he looks at my mouth. His finger strokes gently over my bottom lip but the pain has me flinching back. "I'm sorry I hurt you. You just shouldn't have gotten involved. He needed to be punished for touching what's mine."

"I ...I know. I'm sorry."

"It's okay, he knows now." Dillon gets up from his place on the floor and heads over to the tool cabinet in the corner. He takes a small key from his pocket and unlocks one of the top drawers before removing a first aid kit. He relocks the drawer and returns to his spot in front of me. "What would you like to do after I clean you up?" I flinch at the sting of the antiseptic wipe that he's using to wipe the blood from my lip.

"Sorry, it stings." Dillon's hand stills before he leans forward and gently kisses my lip. I dig my nails into my palm to keep the whimper in my throat. I can't let him know that he scares me. As much as I would love to fight back, I'm afraid of what he would do if he realised that I don't want him. No, it's safer if I go along with everything.

"It isn't too bad now the blood is gone. I just need to be careful when I kiss you." He winks at me in what I suspect is meant to be a flirty way, but it makes me want to be sick. Dillon has already kissed me, and I hate him for it. He removed the feeling of James on my lips, and I don't know if I'll ever get that back.

I relax a little when Dillon starts cleaning up the first aid supplies he used. Having his focus somewhere else gives me a second to compose myself. I take several deep breaths, but my heart is still racing in my chest. "Is James still alive?" The words are out before I know that I'm even thinking them and when Dillon turns angrily towards me, I know I need to make this better. "I don't want you to get into trouble. If you hurt him someone might take you away."

Dillon changes instantly in front of me. His eyes change from dark and angry to happy, and if I hadn't seen the rage a moment before I would never have believed it was there. "He's alive. Don't worry, baby. No one is taking me from you." He drops to his knees in front of me and cups my face. He kisses me gently, obviously trying not to hurt my mouth again but I wouldn't have noticed even if he had. The only thing on my mind is the fact that James is alive. He might be injured but he's still breathing and that fills my body with joy. The knowledge makes me even more determined to ensure my original plan works. Now that I have a moment to let my mind drift, I wonder if there's a way to get both James and me out of this whole thing? If I can get to talk to James again maybe we can make a plan together to get out. I just need to find a way to get Dillon to let James out of that fucking room.

"God, you make me so fucking crazy." Dillon's voice is husky and full of lust. When his hands start to drift down my neck and over my chest, the need to stop him is strong.

"I'm exhausted. Can I nap?"

Dillon's hands stop, and I think he's going to say no, but he finally nods his head and helps me stand up from the floor. He leads me over to the bed, and I collapse onto it, making a show of how tired I am. He strokes his hand gently over my face before picking up the rubbish from where he left it and leaving the room.

I stare at the ceiling for a few seconds before turning onto my side. I curl up facing away from the cameras to pretend I'm going to sleep, but my eyes are open as I stare at the wall. So much has happened today and I need some time to make sense of it all. I should be thinking of the attacks that Dillon inflicted on us, or the need to get James and myself out of here, but the thing that my mind latches onto is the kiss. That kiss was a game changer in more than one way. It showed me that my assumption of James running away after we had sex was wrong. Maybe he still has feelings for me even after all this? I finally close my eyes and let the gentle warmth that those words bring spread through me. It makes me determined to get out of here because I want to see where things with James might go. That is if he still wants me after me causing all this shit.

I GROAN AS I ROLL OVER AND THE MATTRESS PUSHES AGAINST MY painful face. I hadn't meant to fall asleep, but apparently, I wasn't completely lying to Dillon when I said I'd been tired. Now I regret that sleep because my body has become stiff and achy. Shit, I hurt so fucking bad. I push against the bed and sit up slowly. My head's thumping and my face feels like I've fought with a truck. I ease my legs over the edge of the bed and lean my elbows on my knees while I drop my head down. I soon realise that that's such a bad idea when gravity pulls against all my injuries making them scream out in pain. "Fuck me."

"I know the feeling."

My head flinches to the side, and I groan when it feels like my brain connects with the side of my skull. I let out a slow breath and open my eyes. There were a few possible things Dillon could have done while I was asleep. He could have tidied the room to get rid of any evidence of the earlier fight. He could have brought me food, or even fallen asleep in the bed next to me. There is the one thing that I would never have imagined, and that is James being bound to the wall on the opposite side of the room.

Tears fill my eyes, and I have to grip the edge of the mattress to stop myself from rushing to him. The last thing I need to do is hug James and bring more problems for him. "James." My voice is tight and strained as I try to speak through the emotional lump in my throat.

"Hey." The side of his lip twitches up but it vanishes quickly as a look of pain crosses his face. I take a closer look at the injuries that cover his face. His lips are swollen and split in several places, and more damage leads up his face to his black eye. There are cuts over the bridge of his nose, and it's swollen to almost twice its normal size, and I'm sure that's where Dillon's foot connected. "Are you okay?"

"Stop checking that I'm okay. Fuck, James. He hurt you so badly." I make sure to keep my voice low, but I can't tear my eyes away from him.

"He's done worse. I do kinda wish he'd missed the nose. It was one of my best features."

I let out a small laugh that sounds a bit like a sob. After everything James went through yesterday he should be angry and hate me, but here he is trying to make jokes to ease my guilt. "I still think you're gorgeous."

James stares at me, and I can see so many different emotions cross his face. Finally, he smiles and lets out a little sigh. "I'm glad. But you didn't answer my question. Are you okay?"

"I'm fine. I'm better now I've seen you."

Footsteps from above stop our conversation, and I finally look away from James. Watching as Dillon comes down the stairs with a tray in his hands. He smiles as he sees me looking at him and I feel the tension start to build in my body the closer he gets to me.

"Morning, handsome." Dillon approaches a small table that replaces the one broken yesterday. It's the first of my noticing that he had in fact cleaned up after the fight.

How deeply did I sleep?

"Morning."

After he puts the tray down, he walks over and grips the back of my neck. I force myself to relax in his hold and accept the kiss that he gives me. It feels weird to kiss Dillon back but I do it, and the thumb stroking over my pulse point tells me I did the right thing. Dillon's smiling when he steps back and my eyes flicker to James who is now looking at the floor.

"Hope you're hungry." I nod my head as Dillon's serves up some pasta. "You slept through dinner so I thought you might prefer something more filling for breakfast."

Having no windows in the room makes it difficult to know what time of day it is. I've had to rely on Dillon to try and keep track of time. If I go by the meals that I've been served, I've been here for about five days. I'm probably wrong, but it's the closest I'll ever get to know for sure how long he's had me. Five breakfasts in my mind say a five-day stay.

"Thank you." I take a forkful of pasta as I watch Dillon approach James with a small plate. It isn't the same pasta that I've been served, but I'm happy that Dillon isn't going to force James to watch us eat while he starves. Dillon throws the sandwich at James before walking back to sit with me on the bed. We sit in silence while we eat and it feels so uncomfortable. "I need the bathroom."

Dillon puts his plate down and takes a key from his pocket. He unlocks the chain from the back of my collar, and I follow him towards the small bathroom at the side of the room. "Why don't you take a shower while you're in there. There are towels on the shelf." He opens the door and lets me step inside before he closes the door. I never get to lock it, but this little bit of freedom is always welcome. The first time I'd needed to use the toilet I'd panicked because I hadn't known what to do. I had images of Dillon making me go in front of him, and when he'd shown me the bathroom, I had nearly wept in relief.

I strip off my clothes to take a shower like he told me. He hasn't allowed me to shower for a few days so it will be great to finally feel clean again. I tug my t-shirt over my neck and struggle a little when it tangles on my collar. I wish Dillon would let me remove it while I showered, but at least I don't notice it against my skin as much as I used to. I know I'm not allowed to take too much time, so I step into the shower stall and pull the curtain closed. The water comes through cold but it quickly heats, and I wash with the supplied body wash.

I miss the water almost instantly when I turn off the shower, but I push the feeling aside and get out of the stall. I grab the towel and dry myself off as much as possible. I always feel that trying to get myself completely dry in this little room is like trying to do it at a swimming pool. It doesn't matter how much time you spend doing it, you never seem to ever get completely dry. Leaving the steamy room would help, but there's no way that I'm getting dressed in front of Dillon. I drop the towel and search for the clothes that I left on the sink when I got undressed, but they're gone. I frantically look around in case they have somehow managed to fall onto the floor. I even search in the shower because I don't want to admit to the obvious reason they are gone. When I can no longer deny what's happened, I wrap the towel around my waist and walk from the bathroom.

Dillon's face lights up when he sees me coming towards him, and I know this had been his plan all along. He was the one who told me to shower, and apparently, this was the reason. He wanted me naked, and my stomach churns when I wonder why. "You're so fucking sexy. Just like our first night together."

Tears burn my eyes, but I swallow down any emotion that tries to escape. We didn't have a first night together, what we had was Dillon drugging me so he could rape me. I don't think now would be the time to correct him though, not after everything that happened today.

"Come here." He grabs me by the hips and pulls me until we're standing in front of James. I let my eyes flicker to James for a brief moment, and at this angle, I can see that it's not just his hands and feet that are bound. He has a chain around his middle that's connected to a pipe that runs from the floor into the wall. It looks like a drainage pipe that's part of the plumbing system, and if it is, there's no way for James to move from his position. "So fucking sexy."

My eyes go back to James, and I meet his glare. He looks angrier than I've ever seen him, but when Dillon grabs me by the hips and pulls me against his body, James looks like he's ready to rip Dillon apart with his bare hands. Dillon's lips on my jaw pull my attention away from James. I have a good idea where this is going, and I have a pretty good idea why. Dillon needs to prove himself to James, and he's going to use me to do it. I just can't look at James while it happens.

CHAPTER TWENTY-ONE

JAMES

I REPEAT TO MYSELF OVER AND OVER AGAIN THAT DILLON'S trying to get a reaction. He's putting on a little show to prove that he has power over me. I won't let it affect me. I'll just sit here and show him that what he's doing doesn't bother me.

The words all sound fine in my head but putting them into practice isn't as easy. My hands twitch in my binds as I'm forced to watch Dillon's sick play happen in front of me, but I refuse to look away. The rational part of my brain tells me that I should close my eyes and block out what's happening, but there's also a part that says Nicolai might be hurt if I stop looking. That isn't Dillon's plan though. Hurting Nicolai is the last thing he wants to do, but if he takes this whole thing to its logical conclusion, then there's a good chance that Nicolai is going to be hurt.

So I keep my eyes open and watch, even though there's absolutely nothing I can do to help Nicolai. I don't know anything that happened once Dillon knocked me out, but when I woke up I was chained to the stupid fucking pipe behind me, and my hands and feet were bound in tie wraps. I don't know how long I've been sitting here but my arse is numb, and there are raw marks on my wrists from the plastic, but none of that matters as I watch Dillon's hands explore

Nicolai's bare skin. I hadn't been sure what was happening when Dillon had slipped into the bathroom and came out carrying Nic's clothes, but a few minutes later when Nic appeared wearing only a towel, it was clear what Dillon had done. Now he's putting on a pretty show for me so he can show me how powerful he is.

I pull against my restraints again as Dillon bites along Nicolai's collarbone before moving lower over his chest. Nicolai's hands are clenched tightly at his side, but he isn't moving away. That's when I know that he's not going to put up a fight. He can't do that. He has to fight back. "Nicolai." My voice comes out stronger than I thought it would, but it doesn't stop Dillon from what he's doing. It does bring Nicolai's eyes to mine briefly. I want to tell him to stop, that he needs to attack Dillon while he isn't chained so he can get out of here, but the words get stuck in my throat when he shakes his head at me. He silently pleads with me to not argue but I want to get free so I can rip Dillon's head from his shoulders.

The idea of such a young guy being able to do this to two older men is beyond comprehension. He looks young and innocent, but if I'm honest, there was always an edge to the looks he sent my way. I could see he had a thing for Nicolai, and my mistake was putting it down to a simple crush from an old pupil. I never imagined that he posed such a threat and I regret ignoring my unsure feelings about Dillon. Now he's showing me exactly the kind of man he is.

For that reason, I can't do what Nicolai is asking. I can't just sit here while Dillon uses him. "Nicolai, listen to me. You don't have to do this." I don't know what I expect Nicolai to do, but my stomach drops when he gives me a small smile before turning to Dillon and kissing him. "No!" The yell comes out loud, and I see Nicolai flinch in Dillon's hold, but it doesn't stop what's happening.

I try harder to escape, not caring that the plastic digs into my skin until I'm bleeding. I pull until the pain is unbearable, but I don't gain an inch of freedom. I roar in frustration and pull against the chain around my waist, but all I achieve is for the metal to dig into my stomach until the pain becomes too much. All the pain and blood still doesn't compare to the torture of watching Nicolai and Dillon together. The tightness in my chest increases its hold as they both move towards the large bed. I bite the inside of my cheek until I taste blood when Dillon lowers Nicolai onto the bed and removes the towel. "No."

Dillon turns his eyes to me as he licks over Nicolai's stomach, and I can see the joy in his eyes. The sick fuck is getting off on doing this in front of me, like staking his claim on Nicolai is better than actually having Nicolai submit to him.

"I will kill you."

Dillon's smirk increases at my words, and it makes my anger rage through me. I don't care what it takes for me to get free but I will, and when I do that little fucker is going to suffer. Not for what he's done to me, but for what he's putting Nicolai through. I might not know Nicolai as well as I would like, but in the time I've got to know him, I realise he's the kind of guy I've been looking for. Typical that I spend my life looking for the one, and when I find him, there's a chance neither of us will survive to follow our hearts.

"I will kill you." This times my words don't come out with so much strength. There's a sob building in my throat as I watch Dillon explore Nicolai's body. My eyes finally close when Dillon lies entirely on top of a still Nicolai. I can't watch. I can't witness Dillon rape Nicolai again. Dropping my head back against the wall behind me I let my mind drift to try and protect me.

I think back to my first date with Nicolai. I'd been so freaking nervous to walk into that wine bar, thinking that maybe Nicolai would take one look at me and leave. He hadn't though, and I'm sure I'd been half smitten with him before the night was even over. He'd made me laugh more than most people do, and when he spoke about something he liked I could see passion glinting in his eyes. I'd wanted to take him to bed before we'd left the wine bar, and that's the reason I'd made myself wait. Nicolai had seemed like the kind of guy who I could have a relationship with so I hadn't wanted to rush things. I wanted to get to know him before I let my passion get the better of me. I'm so glad I had because the next few times I'd met him had felt like the most extended foreplay ever, and not just for my body. Nicolai is smart and funny, and the more I listened to him talk, the more I knew I needed him in my life.

"Holy shit, Nicolai."

I block my ears, pressing one against my shoulder and using my bounds hands to cover the other, and start humming a random song to block out the sound of Dillon's voice. I feel like I'm betraying Nicolai by blocking this out when he's doing this to keep us both safe, but my heart can't take it. I'm close to losing my mind, and it won't take much to send me over. I need to pretend this isn't happening.

DILLON LEFT A LITTLE WHILE AGO, BUT I HAVEN'T BEEN ABLE TO look at the bed where he left Nicolai. It makes me the shittiest person alive, but I can't look at the remains of them having sex. I should check that Nicolai is okay, that he isn't hurt, but I can't build up the courage to look at him.

A quiet sob sounds through the silence and the ball of emotion I've been trying to swallow down builds. I finally look across the room and what I see there nearly breaks my heart. Nicolai is curled up into himself, his arms wrapped around his knees as he tries to hide in the corner next to the bed. I don't know when he moved from the bed, but he's sitting on the floor between it and the wall. It offers him privacy from the camera but not from me. I want to go to him and hold him, tell him everything will be okay, but this stupid fucking chain is making me stay exactly where I am.

"Nic." He doesn't show any evidence of having heard me, so I repeat his name, this time a little louder. "Nic, please." I feel awful pleading with him after what he just went through, but I need to see his face. I feel a little of my tension ease as he finally looks at me. If I thought he looked broken this morning, I was wrong. There's nothing in his eyes now but sadness, and I can feel the despair flowing off him in waves.

"I'm sorry."

I stare mutely and blink, confused at why he's apologising. He just suffered all the agony, and he's saying sorry to me? What the fuck? "Why?"

"All this."

I refuse to get into this argument again, so I change the direction that the conversation is taking. "Are you hurt?" That's the only thing that's important and the thing I want to focus on.

"No. Just... no, I'm not hurt."

"Just what, Nic?"

Another broken sob escapes him before he speaks. "I feel dirty."

I don't know what to say to him, so I sit quietly as he hides his face in his folded arms and weeps. I want to tell him that he's not dirty, that he isn't the one to feel bad about what just happened, but he isn't in the place to hear that. So I sit and let him break apart, hoping that when he's finally calm, I'll be able to rebuild what Dillon has taken from him.

"IS HE GOING TO BE OKAY?" I'VE SAT IN SHOCK WHILE LISTENING to Nicolai telling me about what happened to Gareth. I can't believe that Dillon did that to him, hurting him in such a bad way especially when he has a family.

"The doctors think so, but it's been a while since I've seen him ..." Nicolai's voice trails off, and I can sense the worry in what he's not saying.

"I'm sure he's fine. From what you've told me about Gareth, he's too annoying to give up the fight to get well."

This finally gets a smile from Nicolai, and I stare at him to enjoy the sight. He's sitting on the floor opposite me, his back leaning against the bottom of the bed. After his tears had dried, he moved to this spot, and we've been talking quietly since. There are so many questions I want to ask him but I don't want to upset him, and I'm worried that I might say the wrong thing.

"What?"

I hesitate for only a second before I ask a question that I can't put off any longer. "How long have I been gone?" I'm met with silence, and part of me wants to tell Nicolai to forget I asked. Maybe not knowing is the best thing in this situation, but before I have a chance to speak he answers.

"From the day you left my house, and that was about two weeks before the police showed up at my door to say you were missing."

"You didn't notice before that?" It stings to hear him saying that he hadn't noticed I was missing. Why hadn't he worried before the police turned up?

"No."

I rub my finger over the dry blood on my hand, so I don't have to look at Nicolai. I've been going through this whole shit show thinking that if we get out, that maybe we could be something to each other. Now he's trying to tell me that he didn't miss me when I vanished.

"James."

I keep my focus on my fingers because I don't want to look at him. I want to hide how much he's hurt me, especially after what he went through to protect us.

"James, please look at me."

I let a mask slip into place before I finally look up.

"I didn't know you were gone. I thought you were ghosting me. I thought you'd gotten what you wanted and were blowing me off."

"I would never do that." I honestly can't believe he thought I would do that. I know we hadn't known each other too well, but did he think that little of me?

"I know that now. But you have to see it from my side. You're amazing, and I couldn't believe that a guy like you would want me. So when you didn't answer my calls or return your messages, it was the logical thought. You just didn't want me anymore."

"That's not what happened."

"Well duh."

His response makes him sound like one of the teens he teaches, and it's so out of place with the situation that I burst out laughing. I haven't found anything worth laughing at in such a long time that now I've started, I'm finding it difficult to stop. I cover my face as much as possible with my restrained wrists and try to muffle the sound of my laughter. The last thing I need is to bring Dillon back down here. It only becomes funnier when I feel tears start to run down my cheeks and I know I can't look at Nic or I will never stop laughing. My stupid emotions fight against the laughter though, and as the tears start to fall faster, it becomes clear my hilarity no longer causes them. A painful sob escapes from around the lump in my throat, and in the blink of an eye, I'm crying. All the fear and frustration I've felt since I arrived escapes in warm tears down my cheeks. It's the first time I've given in to the deep pain I've been feeling, and I'm not sure if I'll be able to stop.

I miss my family. I want to see my cousin again so I can tell her that she needs to stop putting others first and live her own life. I want to tell my parents I love them and ask them if they are proud of me. I want to quit my job as a solicitor and do something I love. I want to get out of here and finally live my life like I should be. Not to make money, but to fall in love and have a family. It took an experience that will probably end in death for me to realise I had only been half living, and now I want it all. I want to be selfish and live for my own happiness ... and I want that with Nicolai. It took me a long time to find someone I connected with, and he's it. I might die in this place, and I'm angry because I won't have a chance to find out if I could love Nicolai.

"James."

I take a deep breath to try and calm down. The tears have drained me, and I've nothing left to give. My fight is gone, and I hate that it has. I need to be able to get out of this, but I know I can't. Even if Nicolai walks away, there's no way Dillon will let me leave this room alive. This is going to be the last place I ever live, and the knowledge is settling. It means there's no point in fighting against it anymore. There is nothing I can do to save Nicolai no matter how much I want to. I'm chained to a wall and bound so I can't move. I was a fool to think that I might be able to do anything important. This is it, and I need to accept it.

"James, please don't."

I open my eyes and stare at a scared looking Nicolai. I look past the fear and focus on the man I met. He's still in there behind all the emotions, and I search to find him. I need the comfort of seeing him.

"Don't give up. We will get out of this, I promise. I need you to keep fighting. I have a plan, and I need you to be ready when it's time to fight. James. God, please stay with me." Nicolai's words come out fast, and I can tell he's starting to panic. I want to tell him that I won't give up, that I'll fight side by side with him when needed, but I also don't want to lie to him.

"I can't do it any more." I want to look away, hide the shame of giving up from Nicolai, but I can't break eye contact. I want to have my fill of Nic before I never get to see him again.

"No, James. You can ... we can. We'll do this together. I promise that we will find a way out of this. You need to stay with me." Nicolai is kneeling up now, and he's struggling against the collar around his neck. He keeps tugging at the chain like he would suddenly be able to get it to break from the wall.

"He raped you."

I see Nicolai flinch and I hate that I caused it. "I know." His voice quiets, and his eyes flicker away like it hurts to admit it. "But I can't focus on that. I will deal with that after we get out, and we will get out."

The determination in his voice almost makes me believe what he's saying. *Almost.* The truth is that we're both stuck here until Dillon decides what he wants to do with us, and in my case, I don't think it will be anything good.

CHAPTER TWENTY-TWO

NICOLAI

HE'S GIVING UP. I CAN SEE IT IN HIS EYES AS HE SITS THERE. There's usually a fire burning behind any emotion he's feeling, but he looks empty. Not the same emptiness I see in Dillon, and truthfully, this one scares me even more. I need James to fight so we can get out of here. Everything I've gone through is to get us out. Having sex with Dillon...

I take a deep breath and swallow down the contents of my stomach that are threatening to make an appearance. It's not the first time I've had sex with Dillon, but this time I remember every single touch. When he was done, I wanted to rush to the shower and scrub my body clean, but he chained me to the wall before leaving me lying on the bed. Even now, sitting talking to James, I can still feel Dillon inside me, and I want to rip my skin off.

"Nicolai."

I open my eyes and look at James. I didn't even realise I'd closed them, but apparently, my mind wants to escape from what happened. "I just need you to keep on fighting, James."

"I don't think I can."

I need to say something to keep him with me. There has to be something that will bring him fully back to me. "If you don't want to fight for yourself do it for your family. Your cousin reported you missing. She wants you home." Tears run down his cheeks, and I worry that I've taken the wrong approach. I tug at the collar again, but just like every other time I've tried to escape it, it doesn't budge.

"I miss my family."

"So do I, and I know they must all be worried. That means we can't give up. We need to fight. If we work together, there's no way that Dillon can beat us." I hope he believes the shit I'm saying because I don't. Dillon has managed to get two grown men tied up and at his mercy. There should be no way for him to accomplish that, but yet here we both are. I don't know if we can get away, I don't even know if Dillon will keep me around once he's gotten what he wants, but I want to at least go out fighting. If he's going to kill me, I want to hurt him before he does. That's the thing I need to focus on. Biding my time until I can hurt Dillon in the worst possible way.

Footsteps on the stairs nearly have me screaming out in frustration. I want to keep talking to James, to get him out of his head, but the chance is gone. I scurry back to the wall beside the bed. I know Dillon has probably been watching us on the cameras so he knows we've been talking, but I don't want to do anything to piss him off. The need to protect James is strong, and I need to focus on that. So I keep my eyes on Dillon as he comes down the stairs. When he reaches the bottom, his eyes flicker to James, but it's only for a second before he looks at me again. That's all I need to do, keep Dillon's attention entirely on me.

"Hey." Dillon's happy voice grates against my nerves, but I force a smile onto my lips. If I pretend to be happy he might let me shower, or at least give me my clothes back.

I'm sitting in just a pair of plain white boxer shorts, and I feel very vulnerable. That's probably Dillon's aim, especially since I only found these on the bed once he'd left after ... that moment. The towel was gone so I couldn't even cover myself with that. It was when I found the boxers that I had finally broken down and cried for what he'd done. I allowed myself a moment to miss what he'd taken from me because it was something I would never have given to him willingly. Once the tears had dried, I pushed the memories away, and I'm glad that James was here to distract me. Unfortunately, the conversation had drifted into topics I'd wanted to avoid.

"I brought you this." Dillon holds out a small book, and I take it from his hand. It's a book full of crosswords and word searches, and clipped to the front is a pen.

"Thank you." I give a small smile before staring at the book. I don't want to make eye contact with Dillon because I'm not sure I'd be able to hide the hatred I feel towards him.

"I thought it might give you something to pass the time. I don't want you to get bored."

It's right on the tip of my tongue to tell him the best way to make sure I don't get bored is to let me go, let me go back to my life and my friends because that way I will have lots of stuff to pass the time. "Can I call my brother?" I don't know where the question comes from, but now that I've asked it, there's nothing more that I want.

"No."

I finally make eye contact with Dillon. I throw the book onto the floor and get to my knees, crawling forward slightly until I'm at Dillon's feet. "Please. I promise to behave. I will do anything you ask. I just want to hear his voice. I won't tell him where I am. *I don't know where I am.*"

"I said no, Nicolai."

I grab the front of Dillon's shirt and pull myself even closer. "Please, Dillon. Just a minute."

I don't expect his hand as it connects with my cheek and I collapse back on to the floor. Dillon follows me down, a look of deep regret on his face.

"I'm sorry. I just ... you can't call anyone. Why do you want to get away from me so badly? I love you, and you just want to run away."

The skin on my cheek is burning with the impact, and I want nothing more than to rub my hand over it to try and ease it, but I return to my position on my knees. It makes me level with Dillon who's also kneeling, and I look deep into his eyes to keep a connection with him. He seems as young as I remember in school, that dangerous edge far away from him. Maybe this is when I can reach him. "I don't want to run away. I just want my family to know I'm safe so they can stop looking. One thing, Dillon. Just this one thing and we can be together." I need him to believe me, so I lean forward and kiss him.

Dillon's hands grip my neck as he takes over the kiss, but I let him. I try to show him that he's in charge and I'll do anything for him. Talking to Andrei is now number one on my list of things to do, and I'll do anything to achieve that goal. He separates us but presses his forehead against mine. "I can't lose you."

"A minute. Just a minute."

"Nicolai, I can't."

"I just want to tell him I love him."

Dillon doesn't say anything before standing and leaving the room. I watch him as he disappears out of sight at the top of the stairs. I drop my head knowing that I've messed everything up. I should have just kept my mouth closed. Footsteps have me raising my head again as Dillon returns. He approaches me and holds something out towards me. It takes me a minute to realise that he's handing me a mobile phone. I take it cautiously, waiting for Dillon to rip it from my grasp.

"You can call, but you only have two minutes."

Tears build in my eyes as I stare at the phone. I'm going to speak to Andrei. He's the one who always looked out for me when we were growing up, and he's the one who'll be able to help me. I told Dillon that I wouldn't say anything to him about where I am, but I plan to give him as much information as possible. I will be punished, but I need the world to know who did this to me. "Thank you."

"Don't do anything stupid, okay."

I don't answer him while I concentrate on dialling Andrei's number. I don't have many contacts memorised but his number I do. I made sure I knew it after losing my phone and my car breaking down. Being stuck in the middle of nowhere with no way to contact anyone, even when someone else stops and offers you the use of a mobile, you quickly learn a few numbers. I close my eyes and listen to the ringing on the other end of the line, praying that Andrei will answer.

"Hello?"

I sob when I hear my big brother speak. He sounds tired and drawn, but it's him, and he's never sounded better to me. "Andrei."

"Nicolai. Is that you? Oh god, is it really you?"

I try to speak, but emotion is clogging up my throat, so I simply listen to my brother as he talks.

"Fuck, I can't believe it's you. Where are you? Tell me where to come and get you. Are you okay? Please, Nicolai, talk to me."

"Andrei. I'm ..." I take a deep breath and try to calm down I don't have much time, and I have so much to tell him. "I'm okay."

"Where are you? Who has you? Someone took you from your house, and I want to know who." There's anger to his words, and I can imagine that he has been going crazy since he heard me pass out on our call.

"I don't know where I am, but I'm ..." I open my eyes and look at Dillon, wanting to watch him as I tell Andrei everything. The words die on my lips when I see Dillon standing over James with a knife pressed against his throat. The tip is pressing hard enough that the skin is dimpled beneath it and I know it wouldn't take much more for it to break through the skin. "I'm safe."

"Tell me where you are."

"How's Gareth?"

"Nicolai, tell me where you are."

"I don't have much time. Please tell me how Gareth is." I try to keep my voice level, but I don't think I'm succeeding.

"He's fine. He got out of the hospital a few days ago. He told us who run him off the road ... is it Dillon who took you?"

I collapse back onto my arse as relief spreads through me at the news about Gareth. Knowing he's home with his girls is fucking fantastic. "Yes."

"Fucker. Do you know where you are?"

"No."

Dillon steps closer to me and holds his hand out, telling me silently that my time is up. I keep my eyes on him as I say my good-bye. "I love you, Andrei. I never told you properly what an amazing brother you were, and I need you to do one last thing for me. Tell mum and dad I love them. That I'm sorry I couldn't speak to them. And tell Gareth to look after the girls. He's the best friend anyone could ask for, and I love him." My voice breaks as I finish speaking. I don't want to hang up, but I have no choice. "I have to go."

"Nicolai! Don't you dare hang up! Nicolai ... Nicolai!" I can hear Andrei yelling as I hand the phone to Dillon and he cuts the call off. He uses his free hand to wipe his fingers over my cheek, drying the tears that haven't stopped falling since I heard Andrei's voice.

"Good boy." I grind my teeth together at his praise. I want to scream that I'm not a boy, that I'm a grown man who shouldn't be held here against his will, but I stay quiet and allow him his moment.

<hr />

I can feel James stare at me as I sit at the table and do one of the word searches in the book Dillon gave me. It's such a strange thing to be doing in this situation, but it's nice to have something to concentrate on. It stops me thinking about where I am and what might happen in the future. "What?"

"Nothing."

I put the pen down and spin on the chair, facing him before relaxing back. "Uh huh." We stare each other out, but it's James that finally gives in and speaks.

"Why didn't you tell your brother where you were?"

"Because I don't know where we are."

James rolls his eyes at my flippant answer. "No, but you could have told him who had you. I'm sure they would be able to find you if they knew it was Dillon. All you had to do was tell him."

"Did you forget about the knife pressed to your throat?" That image will be one I won't forget anytime soon. Knowing that one more press of the knife could have ended James' life, it's too much for me to imagine.

"No. But I'm sure he wouldn't have hurt me. He likes having me around to make sure you behave."

James is probably right, but it wasn't worth taking the chance. "Wasn't a risk I was willing to take."

"Nic."

"Don't Nic me, James. I don't know how else to say this to you so let me spell it out as clearly as I can. I will not risk you. I want to get out of here, but I won't leave without you. If you get out, I want you to run and don't look back. You need to get out of here." My voice doesn't waver as I speak. I feel calm as I talk to James, and it's the most certain I've been about anything since I got here.

"We need to get out of here."

I shrug my shoulders letting him know that I don't agree. I don't want to fight about it though. I want to go back to my puzzle book and forget the world around me for a few hours. With that thought in mind, I pick up the book and sit on the floor at the end of my bed. I flick through the pages until I find a crossword that I haven't done.

"How's Gareth?"

"He's good. Home now, so that will make him happy." Silence follows, and I can feel James stare at me again. I refuse to start some deep conversation with him. I'm too tired for that. "Three down. Six letters. Tasty little bite."

"We need to talk."

"Three down. Six letters. Tasty little bite."

James sighs, apparently realising that I'm not about to talk like he wants to. "Morsel."

I write in the answer before moving on. We're probably going to be here for a long time, so there will be plenty chances to talk. Just not tonight.

ARMS SLIPPING AROUND MY WAIST PULL ME FROM MY DEEP
sleep. I'd been dreaming about going to the dog shelter to adopt a
little buddy. He was a cute little guy with a wonky ear, but his
mischievous eyes stole my heart. James had been there, encouraging
me to give the little guy a home. I relax back into James' arms and
thread my fingers through his. Maybe when we get up in the morning, I should broach the subject of getting a dog. We could get one
together.

The smile I'd had growing on my lips falters when a little more of
the real world slips into my consciousness. My eyes open and I stare
at the now familiar brick wall in front of me. That's right. I'm not at
home with James holding me in his arms. I'm stuck in a windowless
basement, being held against my will by an ex-student who has lost
his fucking mind.

"Nicolai." My whispered name along with the erection that's
pressing into my arse tells me where this is about to lead. I was
hoping that I wouldn't have to do this so soon, but apparently, Dillon
has other ideas.

He works one of his hands free and starts to run his fingers over
my stomach while he kisses my neck. It's a move that I usually enjoy,
but not even that can get me to relax into it. His hand eases into my
boxers, and he cups my flaccid cock. He bites my skin while caressing
my dick. I know he's trying to get me hard, but it's not happening. I
close my eyes and use anything I can to try and get some reaction
from it. I don't want to anger him, and I think him not being able to
turn me on might do that.

I use the memories of being with James to lead my way. The feel
of his hands exploring my body made the hair all over my body stand
up on end, almost like it was reaching for him. God, he'd spent hours
teasing me with his mouth and hands, taking me to the point of
coming, but never letting me go over. He was like the master of my
body, and I just lay there and let him do his thing. I can feel the blood
rushing south as the phantom touches from James make my
body react.

Even the slick fingers at my arse don't pull me from my fantasies, and when Dillon pushes a finger inside me, I moan out in pleasure, picturing James' lust filled eyes staring at me as he slipped inside my body. The ache inside builds when the fingers are removed, and I pant in anticipation as I wait for James to fill me again. I scrunch my eyes closed further as something large stretches me, filling me to the point of pain. Dillon builds up a gentle speed while his hand strokes over my cock. I can feel my orgasm start to build as my mind is filled with the picture of James above me, thrusting into me as he chases his own pleasure.

Fireworks go off as I come in the hand that's gripping me. My muscles tighten as I orgasm, making the body behind me shudder. I can see James' face, the look of sheer pleasure he gets when he finally comes inside me. I smile at the image and let a single word slip from my lips. It's a word I will regret later, but I can't hold it in any longer.

"James."

CHAPTER TWENTY-THREE

JAMES

THERE'S BEEN A STRANGE VIBE IN THE ROOM TODAY. I CAN'T quite put my finger on what's wrong, but it feels like we're sitting in a powder keg and a single spark will set the whole thing off. I'm not sure Nicolai notices it because he's sitting at the head of the bed, his nose stuck in that bloody puzzle book again. He's been doing them most of the morning, and I've enjoyed watching him. When he's concentrating hard, he runs his tongue along the inside of his cheek, making it look like he has a sweet in his mouth. I don't think he notices it and I won't mention it in case he stops. He seems relaxed, the most relaxed I've seen since the day he arrived.

Tension builds in my body when stomping footsteps start down the stairs. This finally gets Nicolai's attention, and he closes the book and gets to his feet. Dillon appears without his usual tray. Instead, he has two paper bags, one of which he chucks in my direction, and it thumps against my chest. He doesn't throw Nicolai's at him, instead placing it on the bottom of the bed before stalking back towards the stairs. Nicolai looks at me like I might be able to give him answers to the questions floating around his head, but the best I can offer him is a shrug of my shoulders.

"Dillon?" Not even Nicolai shouting after him stops Dillon in his tracks, and the door slamming at the top leaves the room in complete silence.

I stare at the bag in my lap, wondering what the hell just happened. I expect that level of hate and contempt from Dillon, but not once have I ever seen him act that way towards Nicolai. Even when he gets angry enough to hurt Nic, Dillon never seemed angry with him. There's still softness in his eyes that said he was sorry for hurting him. Not today though, and it makes me wonder what the fuck happened.

"What do you think's wrong with him?"

Apparently, I'm not the only one who has no idea what's going on with Dillon's mood. "I'm not sure. He seemed fine last night." The last time I saw Dillon, he was all smiles after spending time with Nicolai. He left with a gentle kiss on Nic's cheek, and everything seemed normal, or as normal as this whole cluster fuck can get.

"He came back."

"He came back?" I heard nothing last night after the lights were dimmed. That's usually the sign that it's time to sleep since we have no windows, and even though my common sense tells me I should sleep lightly, I typically fall into a deep sleep that takes me through to morning.

"Yeah, he spent the night." Nicolai takes his now usual spot at the end of the bed. It brings him closer, but he doesn't look at me.

"Oh." I'm not sure what Nic means by Dillon spending the night, but I don't want to ask. The answer would probably fill my mind with images that will put me off my food for the rest of the day. To distract myself I open up the bag that holds my breakfast. I pull out a simple jam sandwich and unwrap the cling film. It's not my choice of breakfast, but I'm at the point I will eat anything to keep my strength up.

"He's pissed off at something."

"Certainly looks like it. You should eat." I point at the bag sitting on the end of Nicolai's bed, and he twists his head to look at it.

"I'm not hungry."

I know how he feels, but after Dillon starving me for so long, it has me eating when I can. "You should still eat." I take a bite of my sandwich, and it turns into a solid lump in my throat as visions of Dillon and Nicolai together invade my mind. I attempt to swallow the food, and I wish I had a bottle of water to help with my struggle. Finally, I get it down, and I watch Nicolai open up his bag, his face scrunching up as he looks inside.

"Looks ... appetising." He gives a little chuckle, but it grates against my nerves.

"I know it isn't up to your usual standards with Dillon. You'll just have to eat it like I've had to." I don't know why I'm being such a bitch to Nicolai, and as soon as the words are out, I regret them. I hate them even more when I see the hurt in Nicolai's eyes. "I'm sorry."

He doesn't respond, his head dropping so I can't see his face. Acid churns in my gut and the few mouthfuls of sandwich I'd managed to eat threaten to make a return appearance.

"Nic, I'm sorry."

He nods his head as he rips off tiny pieces of the sandwich and eats them while ignoring me. I can understand why he's doing it, but it doesn't stop the irritation building again. He's acting like this whole situation is only hard on him. I've been here the longest, and it wasn't exactly a holiday camp before he arrived.

"Great. You just ignore me. Best way to get the fuck out of here." I can't hide the snarkiness from my voice, but with what I just said I don't think it matters all that much.

Nicolai's head whips up and the hurt that was there a moment ago is replaced with anger. "Fuck you, James." I glare at him as he throws his sandwich to the floor.

"Yeah, cause this has been so fucking difficult for you." I need to calm down, but now that the anger has an outlet, I can't get it to stop. It's shitty to take it out on Nicolai, but I have no one else to rage against.

"You think it's been easy for me?" Nicolai meets me anger for anger, and I struggle to get to my feet, thankful that Dillon untied my legs.

The chain pulls against my waist, and I use my tied hands to give myself a little more leeway. "I don't see you tied to a fucking pipe in the wall."

"No, I'm collared and chained to a fucking wall. So much better."

He has a point, but my anger is blurring all the obvious facts. I keep yelling at him as he gets to his feet, and it's the first time I've thought that it's probably a good thing that we can't reach each other. "But you get to move. How's the shower, because I sure as hell haven't been offered one recently?" I've been stuck in the same jeans and t-shirt since I was let out of the room, and they are covered in blood and stink like a sewer. At least I'm now allowed to use the bathroom under constant supervision, but the shower has never been offered. I'm pretty sure the toilet is only provided because I'm now in the same room as Nicolai, so that means Dillon would have to deal with me if I wet myself.

"Fan-fucking-tastic. It completely makes up for everything I have to do."

"Yeah, I'm sure it's so hard."

"I gave him my fucking arse to save yours! You're welcome by the way." His words zap the fight straight from my body, and it takes all my effort not to collapse onto the floor in a heap.

"Nicolai-" I don't get a chance to say anything else as Dillon comes barreling down the stairs. He doesn't stop when he sees me, and his fist connects with my face before I can protect myself. My head snaps back to thud the wall behind me and stars explode into my vision. I can hear someone screaming, and I'm not sure if the noise is coming from me because my head is swimming with pain and confusion. When I can clear it enough, I focus on what's going on above me. I don't even know when I landed on the floor, but Dillon and Nicolai are both above me, and Dillon looks pissed off.

"What is wrong with you?" Nicolai is trying to calm Dillon down, but there's a rage in Dillon's eyes that tell me he's failing.

"He doesn't get to talk to you like that."

I blink a few times to try and clear my head, but I'm still so fucking confused.

"He needs to treat you better."

I must have a concussion or something because it sounds like Dillon attacked me because I was arguing with Nicolai.

Silence spreads through the room, and I'm scared to make a move in case I set Dillon off again. Now is the best time to be invisible.

"It was just a silly fight."

Dillon stares at Nicolai, and I think that he's going to calm down, but suddenly he turns to glare at me. "And it won't happen again."

A cold wave of fear spreads through my body, and a bead of sweat runs down my back. I've seen Dillon angry, and I've seen him when he's been in the throes of beating me, but not once have I ever seen him look so dangerous. He goes for me and because of the chain around my waist and the wall at my back I have no way to escape. I cry out when his hand grabs my hair and pulls my head back, the pain searing through my scalp. I think it can't get worse, but as soon as he has full control of my movements, his fist connects with my nose, and I feel it explode under the attack. Blood instantly flows down over my lips, and I want to close my mouth to stop it filling with blood, but I'm struggling to breathe through my damaged nose.

"Dillon, no!" I can hear Nicolai screaming, but I know it won't stop Dillon.

Another fist lands in the same spot and the bright lights from before return. I cough as blood flows into my mouth, blocking my throat because of my position. I grip Dillon's hand in an attempt to get him to release me, but I barely have any strength.

"Stop! Dillon, you're hurting him." I can hear the panic in Nicolai's voice.

"That's the whole point." The only way to describe the emotion filling Dillon's voice is that it's pure and utter hatred.

He removes his hand, and I drop to my hands and knees on the floor, coughing up the mouthful of blood that I couldn't breathe through. I gasp in loudly to try and fill my lungs, and I'm just at the point of feeling I might not die when I'm kicked in the stomach. Pain explodes out through my muscles as I'm lifted from the ground with the force.

"Dillon! Look at me."

Thankfully this catches Dillon's attention, and I see his shadow move away from where he's standing over me. I grip my stomach as I look towards what's happening. If Dillon's going to attack me again, I want to be prepared. Dillon steps in front of Nicolai, getting close like he has no fear of being attacked.

"Don't hurt, James. Please."

This makes Dillon flinch, and he turns to look at me, making me move back to put more distance between us. It's Nicolai's hand on his chin that finally gets Dillon to look away.

"You don't have to hurt him. He's nothing to me." I can hear the shake in Nicolai's voice, and I hope that Dillon doesn't hear it. It makes my heart ache for all the words I said to him, and I hope I have a chance to take them back.

"Don't lie to me."

"I'm not. I'm here with you, and I thought you knew that." Nicolai smiles, but I can see that it doesn't reach his eyes. He's playing a part just now, and he's doing an excellent job at it.

"You're lying." I can see rage vibrating under Dillon's skin, and I pray that he doesn't give it an outlet because I'm sure that I will be on the receiving end of it.

"Did I fight you last night? Did I stop you?"

Nicolai had mentioned that Dillon had slipped into bed with him last night, but thankfully he never told me what had happened. If anyone had asked me how I thought Dillon would react to the mention of the previous night, I would have told them that it would calm him down, possibly make him melt into Nicolai's arms, but I would have been so wrong. The fury inside Dillon seems to grow, and it only takes Nicolai a fraction of a second to notice.

"No you didn't stop me, but it wasn't me you were with was it?"

Confusion is clear on Nicolai's face at Dillon's words, and even though I can feel that something bad is about to happen, I can't look away. Dillon leans in close to Nic, and with one simple statement, everything changes.

"It was his name you moaned."

Nicolai shakes his head, and his eyes are wide with fear. "No."

"Yes. So now the only way to get you to be fully mine is to get rid of him."

Both men turn to look at me. Nicolai with fear and panic, and Dillon with fury. There's a small smile on Dillon's lips, and I think that scares me more than anything, knowing that there's a part of him enjoying this whole thing.

"No. I'm sorry. Take it out on me. It's not James' fault." The words rush from Nicolai, but it doesn't turn Dillon's glare from me. I want to look away, but I don't want to give him that final bit of control. I will fight to survive, even though I know it's a fight I won't survive.

Nicolai grabs Dillon's arm and Dillon's hand comes up instantly and backhands Nic across the face, knocking him to the ground. Nicolai sits there on the floor in shock, his hand coming up to wipe the blood off his lip. Dillon looms over him, his finger pointing close to Nicolai's face.

"What I'm about to do is all your fault. Everything is on you, and I want you to remember that. I was happy to leave him here, but you had to go and mess it all up."

His words are a lie, and I hope Nicolai realises this. There was no way that Dillon was going to keep me around for much longer. It didn't make sense for me to be here once he had Nicolai in control. I'm completely disposable.

"I'm sorry. Tell me what to do ... tell me how to make this right." Nicolai rights himself slightly, getting to his knees in front of Dillon.

"Do you promise to be with me, as mine? Do you promise never to talk to him again, never look in his direction?"

"Yes. I promise, Dillon. I'm fully with you and no one else."

Dillon leans down towards Nicolai until their noses are nearly touching. "I don't fucking believe you."

Dillon spins instantly towards me, and I barely have a second to react before he's on me. His first contact is with my face again, but this time it's my jaw that feels like it's on fire. I try to block his next blow, but I'm struggling to anticipate where it's coming from. It's almost like more than one man is attacking me, and every time I think I can protect myself, he changes his attack.

I collapse onto the floor and curl my body in the vain attempt to stop some of the pain, but when I roll away from the attack, I'm rewarded with a kick to the spine. I cry out as the contact makes pain radiate through my whole body.

"You had to come along and ruin everything. You can't have what's mine." It's the same thing that Dillon had screamed at me when I first arrived, and he used me to take his anger out on. "Nicolai has always been mine, and you touched him."

The kicks get stronger, and I turn in between them to try and protect my back. I tuck my head into my hands and curl as much as I can, using the tie wraps to keep my hands in place.

"Dillon, stop!"

"Fucking cunt. You couldn't just vanish?"

"Dillon!"

All the words and voices are starting to blur into each other as darkness spreads in my vision. My body is complete agony and with every new hit or kick, I want to let the darkness take me. I want to melt into the quiet warmth that the black void offers. I won't be in pain there and I'll be able to sleep. That's what I want the most. To sleep and wake up and find this is all a dream, but that won't happen. When the darkness claims me, I probably won't wake up again. That's what keeps me holding on, the thought of dying. I want to see my family again even if it's only long enough to tell them I love them. I want to hold my mum and thank her for everything she has ever done for me. I want to tell my dad he made me the man I am today and I love him for it. I want to tell my cousin to take a chance and love with her whole heart, that maybe that guy is exactly what she needs. I want to tell Nicolai that I don't blame him for any of this, and I'm sad that I never got a chance to try with him. I have a feeling that we could have been good together and I regret not finding him sooner.

There's so much I still want to do, but none of that is going to happen now, and that hurts worse than what's happening to my body. Adrenaline is spreading through me dulling the new hits, but it can't take away the ache in my heart. The ache that only spreads as the darkness grows no matter how much I try and fight against it.

CHAPTER TWENTY-FOUR

NICOLAI

HE'S GOING TO KILL JAMES. I CAN SEE IT CLEARLY IN DILLON'S eyes, and I don't know how to stop him. I struggle to my feet and reach for him again. My touch earns me another backhand, and I stumble back, managing to keep my feet this time. I ignore the pain in my jaw and go straight back to trying to protect James. Dillon looks intent on killing him, and I can't let that happen, not over a stupid mistake I made.

When Dillon had told me I'd called out James name the night before I was shocked, but as soon as the reality of it sunk in, I knew that something terrible was going to happen. I just didn't realise how bad it would get. Now seeing James bleeding on the floor, struggling to protect himself, all I can think is I need to stop Dillon. I try to grab Dillon so I can drag him away from James but the stupid fucking collar stops me from getting the strength I need to separate them. I do get Dillon's attention though, but it earns me another fucking slap making me hit the edge of the bed, falling heavily onto the mattress.

I practically growl when I push myself back onto my feet. I look around the room frantically, trying to find something I can use to stop Dillon. There has to be something. I take in the furniture, but there's nothing that can help because it's all too far away. Fuck!

"Dillon. Stop, you're killing him!" I keep my eyes moving around while I scream at Dillon, hoping that he might suddenly take pity on me and stop the attack. It doesn't work though, and when my eyes fall on to the one thing that's lying about, I don't think twice. I grab it before spinning in place and going after Dillon. The only thought in my head is stopping him, and when he steps away from James to get some power into his kick, I grab him by the throat and drag him backwards. He fights against my hold, but I lock my arm tighter, not willing to let him reach James.

I cry out in pain as Dillon's nails dig into my arm, but I don't ease up. I continue to hold him, but I can feel my strength start to give in. Too many days of being inactive and not sleeping is using my energy quicker than I thought possible. I can feel him moving more, his neck slipping from under my arm and I need to do something. I can't let him go, and that means using the only weapon I have. I don't stop to think about what I'm going to do, only focusing on knowing I need to do something. I raise my hand up and use all the power I have to bring it down, stabbing the pen into Dillon's neck.

Dillon screams out as blood covers my hand and arm. His thrashing nearly makes me let him go, but I ride it out like he's a wild horse. I pull the pen from his neck and plunge it back in. Rage drives my next moves as I stab Dillon over and over again.

Blood covers both of us, but I don't stop.

Dillon starts shaking in my arms, but I don't stop.

I can't stop.

I have to make sure this is finished.

Thrust after thrust I stab the pen into Dillon's throat, not stopping when he goes limp in my arms. I follow his lifeless body to the ground, continuing to attack him.

"Nicolai."

I blink a few times when my name is called. I look around, taking a few moments to let the world come back to me. I was so stuck in my head, letting my emotions drive me, that I'm not sure what's happening.

"Nicolai." James shaky voice finally filters into my brain, and I look over at him. He's sitting up, his face a bloody mess, but he's breathing and talking. Relief floods me, but it turns to disgust when I look down at the bloody mess I'm sitting on.

I scurry backwards away from Dillon, and I don't stop until my back hits the wall. I can't get my eyes to leave Dillon's prone body. The bottom half of him is clean and ordinary looking, but from the waist up there's nothing but blood and other stuff I don't want to think about. I know its flesh from his neck and knowing that is making me want to puke. I make the mistake of looking at his neck, not sure how his head is still attached with all the damage I caused, and a loud whimper escapes me.

"Nicolai."

I whip around to look at James again when he shouts my name.

"I need you to keep looking at me." He coughs, groaning in pain as he holds his ribs. I do as he asks, keeping my eyes firmly on him. I want to go to him, let him hide me from what I just did, but we are both imprisoned. "That's good. Are you okay?"

Am I okay? I'm not sure I know what okay means anymore. James doesn't need to know this though, especially since he's sitting there on the floor bleeding and broken, so I nod my head.

"Are you hurt?"

This one I can answer quickly with a head shake. My answer brings a small smile to James split lip, and he hisses a little. "James." I barely manage to get his name out past the lump in my throat, and as soon as it's out, I go mute again.

"I know. It's good now, the danger is gone."

I want to believe his words but reality is flickering back into focus, and I realise how fucked we are. "James, I killed Dillon."

"It's okay, Nic."

It's not though, and he isn't getting what I'm trying to tell him. "I killed him."

"I know. It was self-defence, and everyone will see that."

I shake my head and try to make sense. "*Fuck*. No, I killed him,

and he was the only one with access to keys. We're still chained up."
Bile rises in my throat, and this time I can't keep it down. I get to my
knees, turning away from James, and empty the meagre contents of
my stomach onto the floor. Even when it's empty, I continue to heave,
the images of Dillon seared into my brain and playing on a loop.

"Nic?"

I wipe my mouth with the back of my hand and ease myself away
from the mess.

"You need to check Dillon's pockets, Nic. He might have the keys
on him."

I frown at James' calm rational, not understanding how he isn't
losing it right now. "How are you so fucking calm?"

"Because it hurts too much to lose my shit." Another small smile
graces his lips, but it doesn't settle a single nerve that's sparking
through my body like electricity. "You need to check his pockets."

I look over to where the remains of Dillon lie and I'm not sure I
can touch him. I look down at my hands and notice the blood for the
first time. I scrub them against my legs hoping to clean some of the
mess from them, but when it doesn't work, I rub harder, the pain in
my thighs barely registering.

"Fucking stop, Nicolai!"

I stop instantly and stare at James.

"Stop dicking about and check his pockets." His instructions are
clear, and the strength of his voice has me moving without thought.
Maybe that's the way to get through this, just do as I'm told and not
think about it.

I slip my hands into Dillon's pockets, forcing them deep to reach
the bottom. I come up empty in the first pocket, and I start to lose any
hope of finding anything. I remove my hand and wipe it on my thigh
to give myself a minute to brace for the next search. I don't want to
keep searching, but there's no other option. If I don't do it, then I'm
going to die a slow agonising death while I starve, and then I have to
watch James die too. Of course, there's still a chance of that
happening if Dillon isn't carrying the keys today. I refuse to focus on

that though as I move to check the second pocket. I reach around, and it quickly becomes clear that I'm going to have roll Dillon to get into the pocket. My stomach churns at the thought, and I stare down at the body.

"What's wrong?" James' voice sounds even more strained, but I can't get my eyes to leave Dillon.

"I ... need to move him." I can feel my breathing pick up as I struggle to come to terms with what I need to do. I don't want to touch him any more than I have to, but there's no way to get around it.

"Don't think about it. Just pretend you're moving a bag of rubbish."

He's right. I need to keep my mind focused on the task and pretend its nothing more than the Resusci Anne that I use for CPR training in the school. It's just a plastic doll, and if I concentrate on below the waist, it isn't covered in blood. Taking a deep breath, I push against the legs and roll it, actively ignoring the wet sounds coming from my right. No, it's not Dillon's throat coming apart even more.

I quickly put my hand in the pocket and nearly weep when my fingers connect with something cold. I grip the item and pull it out, not even checking before I turn my back on the gore. I finally look down, and tears eventually fill my eyes when I see a small keyring with a single key. I recognise it instantly as I've seen Dillon use it on the little padlock that keeps my collar locked together. My fingers shake as I pull the padlock to the front of my neck and try to get the key inside the lock. I fumble with it, and it drops into my lap, where I stare at it. *I need to calm down.*

A nervous laugh escapes me as I pick up the key. My eyes flicker over to James, fully expecting him to be laughing at my inability to hold onto something, but that's not what I see. James is slumped to the side, his shoulder pressed against the pipe he's tied to, and that's the only thing holding him up. His eyes are closed, and my heart nearly stops when I see his pale colour. It's the first time I've paid full attention to how much blood is on him. His top is sodden, and his nose is still dripping blood down his chin.

"James?" His name comes out on a whisper, but I can't seem to get any strength into my voice. I automatically reach up and scrape the key over the lock until it slips into the hole. I turn it as I watch James' chest, the sight of it rising and falling making me keep moving. I stare at it convinced that if I look away, he'll stop breathing. I need to get James out of here and quickly.

The metal of the collar slipping from my neck makes my hands still for a fraction of a second. I'm free. I'm finally fucking free. I look at the ceiling and blink back the tears. I'll have plenty of time later to fall apart, but for now, I need to keep it together. I crawl towards James and cup his jaw, nearly giving into my need to cry when his eyes flicker behind the lids. He might not be awake, but he's still kind of with me. I tug at the chain around his waist, growling in frustration when it doesn't budge. I spin it around and see that it has its own padlock. There was nothing else in Dillon's pockets so that means the key must be somewhere else, I just have no fucking idea where.

I look towards the stairs and know that I need to leave James here on his own to get help. I lean in close to his ear and whisper, hoping he can hear me. "I need to go and get help. I'll be straight back so don't die. Please." I brush my lips over his cheek before rushing for the stairs. Taking them as quickly as possible, I use the handrail to propel me faster, and when I reach the door at the top, there's the a moment where doubt kicks in and I fear it won't be open. The handle turns, and I sigh in relief while stepping out into the corridor. Moving cautiously through the quiet house, I keep a lookout in case there is someone else here. My common sense says that Dillon was working alone, but until that's proven, I won't take it for granted.

I pass through a small living room and into a kitchen. The whole place is empty apart from some basic furniture, but it doesn't look like anyone has been living here for a long time. None of that matters when I see the phone sitting on the edge of a small table. Oh god, please let it work. I rush forwards and grab it from the table, my heart rate picking up when I press the on button and it lights up. My finger shakes as I dial Andrei's number and listen to it ring for far too long.

"Hello?"

I lean back against the wall and use it to crumble to the floor. Hearing his voice is something I never imagined I would ever experience again and I can't get words to form. Instead, I cry, hating myself that I'm wasting time that James might not have.

"Nicolai? Is that you? Shit, is that you big brother?"

"Yes." The word is barely squeaked out past my sobs, but he hears me.

"Oh shit. Are you okay? Where are you?"

I use the back of my hand to dry my eyes and breathe deeply. Time to get out of this fucking place. "Andrei, I need you to get help here. James is really hurt, and I'm not sure if he's going to make it."

"James? Who the fuck is James?" Only my brother would focus on that point.

"It doesn't matter. Shit, I should have just called nine-nine-nine. I don't know what I was thinking." My mind had gone straight to calling Andrei instead of using my common sense, and I hope my mistake won't cost James.

"It's fine, tell me where you are, and I'll get an ambulance there. Jodi is calling them, just tell me an address."

Shit. That might be a problem. I search around trying to find something that might have an address, but there's nothing lying around.

"Nic?"

"I'm fucking trying! I don't know where I am."

"Look outside. Is there anything that you recognise?"

Outside. Right, that might work. I head towards the front of the house and find the door, throwing it open and stepping outside for the first time in ... fuck knows how long. I'm surprised to find myself on the top step of a small bungalow in the middle of a street. There are cars driving past slowly and people are standing chatting in front gardens. It looks like the perfect description of suburbia and not one person realised what was happening behind these closed doors. I can't think about that now, and I rush down the garden path towards the two ladies talking in front of a SUV. Their eyes widen when I approach them and I cringe when I picture myself the way they are seeing me. A strange man in nothing but boxer shorts, blood covering most of his body and bruises covering his face. I'm actually surprised they haven't run away screaming.

"Can you tell me where I am?"

Their confusion grows, and I swear they look like they're about to bolt.

"Please. I'm talking to the police, and I need to know where I am."

"Um ... this is Parker Crescent."

I can hear Andrei telling Jodi, his secretary, the street name. "Where is that?"

"What?"

"What area is this? What town?" I nearly collapse to the ground when she tells me that I'm still in my own town. I'm barely a mile away from where I live. How could I be so close and not be found? I thought that Dillon had taken me miles away, possibly to a cabin in the middle of the forest, but the reality is that he hid me right under everyone's noses. I could walk home in less than ten minutes, but the chain kept me trapped like a fucking animal.

I back away from the woman and finally turn to look at the house that was my prison. It looks like the other houses on the street, with bright paintwork and yellow flowers in front of the windows. There is nothing that points to the horrors that happened inside, but I know what's in that basement, and I'm scared to see them again when I go back in for James.

Sirens sound from different directions, but they all stop in front of the bungalow. Police officers and paramedics rush from their vehicles and into the property. A blanket is wrapped around my shoulders, and I stare into the eyes of a sweet woman who's looking at me with sympathy. She is in complete contrast to the policeman who is standing next to her, and panic starts to build as he stares at me without emotion. This is the moment when I'll be arrested for killing Dillon.

"Come on, hun. Let's get you in the ambulance." The paramedic starts to lead me away from the house, and I let her for a few seconds before my mind loses part of its numbness. My eyes keep flickering to the police officer who follows, but he doesn't say anything.

My mind finally clears and my only thought is on the man I left in the basement. "James." I try to turn, but the policeman puts his hand on my shoulder and speaks for the first time.

"The other team is dealing with him. I'll let you know when they know how he is. We want to check you out, make sure you aren't hurt. Then I need to ask you some questions."

Nodding, I let myself be led towards the ambulance. The police can ask any questions they want, as long as they get me information about James. I need to know he's okay. A few steps away from the ambulance someone calls my name and it makes me spin. Before I'm fully turned, a huge set of arms engulfs me and wraps me in warmth. The blanket drops from my shoulder, but I hardly notice it as I throw my arms around Andrei's neck. I hold on like my life depends on it, and finally, allow myself to break. Tears flow down my cheeks, and I let them, not caring who sees me. For the first time in too long, I finally feel safe. I don't care that I'm a grown man, being with my brother makes me feel secure and protected.

"It's really you. I thought I was never going to see you again."

"Sir, you can't touch him." The police officers voice has me pulling from Andrei's comforting embrace, and the scowl on the officer's face tells me that I just made a mistake.

"Why the hell not?" My brother is angry and I lay a hand on his arm to try and calm him.

"Because I killed Dillon, Andrei."

Andrei's head whips towards me and he finally registers the blood all over my body. "Nic."

Noise on the concrete pulls my attention and I watch as two paramedics rush past with James on a stretcher. Suddenly my own situation seems like nothing, the only important thing is James. I try to go after him, but a hand on my arm stops me.

"You can't go with him yet. Come let me check you out, and we can follow him to the hospital. Your friend can come with you." She looks at Andrei as she tries to get me into the back of the ambulance.

"He's my brother. Is James okay?" I sit on the stretcher in the back and let the paramedic start checking on me.

"I don't know, but they're taking him to the hospital, and that's the best place for him. I'll get you strapped in, and then we can follow him. We'll only be a few minutes behind him, I promise."

Sitting back against the stretcher, I watch as the policeman speaks to the paramedic for a few moments. She nods before getting in the back with me, squeezing past Andrei's legs to get to her equipment.

"I will meet you at the hospital. I have a lot of questions for you, Mr Morgan, but I will give you time to get checked out and comfortable."

I relax a little knowing I'll have time to see my brother before I'm arrested, and hopefully I will get information on James before I am taken away.

EPILOGUE

NICOLAI

I collapse into a heap on my couch and look around my new living room. I've spent all day moving in, and my furniture is finally where it should be.

"Are you feeling tired, sweetheart?" Gareth's teasing tone makes me give him the finger, and his returning laughter as he walks past with a box makes me smile. He's recovered well from his crash, his limp barely noticeable now after his three months of physiotherapy.

Thinking about Gareth's injuries makes my fingers rub along the small scar that's still visible along the back of my neck. The collar left me with a sliced neck that I hadn't noticed while I had been held captive, but it had given me the most problems once I got out. Even now I get an ache in the scarred skin when something brushes against it. I shouldn't complain though, because I'm alive and that's the most important thing. All this time after being rescued and the tears still build in my eyes when I think about the fact that not everyone made it out alive.

I shudder in a breath when arms encircle my shoulders.

"You're overthinking again."

I drop my head back onto James' shoulder, thankful that he's always around to pull me out of my head. He's been the rock that's kept me grounded since getting out of that basement, even when he was the one who was injured.

"I'm not." I brush my lips against his cheek and inhale, filling my lungs with his scent. I didn't realise it was possible for someone to smell so good without aftershave, but James smells fucking amazing.

"Liar." He turns his head until our lips meet and he steals my breath with a gentle kiss.

"Oh god, would you two stop it for two fucking minutes."

I laugh against James' mouth, and he bites my bottom lip before standing up. He glares at Gareth over my shoulder, and I can't help but smile at the pair of them. They have become such good friends since I introduced them and it makes me happy. "I'm going to help Andrei with the last of the boxes." He squeezes my shoulder before leaving the room.

Gareth joins me on the couch, sighing as he drops next to me. "I like that guy."

"I know, and he might have mentioned liking you."

"Well of course he does." Gareth gives me a no shit stare before his face gets serious. "How are you doing?"

"I'm good."

Gareth gives me a slow blink that tells me he isn't buying my words. "Again I ask, how are you doing?"

My heart rate picks up but I will myself to calm down. There's no reason for me to get anxious sitting here safely on the couch with Gareth, but sometimes I have no control over my body. "I'm better than yesterday. I think moving will help a lot."

I'd tried to live in my old house, but after the third day, I knew that it was an impossible task. The memories of Dillon and his attacks assaulted me in every room, but the bedroom was the worst. I could barely take a step into that room without having a panic attack. So many memories were in that room, and there was no way to erase them from my mind. I tried to sleep there one night but knowing what Dillon had done to me in there, the thought of him raping me, had been far too much. That next morning I practically moved in with Andrei. It didn't matter that Dillon was dead, I couldn't spend one more night in that house.

"You'll get there. And I have a funny feeling that man of yours will help."

"Hey, fuck face. Any chance you could help at any time?" Andrei's voice booms through from the front of the house and I burst out laughing, the normality of it settling my nerves.

"I hate your brother." Gareth grumbles as he gets up from the couch and I take a second to watch him before I join him. I grab a box from the hall and take it towards the master bedroom where I meet James.

He smiles when he sees me and pulls me into his arms. "Hey, beautiful."

I kiss him gently, enjoying the pressure of his body against mine. I still can't believe that he's here with me after everything we've been through. The memory of him being wheeled past me into that ambulance is going to be stuck in my head forever. I was convinced that by the time I'd reached the hospital James would be gone. He looked so pale, and he'd lost so much blood, there was no way my mind could convince me he was alive, but he had been. Not that he had escaped uninjured but he was alive, and nothing was life threatening. Some broken ribs, a concussion and a broken nose, but he was breathing and would survive.

"Happy?"

"Very." I don't think anything has ever compared to how happy I feel at this moment. Knowing that James has been able to move past everything that happened to him because of me, that means everything. I never imagined that he would be able to forgive me for the torture he endured, but there has never been a moment he hasn't supported me wholeheartedly. I'm the one who struggled to forgive myself, and even to this day I don't think I've managed it fully. I keep expecting him to come to his senses and leave me.

"What side of the bed do you want?" He winks at me before motioning behind his shoulder. I look behind him to see our brand new bed. There was no way that I could bring my old bed here to share with James after what happened in it. No, I wasn't bringing any memories of Dillon into my new home.

"The middle?" I bite my bottom lip and James growls, making my dick harden without too much trouble.

"I like the way you think." He grabs me by the hips and pulls me towards the bed. I laugh as he pushes me down onto it and straddles me. "Oops, you fell."

"Seriously you two. Get a fucking room." Gareth puts a box on the floor and shakes his head. James turns towards Gareth, a fake frown on his face.

"We have a room. It's not our fault you're standing in it."

I lie there and listen to the pair of them bicker back and forth, but I smile at it. This is my life now, and I couldn't be happier. I never imagined that I would ever reach this point, especially after what I had to do to save James' life.

My stomach drops when I think about the lengths I had to go to to get out of that place. Knowing how insane and dangerous Dillon was can't take away the fact that I killed him. I took someone's life and I'll have to live with that forever. I'd been convinced I was going to jail. You can't kill someone and not go to jail, or at least that's what I'd thought. The whole investigation against me had barely begun when they had concluded I'd acted in self-defense. It doesn't take away the guilt I feel but it helps, and now I can have the life I've always dreamed about with James. He's the best thing that's ever happened to me, and I don't know how to live without him anymore.

JAMES

I know he's disappeared into his head when I feel his body tense under mine. I've spent the last few months rescuing him from his thoughts. He struggles to get out of his head sometimes, but I'm only too happy to help him escape. I nod at Gareth, and he gets instantly gets what I'm trying to say. We have developed a close friendship since we met and I think that's based mainly on Nicolai. We both love him and want nothing but the best for him. Gareth leaves the room quietly, closing the door behind him.

I relax my body until I'm lying on Nicolai's chest. His eyes focus, and he smiles at me, finally back in the present. "Oh, there you are."

His cheeks heat, and it makes him look so fucking cute. I don't tell him that though because he hates it. He keeps telling me that a man of his years doesn't blush and I love being able to correct him.

"Sorry."

I brush a piece of hair off Nicolai's forehead. "Don't ever be sorry. Want to talk about it?"

"Not really." Instead of talking he leans up and kisses me. I know he's using his lips to distract me, but I'm okay with that. There was a time I thought I'd never kiss Nicolai again, so I will accept anything he's willing to give me.

Waking up in the hospital had been scary. I didn't know where I was or how I go there, but when I looked to the side and saw Nic sitting next to my bed, I knew I'd be okay. That was the moment I knew I wanted more with him if he would have me. He'd been worried at the start that I was only wanting to spend time with him because I was grateful to him for saving my life, but it was so much more than that. I had survived something horrific, and I refused not to grab hold of the things I wanted. Just happened that the thing I'd wanted more than anything was Nicolai, so I grabbed hold of him with both hands.

Watching him struggle with the aftermath of the attack has been difficult. There have been nightmares that end in him screaming, and the fear of leaving the house has been hard to overcome, but he's getting better every day. When he wakes in the middle of the night, his eyes wide with panic, I'm only happy to hold him until the fear passes. The times he vanishes into his head are getting fewer so it makes me feel like there might be peace for him in the future.

I ease back from his distracting kiss and stare into his eyes. I still can't believe that this man is mine. He can't see how amazing he is, but I will spend the rest of my life telling him. "I love you." No matter how many times I tell him how I feel, it never seems enough. We've been through more than most couples will ever have to endure, but instead of it ripping us apart, it's just made us tighter.

"I love you too."

Those are the words I've spent my life waiting on. Not once did I think joining a dating app would lead me here. I'd thought I would find nothing more than someone to warm my bed, but after so long on my own I was willing to give it a shot. Reading Nic's advert had made me smile, and since the day I met him he's had me hooked. It took me thirty-two years to find the one, but I wouldn't have it any other way. He's my other half, and he sees the real me more than anyone ever has before. I don't even have to talk to him for him to know what I'm feeling or thinking. He just knows.

"Nic, Gareth needs to leave." Andrei's voice booms through the closed door and I feel Nicolai sigh underneath me.

"I better go say goodbye." With a brush of his lips, he pushes me to the side and smiles as he leaves me lying on the bed.

I stare at the ceiling and listen to the voices outside the bedroom door. As much as I appreciate everyone's help, I wish they would leave. I want to get my man alone so I can spend the night holding him in our home. That sounds amazing. Our home. When Nicolai first told me he was selling his house, I understood his reasons, especially after everything he'd been through under that roof. What had shocked me was when he asked me to move with him, get a place together. I didn't hesitate for a second to say yes because, after everything we'd been through, I just wanted to be with him as much as possible. Moving in seemed the perfect solution for that.

I jump when hands land on my thighs. I look down my body and see a smiling Nicolai climbing up my body. "Hey, sexy."

I drag him up the final length of my body and attack his mouth. I try not to get carried away knowing that Andrei's still somewhere in the house, but it's difficult when I feel Nicolai's erection against my thigh. I groan into his mouth as he rubs against me. "You're not playing fair. Behave while your brother's here."

He doesn't stop moving, and I grip his arse tightly in my hand, pulling him tighter against me. "Lucky he left with Gareth then. Thought maybe we should test out this new bed."

I stare at him, and my mouth hangs open a little. I want to ask Nicolai what he means, but I don't want to put any pressure on him in case I've misunderstood what he means. We have been intimate before today, but Nicolai hasn't felt comfortable enough to take things too far. Some kissing and mutual hand jobs has been his limit, but even that is more than I could expect. Any little attention he gives me I'm grateful for because if I had gone through what he had, I'm not sure I would be able to trust anyone again. This is why Nicolai amazes me every single day.

"You've gone quiet." Nic's voice is almost shy, but there's still a fire burning in his eyes.

"I'm not sure what to say. I don't want to get this wrong."

Nicolai brushes a finger over my lip, and I sigh against the skin. My eyes flutter as I enjoy the movement, the simple touch sending electric sparks through my whole body. "I love you, James. This house is our new start, and I want all my memories to be good."

His words send a thrill through me because that's what I want. This is the start of the rest of our lives together, and I can't wait to make memories with him.

"And that means I need to get rid of a few demons. I don't want to take them with me any longer."

My heart is racing, but I try to keep calm. I think I know what he's trying to say, but he's going to have to say the words himself. I refuse to voice what's in my head because if I'm wrong, it might make Nicolai feel pressured. "You have to say it, angel."

"I'm ready."

"I need more words." I'm close to hyperventilating with excitement, and there is no way to hide the raging hard on that pressing against Nic's hip, but I still won't take anything for granted until he tells me.

"I love you Mr Kaine, and I'm ready to move on. I want your lips to be the only ones I can feel on mine. I want it to be the memories of your touch that is on my body all day, driving me crazy until I can see you again." He leans down and kisses me gently before dropping his forehead onto mine. He closes his eyes, and his words come out soft, but I know he means them. "And I want your body to be the only one I can remember inside me. I want you to erase his touch. I don't want to feel him anymore."

Joy and anger go to war inside me. Anger at Dillon for what he did, for the pain he left Nicolai to deal with long after we got out of that basement. If he weren't dead, I would want to kill him all over again. Nicolai has spent so long struggling to recover from what happened to him, and every time I think of Dillon, I think that it's a great thing that he's dead.

"If you don't want to, I understand." Nic's voice doesn't sound so confident, and its only then that I realise my anger at Dillon has dragged me away from what should be an important moment.

Nicolai starts to lift himself off my body, so I grab him and twist us until I'm now on top. When I have him fully under my body, I relax so my weight is holding Nic in place. I want to explain to him how much he means to me, how much I love him, but I decide to show him. So I kiss him, claiming his lips and hopefully showing him how much I need him. Reading Nicolai's body is easy, and when he relaxes under me, I use it as an invitation to keep going. My hands roam over his body, and when Nic grinds his cock into me, I press down harder until we both groan in pleasure.

Tonight is important, and I need to make sure I do everything right. I'm going to remind Nicolai how amazing it can feel to let someone else control his pleasure. To remind him that I will never hurt him. I will prove to him that he's the most important thing in my life, today and always. And I will prove it with every gentle touch he allows me.

The End

ACKNOWLEDGMENTS

I love my tribe! The only reason I can do this job that I love is because of the people who have my back...and I have the best people behind me.

Claire Booth: You listen to me complain and stress...but then you just tell me to get on with it. I always write with you in mind...especially the best friends!

My Scary beta Marie Mason: You read my stories and make sure that it's as good as it can be. You will tell me how it is...and for that I am forever thankful....even if it usually means adding a chapter or two!

My betas: Jax, Mildred, Sooz, Anita, Rachael, and Rhiannon. Thank you for taking time out of your lives to read this story for me. Knowing what you think is so important, and I hope people love it as much as you did.

My proofreader Chele: Again...just thank you!

To Nicola: You allowed me the pleasure of being in your life...for that Im always thankful!

To my Minxes...thank you for all you do. You help with my dilemmas and push me when I need it...so a huge THANK YOU!!

ABOUT THE AUTHOR

For more information on T.a. McKay

www.authortamckay.com
tamckayauthor@gmail.com

ALSO BY T.A MCKAY

Leaving Marks series:

Leaving His Mark ~ Out now

Leaving Her Mark ~ Out now

Hard To Love series:

Worth The Fight ~ Out now

Make Me Trust ~ Out now

This Isn't Me ~ Out now

Undercover series:

Undercover ~ Out now

Unsuspected ~ Out now

Clay ~ Coming soon

Standalone Novels:

Someone To Hear Me ~ Out now

Rescue Me ~Out now

Coming Soon:

Satan's Crush

Maxed Out

·

26957633R00137

Printed in Poland
by Amazon Fulfillment
Poland Sp. z o.o., Wrocław